CLASS OF '99

TORI BEAT

First published in Great Britain in 2025
by Indie Novella Ltd.

INDIE NOVELLA www.indienovella.co.uk
Hackney, London

Editorial: Damien Mosley; Sam Burt; Gina Adams

A CIP catalogue record for this title is available from the
British Library
Paperback ISBN 978 1 738 44215 7

Printed and bound by in the United Kingdom.
Indie Novella is committed to a sustainable future for our readers and the world
in which we live. All paper used are natural, renewable and sustainable products.

Indie Novella is grateful that our work is supported using public funding by
Arts Council England.

For those who silently battle with their thoughts

CHAPTER ONE

I roll over and squint at the alarm clock. 5.45am. I groan and rub my stinging eyes, swing my legs from beneath the warmth of the duvet and stretch as I come to standing. My back is stiff as hell, these days.

'Daddaa, daddaa!' sings Emilia from the cot in her room across the hall. She almost always calls for me as soon as she wakes up, rather than my wife.

'Good morning, my angel,' I greet her with a warm smile as I poke my head around the door into her room. 'It's very early!'

'Dadddaaaaaa.' She grins and reaches towards me with both arms outstretched. We're definitely not going back to sleep.

'Come here, poppet.' I lift her out of the cot and sit with her in the rocking chair next to the window. She snuggles into my chest and I melt into the scent of her soft hair. I can't remember what life was like before she came along. Wednesday 3rd September 1997, 3.45am. The moment my life changed forever.

As a teacher, I was secretly chuffed that she arrived eight

days late, at the very beginning of the academic year. Lisa just wanted the baby out as soon as possible. In the scheme of things, as long as she was healthy, it didn't *really* matter. But I must admit I was keeping my fingers crossed that she'd be one of the oldest in her year, rather than the very youngest.

I lie Emilia down on the changing table as she chats away happily. I wonder what she's trying to say to me but I nod and respond encouragingly, doing all the things I've read in the pile of parenting books we bought when we found out Lisa was pregnant. Her babble gets louder as I pull the vest over her head, playing peek-a-boo as she emerges.

'Let's try not to wake mummy!' I whisper gently as I glance towards our bedroom. I can see through the slight gap in the door that the room is still in darkness. She's probably still asleep.

Lisa went back to work on her freelance contract at the advertising agency a few months ago, just before Emilia's first birthday. It took a while to settle her into nursery but we were lucky to find one not too far from school that allows term-time only childcare. And the day-rate Lisa gets from the agency is too good to turn down, until I make head of department, anyway.

———

'Morning, love,' I call to Lisa as I wipe porridge from Emilia's chin with the spoon.

'Morning, what time were you up?' She heads over to the table in our open-plan kitchen and kisses the top of Emilia's head.

'She was stirring about quarter to six.' I lift my head for a kiss but she goes to the sink and fills the kettle.

'Didn't you try and leave her to settle herself?'

'Well I was awake anyway, so...' I lie.

'Even so, we've got to try and get her to sleep beyond six at least. She should be doing that by now.'

'I know, I know,' I admit. 'It's just so hard when she's shouting for me. I can't just *leave* her.'

Lisa sighs through her nose. 'Tea?'

'Yeah, go on then, I've got time for a quick one before we head off.' I check my watch: it's 7.30. I managed to get on top of my marking on Saturday night while Lisa was out with her friends at the wine bar in town.

'You got a busy day?'

'Not too bad,' she says as she takes the lunch I prepared for her out of the fridge. 'Thanks for this,' she smiles, holding up the green Tupperware.

'That's OK.' I get up and take a sip of the tea she's left on the side for me. 'Just watch Emilia while I go and grab my bag, will you?'

'Did you enjoy your porridge, poppet?' she chirps as she takes off Emilia's bib. 'What are you doing waking Daddy up before six in the morning, hey?'

I run upstairs and grab my brown leather satchel from the back of the door in the box room. We've converted the fourth bedroom of our new-build house into a shared office space, for me to use for marking and prep and for Lisa while she's studying for her master's. I check I've got my lesson plans and head back downstairs, plucking my navy blazer off the row of coat hooks by the door. I glance in the hall mirror and try to neaten my unruly salt-and-pepper hair. I probably ought to have shaved.

'Come on then, little one.' I pull Emilia's tiny arm through the sleeve of her thick, rainbow-coloured coat. 'Off we go to nursery!'

She beams at me as I pull on the hand-knitted hat my mum made for her birthday. 'Give mummy a kiss,' I say, as I hold her up towards Lisa. Lisa cups her face as she says goodbye.

'Do you think she'll be alright in this massive coat in the car seat?' I worry out loud to Lisa. 'It's just way too cold in here for her to be without a coat and it'll take ages to warm up.' I pause buckling up her harness whilst I contemplate taking the coat off.

'She'll be fine, Paul.' Lisa frowns at me, shaking her head. 'You're only going round the corner.'

I begrudgingly agree. She'll be fine.

Emilia waves to Lisa as I strap her into the freezing cold car, still bundled up in her enormous coat. Should have known it would need de-icing. I run around to the boot and grab the scraper as I run the engine to warm it up. Now I'm cutting it fine.

'Morning, Martin!' I do an awkward saluting wave in the direction of our headteacher as I make my way to the kitchenette in the staff room for coffee. We all chipped in and treated ourselves to one of those snazzy espresso machines at the beginning of term, to celebrate our latest Ofsted rating.

'Alright Paul, good weekend?' he asks in his usual cheerful tone.

'Yeah, not bad ta, just the usual. How about you?'

'Very nice, very nice.' He runs a hand through his impressively thick head of silvery-golden hair. 'Had a very pleasant evening with Mrs Taylor at the jazz club in town on Saturday.'

'Lovely,' I say, with only a hint of jealousy.

I'd say Martin is only in his mid-forties but his eldest has just started her first year at Manchester Metropolitan University. He was a young dad, so his life seems at a totally different stage to mine, with kids flying the nest already, no babysitting issues.

'Now, no pressure Paul, but I want you to treat that application for head of department as a priority before the end of this term.' He nods knowingly at me as he peers over his square-rimmed tortoiseshell spectacles, in a classic headteacherly fashion. I feel fifteen again.

'Yep, will do Martin, it's top of my list to do before Christmas.' I shoot him double trigger fingers and instantly regret it. What's with all the weirdness this morning?!

He doesn't seem to notice. 'You're the best man for the job Paul, but you've got to be in it to win it!'

'Thanks Martin, leave it with me.' I grab my coffee and sling my satchel back over my shoulder. I realise I've inadvertently nicked Julia's Sheffield United mug. I'll get some stick for that later – from Julia *and* the kids in the class. And I don't even like football.

'Happy Monday, team!' I announce energetically as I enter our tutor group classroom. I'm met with some groans and a couple of more polite greetings as I sit down on the red plastic chair at the front of the room. I place my coffee on the grey vinyl coated desk and grab the register I'd just picked up off the staff room printer out of my satchel. 'How we all doing, then?'

'Alright thanks, sir!' chimes Sarah, one of my chattier students.

They're a good bunch, my tutor group. I'm lucky enough to have been with them since they started in Year 7, which was exactly when I started too, in September 1994. They've all got their GCSEs next summer and some are coping with the pressure better than others. It's a fairly mixed demographic, socio-economically if not so much racially, being the only comprehensive in a working/middle-class suburb to the west of Sheffield. There are pockets of poverty, with some families still feeling the effects of the mine closures. Some of the students' dads were on the picket lines in the miners' strikes in the mid-eighties, while the kids were just babies. But the majority of parents are in middle-management or professional roles, maybe a handful of teachers and nurses. Then there are some, despite having the privilege of a middle-class background, who just don't get the support they need at home.

'Right let's crack on then, shall we?' I get up and close the door; it's 8.50 and most of the class are assembled.

'James?'

'Yep.'

'Erin?'

'Yes.'

'Jo?'

'Yeah.'

'Laura?'

I look up. 'Laura?'

'Er yeah, sorry sir.'

I continue down the register and read the bulletin to start the week, then pack them all off on their way to their various lessons. All except Laura.

'Laura, you got a minute?' I say quietly as she gathers her bag and coat.

'Yep,' she sighs, indignantly. 'I'll catch you up, Manny.'

I perch on the edge of my desk to try and put her at ease. She's been quiet and withdrawn for a couple of weeks now and other teachers have commented that she's been falling behind with her work, which isn't like her.

'Everything OK?' I ask as she frowns at me from under her thick, chestnut coloured fringe. She softens slightly as I give her a questioning smile. Her hazel eyes reveal a depth that's unparalleled in her peers.

'Yeah, I'm fine sir, thanks. It's just a bit... tense, at home, that's all.' Laura's parents have recently decided to separate but from what I can grasp from snippets of overheard conversation, her dad is still living in their five-bedroom terrace on Chatsworth Road. Her older sister left a couple of months ago to study design at Leeds University.

'Anything you want to talk about?' I ask, walking a tightrope between approachable and irritating.

'Not unless you want to hear all about the *blazing* row my mum and dad had this morning?' She raises her eyebrows and sends a sarcastic grin my way.

'Listen, Laura, that's none of my business but I want you to know I'm here if you need any help with anything school-wise. And if you want me to put you in touch with the school counsellors to talk through your family stuff, just let me know, OK?' It doesn't feel like that long since I was in Laura's shoes, although it's actually been at least twenty years.

'Thank you.' She smiles unconvincingly. 'I'd better get going.'

'OK, see you after lunch.'

I don't have any lessons for the first two periods so I sit in the peace of the classroom and make a start on the head of department application. I wonder if I'm doing the right thing. But the extra money will come in handy and it'd be good to put some more energy back into work. I'm better when I'm busy. Plus Martin's not going to stick around forever, so I could even be looking at the headteacher position before too long. Maybe. Ambition has never been my strong point but maybe I could make this work.

CHAPTER TWO

I take the short walk from school along the leafy rows of three-storey terraces to collect Emilia from nursery. She's had a great day, they tell me. She seems to be settling in a lot better now she's been there a few months. I'm relieved. I know there's not much I could have done about it as Lisa wanted to be back at work when Emilia turned one, but leaving her so upset at drop off used to kill me.

We head out to the car which I'd left parked outside nursery. At least that way I get a bit of exercise rather than parking in the school car park. And there's less chance of your car being wrapped in cling film by the kids when they finish Year 11. I have to de-ice it again because it's so bloody cold. I strap Emilia into her car seat. It's pitch dark already and I can see my breath in the orange glow of the streetlight as I scrape the thin layer of ice off the windscreen. I open the driver's side door to jump in, before deciding to check Emilia's harness one more time. She's fine. We make our way home through the backstreets, avoiding the building traffic on the main road, before turning off for the two mile drive out of town towards the new estate.

A wave of warmth from the central heating hits us as we bundle in through the front door. I flick on the radio and make a start on tea while Emilia plays in her playpen next to the dining table. The house we bought when we found out Lisa was pregnant is what an estate agent might call a 'generously proportioned suburban family home'. I never thought I'd be the sort of person who lived in a house with an en-suite. Or a utility room for that matter. But there's been so much development around here in the last few years, so it was easy to get a part-exchange on our first house, a two-up two-down in the centre of town that we bought about a year before we got married. Lisa's parents helped us with the deposit on the first house as I was only a couple of years qualified and she'd just started a post-graduate junior position. I was reluctant, but I knew they wouldn't like the idea of us getting married before we were on the property ladder, as they put it.

I slice the peppers into thin strips and set them aside before starting on the onions, chatting to Emilia as I go. If I'm talking, it stops the thoughts creeping in. I hear the front door close and Lisa kicking off her shoes into the hallway.

'Hey, you OK?' she asks cheerfully as she dumps her bag on the sofa in the corner of the kitchen.

'Mummy's home!' I put the knife down carefully and wander over to give Lisa a kiss. She leans her cheek towards me and takes a hairband from her wrist to bunch together her mass of straw-coloured curls. She looks lively. I ask how her day went.

'Yeah, good thanks. Really good, actually. The agency bagged a new client so Richard asked me to go along to the 'creative direction' meeting.' She makes air quotes with her fingers as if it's a new thing. 'They're a new internet-based company and they want us to lead their UK launch campaign so it's a pretty big deal. Richard said I'd be the best writer on the team so he's offered me another contract to include this project. It'll mean an extra day in the office but I think it'll be great.'

'Oh well done love, that sounds amazing! Internet-based company, what does that mean? Doing what?' I haven't really got up to speed with all this new technology that everyone's talking about but Martin's booked me on a course for next term.

'Well, it's like a shop but you browse online and buy products through their website, a bit like mail order I guess but it's all done over the internet.'

I raise my eyebrows and pull a mystified face. 'What a time to be alive, hey Emmy?' I jokingly call in Emilia's direction as I stir the onions sizzling in the pan. 'That's great Lis, I'm really pleased for you.'

'So I'm going to need to start working full time to pull the hours in. Can you have a word with nursery and see if we can get her in an extra day?' Lisa takes a glass from the cupboard and pours from the bottle of merlot on the worktop. 'Ooh what's for tea?'

'Fajitas,' I answer, still catching up with what she's saying. I wince as I feel a slight churn in my stomach. I clear my throat to make sure I strike the right tone with what I'm about to say. 'Are you sure about this, you know, working full time *and* doing your MA? It's a lot to take on - with Emilia, I mean.' I breathe out silently and turn to the fridge to take out the sour cream.

'*Yes*, I'm sure, Paul. Loads of people do it. I'll just have to knuckle down. Besides, your job's pretty flexible, you know with the short days and stuff and you get all those holidays. We're hardly *abandoning* her.' She pulls up a stool to perch at the breakfast bar.

I try and brush off the 'short days' remark for the sake of

not getting into an argument. OK, the school day is 8.50 until 3.40 but there's a lot more to it than that. Especially if I'm going to go for head of department.

'No, no, I know,' I concede, strategically. 'I just don't want us biting off more than we can chew, that's all. And I had some news today actually, about work.'

'Oh yeah?'

'You know how I mentioned I might like to go for head of English? Well Martin has basically said the job's mine but I've got to get the application in before the Christmas break. I was working on it today actually; thought maybe you could see if it reads alright?'

'Ah OK, yeah,' she mumbles into her wine glass. 'Leave it out for me then and I'll take a look.'

She places her glass down before wandering off upstairs and I start to notice that familiar knot tightening in my stomach. I swallow hard and take a deep breath in, to try and stop it rising. *We're all here, we're all safe,* I repeat in my mind like a lullaby, soothing myself back to calm.

CHAPTER THREE

I set an early alarm but I needn't have bothered as Emilia is awake before six again. Lisa gets up with her on a Tuesday – her day off, for now at least – and I usually get into school early to do paperwork before class starts.

It's still dark when I arrive at school and I can see through the window that all the lights are off in the staff room. I approach the main entrance and pull the huge bunch of keys from out of my satchel to let myself in. The fluorescent lights above me flicker into life before settling with a ping, illuminating the long corridor in front of me.

Silent moments like these, when no one else is around, are when the thoughts start creeping in. *Please keep us safe*, I repeat in my head, not entirely sure whom I'm asking. I'm not a religious man but these mantras somehow calm me down, distract me from the dark intrusions into my stream of consciousness. I count my steps as I head down the corridor to the staff room at the far end. *One, two, three, four. One, two, three, four.*

You can't keep them safe. I shake my head as the whispers take over and I realise I just stepped on a crack in the parquet floor. It didn't feel right. An uneasiness sticks in my chest. *Go back; you have to go back.* For fuck's sake, not again. I turn around and tread on the same crack but this time repeat my positive mantra to balance out the negative, a vain attempt at eradicating any possibility of the horrors of my imagination actually happening. My pulse quickens and I feel a tightening in my chest.

Please keep us safe. I carry on walking, faster now, humming to myself to try and block everything else out. I thought I'd got the compulsions under control after my counselling last year. I guess I'm just tired, I tell myself. It always gets me when I'm tired. Suddenly I'm fourteen again, the same anxiety overpowering me like an arm-wrestle I've no chance of winning. The terror of wondering what the hell is wrong with me and why my mind behaves this way. The obsessions might be different now but the constant dread resting in my stomach remains the same. And the compulsions are just a variation on a theme.

'Alright mate?' My heart stops and I jump backwards.

'Jesus, Julia! You scared the shit out of me!' I catch my breath as Julia, Head of Art, emerges from the ladies' toilet block adjacent to the staff room. 'Where did you come from anyway? The main entrance was locked when I came in?'

'Oh I came in t'back way, through the art block. Sorry, didn't mean to give you a heart attack!' she laughs and slaps me on the back as she follows me into the staff room.

'What you doin' here so early anyway?' she asks, heading over to the kitchenette. 'Coffee?' Her glossy black bob follows her as she spins around and waves a mug in my direction.

'Yes please, make it a strong one, will you?' I let out a sigh, sitting myself down at the long wooden table in the middle of the room; one of Martin's castoffs when he moved house last year. 'Lisa has Tuesdays off so I didn't have to do the nursery drop off.'

'Oh yeah, course. How's it all going with her back at work an' that?'

'Yeah, it's alright. We're knackered and don't see much of each other, properly, but we're managing.' I start to lose my neutral accent as I subconsciously mimic Julia's thick Yorkshire twang.

'God, I remember them days. It don't last forever you know!' She winks and sends a sympathetic smile my way. It was Julia's fortieth last year but her youngest is in Year 9. She places a black coffee down in front of me that looks like pure tar. 'Just the way you like it!'

'Cheers, Ju.' I lift the mug and wrap my hands around it, grateful of her company. 'How you doin' anyway, alright?'

'Yeah, can't grumble, you know. I were gonna ask you actually, what's goin' on with Laura Michaels these days? She stormed out o' my class yesterday afternoon, sobbing her eyes out. I had to send Manny Dhindsa out after her.'

'Yeah, she's struggling a bit lately, her mum and dad have separated but sounds like he's still living at home so I think it's a bit...tense.' I scrunch up my nose in sympathy with Laura, having a pretty good idea of what she's going through.

'Shit. I've seen that boyfriend of hers picking her up a few times recently, in that battered old red Punto.' Julia nods out towards the car park.

'Yeah, Jay Goodwin, he was in Year 11 when I started here so must be four years or so older than her. I think they got together last summer, from what I've heard.'

'I thought I recognised him! Bloody 'ell, he must be, like, twenty now?!'

'I know, bit weird. But Laura's pretty mature for her age, so...'

Julia's eyes widen as she processes it all. 'Right, well I'd better get off and set up the studio. Still-life drawing today!' she declares, downing the rest of her coffee. 'I saw you using my Blades mug the other day you know.'

'Yeah sorry, picked it up by mistake.'

Julia winks at me. 'Yer alright, Johnson, dunna worry. We need all the fans we can get at the minute, anyhow!'

I laugh and give her a wave as she heads out of the class-room, feeling calmer having spoken to her. She's been here for years so she took me under her wing when I arrived from my last job and we've been good friends ever since. But I've never told her about my obsessive-compulsive disorder. I've never even gone into any real detail with Lisa. What goes on in my mind is sometimes so disturbing I think people will recoil in horror if I tell them the truth of it.

'Oh, by the way...' She pokes her head back around the door and gives me the same look Martin did the other day, over her red cat-eye glasses. 'You gonna go for head of English, or what? Martin's been pestering me to chivvy you up – the job's yours, mate! If you want it, that is.'

I look down at my empty coffee cup. 'Yeah, I'm gonna go for it, I think. I just need to get my application polished then I'll hand it in.'

'Well, if you want me to give it the once-over, just let me know, won't yer?'

'Cheers Ju. I'll bring it in tomorrow.'

I gather my things and head over to the classroom, feeling lighter than I did when I arrived.

'So, don't forget, guys,' I raise my voice over the din that starts to ripple through the classroom after I've taken the register. 'We've got our Christmas talent competition rehearsal at lunchtime on Thursday this week, no excuses!'

They collectively groan. 'That's the spirit!' I declare sarcastically. 'Come on, we were *robbed* last year when Mr Patterson's Year 10s did that wild dance routine. No one saw that coming. We've got to reclaim our status as the most talented tutor group in the school!'

'Yeah they were pretty good though, weren't they sir? I mean, I think we just looked a bit average really, in comparison,' Erin Robson chimes in.

'*Average*?! Erin, you've wounded me!' I stagger backwards playfully clutching my chest as they all laugh. 'But yeah, they were pretty good, to be fair. This year is our year though, I'm sure of it! We're gonna smash it!' We're doing a choral rendition of *Disco 2000* by Sheffield's finest, Pulp. I seem to be more enthusiastic about it than the kids though.

'Where are we doing the rehearsal, sir?' Sarah asks.

'We'll be in the drama studio, 12.30 sharp. And don't forget your song sheets! Oh and James, can you bring your guitar in for your solo please? I want to hear the whole thing all the way through before the big day.'

'Yeah, course,' James mumbles in agreement.

'And Laura do you think your dad will be able to bring in that amp we're going to borrow, maybe early next week?'

'Yeah I'm sure he will, I'll ask.'

'He won't be too busy will he?' Andy Smithurst sniggers with a snide remark in Laura's direction, nudging his mate next to him. 'With his new *girlfriend*?'

'Oh piss off and mind your own business will you?!' Laura retorts with a sigh. She looks tired.

'Alright, that's enough,' I say wearily. It's sometimes more like dealing with toddlers than teenagers. Especially when it comes to the likes of Andy Smithurst. 'Andy, I don't want to hear any more comments like that from you, OK?' My tone switches to stern in an attempt to nip his nonsense in the bud.

I glance at Laura to try and catch her eye but her gaze is fixed on her feet.

'So we've got English Lit together for last lesson, I'm sure you'll all be thrilled to hear!' I address the class, met by more groans.

'Come on, it's not that bad is it?!' I laugh as the bell rings to indicate the end of registration. 'Right, go on then you lot, I'll see you all later.'

CHAPTER FOUR

'So what do we think Duffy is getting at in this stanza?' I pick up the textbook and read aloud from Carol Ann Duffy's *Valentine*.

I look out at the sea of blank faces. I swear some of them are asleep with their eyes open. To be fair, it's fifth period and there's an air of 'can't be arsed' hanging in the room, even from me. Laura puts down her pencil and raises her hand, a look of disdain from under her fringe.

'Yes, Laura.'

'She's likening the effect of the onion to the emotional effects of a relationship. When you cut an onion, it stings your eyes and brings you to tears. And sometimes a lover will bring you to tears.'

'Good! Anyone else got any thoughts they want to share?' I ask, in hope.

'Is that what happened to your mum when your dad shagged her best mate?' Andy pipes up from the back of the class.

'Fuck off Andy, you prick!' Laura screams as she rises from

her chair. Marching over, she takes a handful of his greasy black hair and in one swift movement slams his forehead down on the desk. The whole class collectively gasps as Laura runs sobbing out of the classroom, the door slamming behind her. I dash out after her and ask Erin Robson, one of my more sensible students, to check on Andy.

Laura sits in the corridor, back against the wall with her face buried into her raised knees, crying.

'You OK, Laura?' I sit down next to her. I need to balance reprimand with sympathy if I'm going to get through to her.

'I'm fine,' she spits through gritted teeth, rubbing her eyes as she takes a breath in through her nose. 'I'm not taking any more shit from that fucking prick Andy Smithurst.'

'I know, he was out of order. And I'll have a word with him. He's just trying to get a reaction from you, you know what he's like. But I can't have you attacking other students, Laura. No matter how much of a prick they're being.'

She laughs and pulls a crumpled tissue from out of her blazer pocket. 'I know, I'm sorry, I just...' She sighs slowly through pursed lips. 'I could do without him talking bollocks about my dad in front of everyone. He's been on at me all day.'

'I'll speak to him, OK? But I'm going to have to keep you behind after class. We can't tolerate violence. OK?'

'Fine, whatever.'

'Come on.' I nod towards the classroom.

I follow Laura back in and summon Andy Smithurst outside with my most severe tone for a dressing down loud enough for everyone to be able to hear. When we go back in, they've descended into missile throwing, a couple of the girls gathered around Laura's desk.

'Alright, let's get back to it.' They quieten down and

everyone files back into their seats before the bell rings with perfectly comedic timing.

'Well it must be your lucky day. Off you go! See you all tomorrow,' I raise my voice over the hubbub. 'Laura, you're staying behind this afternoon I'm afraid.'

Laura remains in her seat, picking at the skin around her thumb. I get up to close the door once the others have filed out and take a seat at one of the desks next to her.

'Is there anything you want to talk about Laura? Sometimes it helps to talk things through with someone outside of your situation. And whatever you tell me will stay between us, unless you want me to get you some extra help,' I offer, trying not to sound overbearing.

'It is what it is, I can't change what's happening to my family so I've just got to suck it up.' She shrugs her shoulders and looks up at me. 'So I'm not sure how *talking about it* will help.' She uses air quotes and rolls her eyes.

'When I was about the same age as you, my parents split up. My dad left us for his secretary at work. It tore me apart; I was so angry. But most of all, I was scared for my mum. She was in a right state and I had nowhere to channel that anxiety. So it started to take over and every day I was plagued with worry. And I'm pretty sure that was the trigger for some issues I still struggle with a bit today. I've not told many people about this but I want you to know I kind of know what you're going through.'

'Did it ever go away, this anxiety?'

'It got better.' I try not to think about this morning. 'But sometimes if I'm stressed or tired or whatever, I still get these awful thoughts. And when it gets me, it feels like a huge wave has knocked me off my feet and dragged me under. Every thought is tossing me around and pulling me further and

21

further away from the shore, and I'm fighting desperately to get back to safety. Sometimes the more I fight, the harder it is and I'm drowning.' I realise I've gone way deeper into this with Laura than I intended to, but I figure I need to show her this is normal if I'm going to get anywhere. 'But, you know, with proper counselling and stuff, I got much better than I was in the really dark days. I just...I don't want you to feel like you have to struggle on, on your own. If I'd have spoken to someone about how I was feeling at the time, there's no doubt I could have avoided years and years of pain.'

Tears spill over Laura's eyes and roll slowly down her cheeks. She bites her lip and breathes in through her nose, as if trying to stem the flow of sadness from escaping to the point of no return. 'I'm fine, sir, really. Thank you,' she says with a deep exhale.

'It's OK to not be fine though, Laura. You're grieving, you're allowed to feel this. Sometimes allowing yourself to connect with your grief, your anger... it's the only way through.'

'It's easier not to. I'm scared of where it might take me.' She looks away, towards the window overlooking the car park and pulls out her phone. 'Sir, can I go now? Please? Jay's outside and if he's going to give me a lift home we need to leave now. He's got a shift at the chippy at five.'

'Alright,' I sigh, 'but Laura, we can't have a repeat of what happened this afternoon, OK?' Laura gets up and wraps herself up in her black cropped puffer jacket. I hesitate, wondering if I should ask her about her relationship with a grown man.

'Laura, this Jay, he's...he's a bit older than you, isn't he?'

'Yeah, he'll be twenty next week, why?'

'Well, it's just...it's my job to look after you, you know, and, well you've only just turned sixteen and he's an adult so, I'm just saying...' I don't really know what I am saying, as technically she's old enough to be doing what she likes. I regret saying anything at all.

'Look, Jay's good for me. He's all I've got at the minute. He looks after me.'

I look at my watch. If I keep her behind any longer it will probably mean her walking home on her own, in the dark.

'OK, off you go. Just...just be careful Laura, OK? I'm here if you need anything.'

'Thanks sir, it means a lot, really.' She smiles and heads out of the door.

CHAPTER FIVE

It's a crisp, icy day and the cold is biting at my face. Blinded by the rising winter sun, I pull down the visor before turning the corner to pull up outside nursery. I do a little dance to fend off the cold as I get out of the car to unload Emilia. We rush across the road into the warmth of the inner porch and ring the bell to be let in.

'See you later then, poppet,' I kiss her cheek as I hand her over to Melanie, her carer, before dashing back out to grab my satchel from the car. It's a glorious morning for the short walk to school and the sun gives me an energy I've not felt in a while. I've got the head of department application in my bag, ready to give to Julia to read before I hand it in to Martin. Lisa had Emilia yesterday so didn't have a chance to read it before she went out to a lecture when I got in from work. We're like a tag team at the minute.

I breeze into the staff room and greet Julia, Martin and Chris, Head of Science. 'Morning guys, how we doing?'

'Paul, take a seat.' Martin gestures to an empty chair next to

Julia. She looks like she's been crying. I panic. Martin looks like he's seen a ghost.

'What's going on? Is everything alright?'

'It's about Laura... Laura Michaels.' He pauses and my mind races. I search their faces for clues as to what's going on. 'I'm sorry Paul, she died in a hit and run accident last night.'

My whole body feels like it has frozen over. 'What?!' I must be dreaming, I tell myself. My ears are ringing. There's a surreal notion hovering over me; a part of my consciousness has already – in those split seconds just passed – realised that my life will never be the same again, but I'm still searching the depths of my reasoning to try and process what Martin has just said.

I try and catch my breath. I need to keep talking before this familiar panic catches me and pins me down. I look at Julia. Her face cracks as she squeezes my shoulder. I glance over at Martin, the look in his eyes quite possibly the saddest thing I've ever seen. I never expected to see this expression on his face. I never expected to share such an inconceivable loss with someone I've never seen without a tie on. This wasn't meant for us.

'How?' I ask, still stumbling over my words. 'I mean, when?'

'Yesterday evening, about 4.30, her boyfriend had just dropped her off near her house. Apparently she got out of the car into the road and was hit by an oncoming van. The driver fled the scene and Laura died in hospital about eight o'clock last night. I got a call from the police this morning.'

'I shouldn't have let her go,' I mumble, shaking my head in disbelief.

'What do you mean?' Julia asks, lifting her glasses to wipe her eyes.

'I had her in detention yesterday after last lesson, Andy Smithurst was winding her up about her mum and dad and she went for him. I had to keep her behind, and anyway we were having a good chat, she seemed to be…listening to me. I let her go early because her boyfriend was giving her a lift back. Oh God, I shouldn't have let her go!' A sickening sense of remorse descends on me and I put my hand to my forehead. It's clammy and cold. I think I might throw up.

'Don't be daft, Paul, none of this is your fault. How were you to know? Anyway it was an accident, it could have happened at any time. The only person to blame is the driver who hit her and left her for dead!' Martin tries to reassure me but my thoughts gallop away from me. This should never have happened. I have an ineffable, fleeting belief that I can somehow rewind time; some childlike response to a regretted action that I can surely make right again. This can't be happening. I won't believe it.

'Have you spoken to her parents?' I ask, grasping for some normality.

'Not yet. They'd asked the police to call and let us know. The officer I spoke to said I should probably write to them instead of calling, just whilst they process everything.'

'Christ!' I blurt out as the reality of it all starts to sink in. 'What are we going to do?! Today, I mean. Do the kids know yet? How are we going to tell them?'

'The police have been in touch with Manpreet Dhindsa's family. Her and Laura were close so her parents asked them to let her family know last night. They usually walk to school together so they didn't want her to find out this morning. I imagine the news will have started to filter through to some of the kids in your class, Paul, but we're going to have a special assembly straight after registration this morning and offer sessions with the school counsellor to anyone that wants them. A news reporter has already been on the phone wanting me to give an interview later on as part of their coverage of the incident, so I'm going to need to deal with that.'

'What about the driver? Have they found anyone yet?' Chris asks, a look of sheer incredulity on his face. 'How can anyone do that and just drive off?!'

'The police are still looking for the driver and they're appealing for witnesses. It's a dark bend in the road where Laura lives but it's a busy stretch so you'd think someone would have seen something at that time in the evening.' Martin sighs, shaking his head. 'I just feel for the family, for that to happen so close to their home. It's a tragedy.' He purses his lips and clears his throat, before turning towards the window.

I bring my hands together and press my thumbs into the bridge of my nose. I close my eyes and sigh out through my mouth, trying to regulate my heartbeat. I've no idea how I'm going to get through today; the kids, the inevitable gossip. The *grief*.

'Can I just give Lisa a quick ring, Martin? I just need a minute before the kids start arriving.'

'Course you can, Paul, take your time,' he says, giving me a friendly pat on the shoulder.

I call Lisa but she doesn't pick up. In fact, it goes straight to voicemail so I try her work number too. Same. I leave her a message at home and ask her to call me when she can. I don't know why I'm so desperate to talk to her, it's not like she can do anything to help. But I just need to speak to someone outside of this sphere of shock and disbelief to make sure I'm not losing my mind. Or imagining it all. It all feels so surreal. I'm not sure I can trust my own mind at the minute.

27

The kids start arriving and, amongst the tear-stained faces and uncharacteristic quietness, I can gather that most of them have already heard the news. I speak to each of them quietly, confirming their fears that there is truth in the rumours doing the rounds outside of school. This is not how I expected this morning to pan out. There's something calming and grounding about being the only adult in a room of kids just learning that their friend and classmate has just died in tragic circumstances. A sort of anaesthetic that is helping me keep it together. For now. There's a familiar sense of dread that something is bubbling within me, just beneath the surface, but I need to keep it under control for the sake of the kids. I can't help but think that no one ever trained me for this.

After registration, we all file quietly into the assembly hall, one by one. The glistening sun streams in through the skylight, making playful shadows dance on the walls, incongruous with the mood of the room. My eyes hurt. I can't shake from my mind Laura's sad smile when she left yesterday afternoon. I look around. Manny Dhindsa is sobbing and I notice Julia heading her way, then leading her to the edge of the hall, an arm around her shoulder. Some of the kids look completely bewildered; they've all heard what has happened by now but it's beyond their comprehension, yet. Aside from a few quiet mutterings, the room is almost silent as they all exchange nervous glances. My heart is racing. How does something as catastrophic as this just come out of nowhere, with no warning? That thought makes me panic, selfishly, about Emilia and Lisa. A heat rises through my body and into my face as I realise the futility of me battling to keep them safe. I berate myself for being so self-absorbed. Laura is dead. And all I can think of is my own family. Thank God it's not my daughter.

The sun disappears behind a cloud and a morbid gloom

shrouds the hall. It feels strangely comforting, like the weather has finally got the memo. Martin enters, walking slowly from the back of the room towards the raised stage and the room falls eerily silent. My abdomen tenses up as the enormity of what has happened hits me and I audibly try to catch my breath. Julia looks over in my direction and gives me a reassuring look. I clench my fists, digging my nails into the inside of my palms – my well-rehearsed method of stopping any outward display of emotion. I watch Martin walk up the steps and onto the stage, before clearing his throat. I swallow hard as hot, briny fluid rises up from under my tongue. I breathe out through pursed lips to stem the waves of nausea.

'Most of you will already know why we're gathered here this morning,' he begins, before pausing. I notice his jaw clench and his chest expand. 'And it is with great sadness that I must inform you all of the death of one of our students and dear friends, Laura Michaels.' I feel my shoulders trembling as I fight the threat of tears. Julia wipes her eyes from underneath her glasses.

'Laura was an extremely promising and talented student in Mr Johnson's Year 11 tutor group and had many, many friends throughout the school...' Martin's words fade out as I focus on the whirr of the heater behind me, its rhythm calming me.

'For many of you, this will be your first experience of bereavement and it is, of course, particularly difficult to deal with under such tragic circumstances.' Several of Laura's friends are sobbing and consoling one another. Some of the younger students look baffled, some smirking in that way kids do when they've no idea how to process their emotions. *This is your fault. You should never have kept her behind. She wouldn't be dead if it wasn't for you.* I shake my head to try and reset my thoughts.

'Whilst we all deal with the initial shock and anger at what

29

has happened, the school counsellors will be available to anyone who feels they need their services. For now, school remains open but lessons will no doubt be taking a more relaxed format for the rest of the week whilst we all gather our thoughts.' I've no idea how I'm going to gather my thoughts, let alone try and help thirty teenagers navigate the sudden death of one of their peers. Twenty-nine, now.

Martin gestures with a hand towards the exit in the far right-hand corner of the hall that everyone is free to go. Chris props the double doors open and the Year 11s on the back row start filing out slowly. The room is still dark and I notice that it has begun to rain. My eyes well up as I watch my tutor group leave the hall, united in their collective grief. *They'll all figure out Laura died because of you. Everyone will know.* I shake my head again and smooth down the front of my blazer. Once, twice, three times. I start counting my steps, trying to leave no space for the thoughts. *One, two, three, four. One, two, three, four.*

I head back to our tutor group room for the lesson I have with the Year 8s. At least I don't need to face my own class just yet. *That's right, coward, don't worry about those grieving teenagers. You just look after yourself.*

All I can think of is what Laura's parents must be going through. I need to speak to Lisa. And hold Emilia in my arms. Although I'm worried I'll never be able to let her go.

CHAPTER SIX

The rest of the morning is hell. I've got a blinding headache and I can barely string a sentence together, let alone act as grief counsellor.

I head back to my tutor group room between third lesson and lunchtime to check on the kids. A few of them have come back to drop their bags off before heading to the canteen. I try and think of something philosophical and erudite to say to those who come to me in tears but it takes every ounce of my strength not to sob with them. There is no logic to this. No 'everything happens for a reason'. Just rage and desperate sadness.

'I just can't believe she's never coming back,' Manny cries, wiping her nose with a sleeve before I hand her a tissue.

I bite my lip and sigh out through my nose. 'I know, Manny,' I say softly, as I perch on the desk in front of her. 'It's going to be a long time before it sinks in properly, I'm sure. I know how close you two were.'

'It's not fair! Why her? Why now?! And what was the driver thinking, leaving her like that?!' she shouts, exasperated, before falling back into silent sobs, closing her eyes and covering her mouth with her hand. Laura's empty desk fills the room.

'You're right, it's not fair. And I know it's hard to see how you're going to get through this but remember we're all here for you Manny, OK? Have you seen the school counsellors yet?'

'Not yet, I was maybe going to go and see them after lunch,' she says, wiping underneath her eyes with her finger. 'I don't know if there's much point though, really.'

'Well, it might seem like that, but I think it will help to talk through how you're feeling with them. They know how to handle these things properly, I mean.'

'Yeah, I guess,' she sighs.

'Maybe try and eat something and then go and see them? Don't worry if you're not back for fourth lesson. And if you'd rather just head home, just let them know in the office, OK?' I give her a soft smile. 'My door's always open though, Manny, OK?'

'Thanks, sir.' She smiles but her eyes can't hide her despair.

I catch Julia in the staff room at lunch.

'How's it going mate?' she asks me with a sigh, her eyes bloodshot and puffy.

'I've no idea to be honest, Ju. It still feels like a bad dream, really. I don't know what to say to the kids, they're in bits.'

'Yeah, it's shit, int it?' She squeezes my shoulder then picks up the red plastic kettle. 'You wanna brew?'

'Ah, yeah please.' I sigh and slump back into the blue plastic chair, rubbing my eyes. 'I'm pretty sure it's my round though?'

'Dunna worry, pal, you can mek t' next ones.' She takes two mugs out of the cupboard over the sink and puts teabags into them before taking out the milk bottle from the fridge. If there was ever any doubt, I know Julia is one of my people as she pours the boiling water into the cup before putting the milk in.

'Yer know what you said this morning, about letting Laura go last night? You do know that's bollocks don't yer?' She squeezes the teabags against the mugs with the back of the teaspoon and leaves them by the sink before pouring in the milk and placing the World's Best Teacher mug down in front of me.

'I just can't help but think I should have kept her behind longer. I knew she was going with that boyfriend of hers, why did he pull up on that bend?! What a stupid thing to do! I should have given her a lift myself.'

'That's not really the done thing though is it?' Julia takes a sip of her tea and looks at me over the rim of her mug.

'At least she'd still be alive!' I blurt out as the wave crashes down over me. I can't hold back the tide any longer and tears escape down my face. I try to stop them but Julia's noticed and hands me a tissue. She pulls her chair in closer and puts an arm around my shoulder.

'You can't blame yerself, Paul, it'll eat you up. You know that's not how the world works. How were you to know what was going to happen? Any of them could be hit by a bus at any time, we can't watch their every move.'

But my dysfunctional mind thinks otherwise, I should have kept her safe. My thoughts taunt me. *Well you failed, didn't you? You're only concerned about yourself. You and your perfect little life in the leafy suburbs. And if they find out about the time you* did *give her a lift...*

My stomach churns as I think back to the night I'd spotted Laura around the corner from school, just before October half term. It was already dropping dark; I'd stayed behind to catch up on my marking. It was Lisa's day off so I didn't need to rush

33

off to collect Emilia. Laura had been at netball practice. She was sitting on the wall that backs onto the school playing field, waiting for her boyfriend to pick her up, but he'd called her to say his plans had changed and she'd have to make her own way home. She looked upset. I just wanted to make sure she was OK. I didn't think we were doing anything wrong. Better that she gets home safe, surely? This is what I'd told Lisa when she found Laura's scarf in the passenger side footwell of the car. Her name was written on the tag. She asked me why. I said I just wanted to keep her safe.

I wipe my eyes with the heel of my hand before blowing my nose, pushing my thoughts aside. 'I just... God, I don't know, Ju. Why do things like this happen? She had so much going for her. It's such a waste.'

'I know, mate. I know.'

I'm nervous on the walk back to nursery to collect Emilia. I need to try and keep it together; I can't face a load of questions from the nursery staff. I know they'll have heard the news. I start to count my steps but even that fails to keep the thoughts from seeping into my mind, suffocating me like carbon monoxide. *One, two, three, four. One, two, three, four. It was your fault. One, two, three, four. One, your fault. One, two, how are you going to look her parents in the eye? One, you shouldn't have let her go.*

I step on a grate in the road and it doesn't feel right. *Go back, turn around. If you don't go back Emilia will die. And that'll be your fault, too.* I try and catch my breath. I'm exhausted. I don't want to give in to this poison in my head but I can't take the risk. I'd never be able to live with myself. There's a whisper in my ear from the rational part of my mind that reminds me I have no control over what happens in the world, but my ability to listen to reason fails me. I turn around and step on the grate again, concentrating hard to think of something good, something positive. *Keep us safe, please keep us all safe, especially Emilia.* That's better. I look up and a woman walking towards me crosses the road. I'm freaking people out with my weird to-ing and fro-ing in the dark.

I start to count again and it helps me to concentrate. *One, two, three, four. One, two, three, four.* I try and synchronise the counting with my breathing. In for four, out for four. Relief arrives as I turn the corner and walk up to the front door of the nursery building. The smell – a mixture of shepherd's pie, talc and dirty nappies – is strangely comforting, as I enter the porch and ring the bell. I close my eyes and inhale deeply, feeling my shoulders drop as I breathe out through my nose. I've made it. Back to the safety of other people. The thoughts can't get to me as easily when I'm not on my own.

I bundle Emilia into the car as she giggles, trying to pull off my hat while I tighten up her harness. Her nose is red from the biting cold. I pause for a moment to take in the sheer beauty of her tiny face. Laura was a baby once. With loving parents, adoring her every move.

'Let's get home shall we, poppet?' I say softly to Emilia, glancing in the rear-view mirror. She kicks her legs excitedly and giggles as I start the engine.

The radio comes to life and I instantly recognise the second bar of Jeff Buckley's *Hallelujah*. This song gets me every time, but there's something about hearing it now, after the horror of today, seeing the Christmas lights twinkling through the misted windscreen that leaves an ache in my heart. We're all living on a knife-edge, I realise. A frantic, yet unacknowledged battle just to get through life without getting hurt. It seems impossible, but at the same time we're convinced the worst will never happen to us. I'm holding back what feels like a tsunami, desperate not to let Emilia see me upset.

I'm brought back by the vibration of my phone in my satchel on the passenger seat. It's Lisa. I can't face breaking the news to her now so I ignore the call and send her an SMS.

'Just leaving nursery, be home in 10. X'

Lisa is standing at the hob, cooking what smells like spaghetti Bolognese and sipping a glass of red wine as I walk through the hall into the kitchen. I put Emilia down and let her wobble over to Lisa, both arms in the air for balance.

'Hello baby girl!' she smiles as she bends down to kiss Emilia's cheek. 'Did you have a lovely day?' Lisa rises to greet me with a kiss on the cheek too. 'How was your day love?' she asks cheerily. She obviously hasn't seen the news.

My face crumples. 'Paul? What? What is it?' She scans my face, panicked.

'One of my students, Laura Michaels, died last night,' I tell her, bringing my hands to prayer under my nose and breathing in deeply. I feel the blood drain from my face as I say it out loud. Lisa's eyes are wide as she takes hold of my shoulders and pulls me towards her.

'Bloody hell, love. I'm so sorry. Jesus. That's awful. So you've had a bit of a shocker then?'

'You could say that, yeah.' I sit down on one of the stools at the breakfast bar. 'It's been... intense.'

'What happened?! I mean, how did she die?' I reach for the evening edition of the local paper that's piled up with today's mail, untouched.

'TEEN DEAD IN A57 HIT AND RUN' reads the front page alongside a photo of a police sign by the road, appealing for witnesses, and one of Laura. It looks like last year's school portrait from the end of term. She's smiling. I'm numb. I hand the paper to Lisa for the details. I can't bring myself to talk about it anymore.

She unfolds the paper and scans the front page, eyes widening, her hand to her mouth in disbelief. It's almost cathartic to witness someone else's reaction to the news. I notice a glassiness to her eyes, a moment of imagination. She swallows hard and turns to me.

'I'm so sorry, Paul.' She reaches for me and pulls me in. I slump into her and clutch at her back as the shock catches in my chest again. *Breathe, Paul, just breathe.* The lump at the top of my ribcage solidifies and I splutter as tears start to tingle in my eyes again. 'I know how much you thought of her,' she says, without the usual derisive tone she slips into when I talk about Laura.

'I just can't imagine what her parents are going through,' I manage, as I wipe at my eyes with my sleeve. 'I mean, I *can* imagine it, I suppose that's the problem. I just don't want to. She had so much promise, Lis. She was so... different.'

'So how was it at school today?' she asks, taking a sip of water before reaching down to pick Emilia up, who's trying to hand her a toy carrot. She holds her close to her chest, closing her eyes as she kisses the top of her head. 'Stupid question, I guess, but... I mean, how are the kids coping?'

'They're still in shock I think, to be honest.' I pinch the bridge of my nose. 'Manny is obviously in pieces. And the

37

whole class is just at a loss to comprehend it, really. Death at this age is such an alien concept, especially when it comes so out of the blue. I guess some of them will have lost grandparents, but this... it's just unnatural.'

'Have you heard anything about the driver?' Lisa asks, shaking her head, her eyes narrowing. 'Who does something like that?! Just says here the police are 'appealing for information'. How can anyone do that and just keep quiet?'

'Yeah, I know, that's what the kids keep saying.' I close my stinging eyes. 'They're so angry. I just don't know how we're going to get through these next few weeks.'

CHAPTER SEVEN

My hands are shaking as I pick up the receiver and sit on the leather seat beside the telephone table. I realise I don't know the number for the doctors' surgery so I put it back down and take out the telephone directory from the drawer underneath the phone. I flick through the flimsy pages to 'W' and work my way down the list of numbers to White Peak Surgery. I keep my finger at the position in the directory as I lift the receiver again with my other hand and punch in the numbers with my thumb. A feeling of dread churns in my stomach as I clam up, trying to quickly rehearse what I'll say when they answer.

The line rings. It's 8am and the surgery has only just opened. Lisa has already left for work with Emilia and I'm alone in the house. It feels cold. The line clicks and the receptionist answers.

'Good morning, White Peak Surgery,' she sings cheerfully.

I panic. What do I say? 'Err, morning, I erm ... I was wondering if I could get an appointment, er, today, if possible? To see a doctor?' I kick myself at being apparently unable to string a sentence together. *Breathe*.

'Of course, let me have a look. Could I start by taking your name and date of birth?'

'Yes... it's Paul Johnson. Tenth of June 1967.'

'Let's have a look for you... Could I ask for a brief description of what the problem is?'

I don't know what to say. 'I, er, well...' I choke up as I struggle to finish my sentence. 'I just really need to talk to someone,' I blurt out, fighting to hold back tears surging behind my eyes.

'OK, love, let's get you in with Dr Rowley. Is 10.40 OK?'

'Yes, yes, perfect, thank you.' I clear my throat and a wave of relief washes over me, knowing I can finally talk openly to someone about how I've been feeling these last few weeks.

'Okey dokey, we'll see you at 10.40 then Mr Johnson. Bye bye.'

'Thank you, bye.' I put down the receiver and my heart feels as though it might stop as the pain rises up from my chest and constricts around my throat. I need to lie down.

I wake to my alarm clock buzzing and I could have been asleep for a week. I squint at the red numbers – it's 10am. I'm amazed that I had the good sense to set an alarm ahead of my appointment; there's no way I would have pulled myself from such a deep sleep. I pull myself up and head over to the bathroom.

The doctors' surgery is only a ten-minute walk. The cool breeze is refreshing on my face, giving me a dose of optimism. I turn the corner and enter the surgery through the automatic double doors. The reception area is stuffy and I take off my coat before approaching the reception desk. The receptionist regards me with kind eyes; it must be the woman I spoke to on the phone, I think.

'Paul Johnson to see Dr Rowley at 10.40.' I smile, not quite meeting her gaze.

'Take a seat Mr Johnson, thank you.'

I head over to the waiting area and sit down on one of the light blue faux-leather chairs which makes a strange puffing sound as I lower myself into it. I drape my coat across my lap and look around at the other patients waiting. It's a while since I've been here.

Energy looks for an escape as I wait for my name to be called. I take out my mobile phone and see that Julia has messaged me.

'*Hope ur OK, pal. Let me know if u need anything. Ju x*'

It sometimes feels like she's the only person who knows me.

'Paul Johnson please, room five,' says a well-spoken voice over the PA system. I get up too quickly. *Room five. Room five. Don't forget, room five.*

I walk through the door, which has been propped open with the fire extinguisher, and along the corridor, past the other consultation rooms. Room five. I knock and enter. Dr Rowley is sitting at her desk facing an enormous computer with a black screen and green text that looks like it belongs in the eighties. She turns on her swivel-chair to greet me and smiles warmly.

'Mr Johnson, hello. Take a seat.'

I sit without speaking. Fear sets in and I feel like as soon as I do speak, I'm going to cry. *Just pull yourself together.*

'What seems to be the problem?' she asks, looking at what I assume are my notes on her screen.

I take a deep breath through my nose to try and prepare myself for speaking. Words are lodged in my throat.

'Mr Johnson?' she asks gently as she turns to face me.

41

I put my face in my hands. Dr Rowley takes a tissue from a box on her desk and hands it to me. 'Take your time,' she says.

I'm conscious of the ticking clock. I inhale and exhale sharply, looking her straight in the eye, as if I'm preparing myself for a 100-metre sprint. She has a welcoming face, a good feature for a doctor, I think to myself. Her wavy dark hair, peppered with grey strands, sits just beyond her shoulders. She looks like she might be a bit younger than my mum, maybe late forties.

'I'm really struggling at the minute,' I manage to say and I'm out of the starting blocks. 'Mentally, I mean.' With that, there's freedom, like I might just be able to hold it together. The hardest part is over. Now we know what we're dealing with.

'OK, and how long has this been going on?'

'This time, for about the last month or so, maybe six weeks.'

She types noisily on the grubby-looking keys of the long cream-coloured keyboard. 'And is there anything in particular that has triggered this episode?'

'Erm, well I'd been feeling a bit more anxious than normal for a few weeks and now...' My voice cracks as I trail off. I clear my throat. 'It's been a bit of a tough time at work. I'm a teacher, at Melbury High.'

'I see.' She makes more notes. She doesn't need me to elaborate. 'And can you tell me more about how you've been feeling? What symptoms are you experiencing?'

I find it easier to talk in a matter-of-fact way about my symptoms, as if I'm talking about someone else experiencing them.

'I've been getting a lot of intrusive thoughts. Like, really dark stuff. I'm finding it all quite exhausting, this constant internal battle.' I pause for breath. 'I had some counselling for OCD around this time last year but I've suffered generally with... stuff, since my teens, I guess. But the thoughts have been getting worse and I'm finding it harder and harder to function day-to-day. It's starting to affect... everything, really and... well, my wife and I don't get a lot of time together at the minute, so...'

'You've had a lot to deal with over the last few weeks then? And you've got a little one, too, is that right?' She glances again at the screen.

'Yeah, Emilia.' I smile at the thought of her. 'She's amazing. But yes, it's a bit... full on, you know?' Guilt creeps in, as I sit here complaining about life when I don't have very much at all to complain about. We've got a roof over our heads – and a comfortable one at that – a beautiful, healthy daughter, steady jobs and no real money worries. I point this out to the doctor but she quickly sets the record straight.

'Mental illness doesn't discriminate, Mr Johnson. You can lead a charmed life but still struggle with mental health issues. And it's important to get the help you need, when you need it. So you're doing the right thing, coming here today. Now, did this course of counselling seem to help you, last year?'

'Yes, it did, I think. But I only had the three free sessions you get with the NHS. I meant to carry it on as it did seem to be helping but... well, you know. I just never got round to it. So it didn't take much to tip me over the edge again and now I'm back to square one. I feel like I'm just on a bit of a merry-go-round; I start to feel better and think I'm 'cured', then it hits me and I'm out of control again.'

'OK.' She nods sympathetically. 'Well, I think the first thing to do is to start you on some medication, to help settle the chemical imbalance in your brain. That will start to make you feel better generally, less overwhelmed. And more able to cope with the day-to-day. They'll take two to three weeks to kick in and there might be a few unpleasant side-effects to start with but that should all settle down after a little while.'

I'm not sure about this. I'm not keen on the idea of changing the chemicals in my brain. What if they totally change my personality? I don't like the idea of being out of control. Or getting addicted. That's why recreational drugs have never appealed, apart from the odd spliff at a festival. I can't even cope with much more than a glass of wine these days.

'I don't know… I'm not keen on the idea of medication, really. I'd probably rather just try the counselling again,' I protest, despite realising what she's saying makes a lot of sense.

'Yes, I think that would be helpful. But I would recommend you try the medication as well; it will take the edge off the anxiety, so you can start to get back on track. And I think a few weeks off work will do you the world of good. I'm signing you off for three weeks – that should give the medication time to kick in – then you can come back and see me after that, to see if you're ready to go back.'

Shit. My heart races. Three weeks off work? I start to worry about what they'll be saying in the staff room. How will they cover my classes at such short notice? I suppose that's what the supply teacher agency is there for, but what an arse ache for Martin. Guilt sets in, like I'm making a fuss over nothing.

'I don't know if that's necessary…' I start.

'We need to get you back up to strength, Mr Johnson. Now, I can't make you take the meds, but I would strongly recommend it. You're an intelligent man, you can make up your own mind.' She clicks a button on the screen with her mouse and the printer whirrs into action. 'I've referred you onto the local therapists' rota so they will be in touch shortly. And here's the prescription for the medication.'

I take the piece of paper from her and stare down at the

print of the prescription. The medication is a long word that I can't even begin to try and pronounce.

'I do hope you're feeling better soon, but you know where we are if you need us, OK?'

'Thank you, doctor,' I say weakly as I get up from my chair and turn to leave the room, wondering how I'm going to tell my wife.

CHAPTER EIGHT

I feel like I've been hit by a train as I wake from the deepest of sleeps. The kind you can't pull yourself out of. It's probably just the exhaustion. But I feel like I'm inhabiting a world where there's something just ever-so-slightly beyond my recognition and no matter how hard I try to focus, it doesn't arrive. Like a forgotten dream, just out of reach.

I walk down the corridor to the staff room and flick on the lights. It's just starting to get light outside and, through the window, I can see the pale-yellow glow of the sunrise creeping out tentatively from under the horizon, beyond the car park. Wisps of grey cloud are shifting slowly across the milky morning sky and I take a deep breath to try and steady my heart rate. My mouth feels dry. Coffee, I decide.

I run my thumb and middle finger across my eyes, meeting between my eyebrows as I take another deep breath in through my nose. The steam from the first drops of coffee stings my nostrils as it trickles through the machine and into my cup. The loud whirring that follows makes me jump and I feel someone enter the room behind me. Julia, I think. It's only usually me and her in the staff room so early. I turn around to offer her a coffee.

'Laura?!' My heart races and the dryness returns to my mouth. I stumble back against the worktop and a spoon goes crashing into the sink behind me. I turn around to retrieve it and in the process knock over an empty glass milk bottle which starts rattling around like a bowling pin. 'Fuck!' I mutter under my breath as I try and gather myself then realise my coffee cup is about to spill over. I quickly stop the machine and the whirring stops as the steady trickle of coffee turns to drops.

'Sorry sir,' she giggles, putting her hand to her mouth. 'Didn't mean to startle you! I probably should have knocked.' She's standing in the doorway in opaque black tights, shorter-than-regulation grey pleated skirt and white blouse, which is open at the collar as she's not wearing her tie. Her blazer is draped over her right arm and a brown leather satchel sits awkwardly on her left shoulder as if it's about to fall off. She leans down to one side to hitch it back up.

'What are you doing here?' I look at my watch. 'You know it's only 7.30?'

'Sorry, I know we're not meant to come to the staff room but I got here early hoping I'd be able to talk to you. I could see you were in here alone, so...' Her voice trails as she looks down at her Doc Martens.

'Is everything... OK?' I ask, as I turn to the sink to fill a glass with water. She closes the door behind her and walks over to the table in the middle of the room. 'You weren't in class yesterday?'

Laura puts her bag down on the table and pulls up a chair. 'I just needed a bit of time, you know, after...' She ruffles her

47

fringe and tucks some stray hair behind her ear. 'Well, anyway, I wanted to talk to you about what you said to me, the other night, when we... were talking.' Her gaze meets mine and I feel myself starting to relax. I still have this fogginess that I woke up with, an unsettling feeling that I'm forgetting something, something I can't reach.

'What is it?' I ask, clearing my throat.

'Well, I just wanted to say thank you, really, because our chat helped me figure some things out and I'm in a better place now, I think.'

'That's... good,' I manage to say, swallowing hard and breathing out through my nose. 'So how are things, you know, with your parents?' I reason that if I just carry on as normal, then maybe things will start falling into place and I'll regain my grasp on reality. I grip onto my coffee cup in my right hand and feel the heat starting to scald my fingertips. Nervously, I examine my left hand, stretching out my fingers and focusing on the three-millimetre platinum gold band on my third finger. It's lost its original shine and there are tiny little scuff marks all over it from having worn it every day for the best part of the last five years. Meditating on it helps to bring me back to what's real.

'Well, things are still shit, you know,' she laughs. But I've come to a sort of... acceptance, I guess. Life's complicated, I suppose, and... I don't know, I guess we have to work through these tough times to really value what's good in the world. What's actually good in our lives. We all suffer, don't we?' She shrugs one shoulder nonchalantly as she picks at the skin around her thumb.

I nod and sigh through my nose. 'You're wise beyond your years, Laura.'

'That's what my dad said,' she laughs. 'I don't know, I just don't want my parents to be stuck in this... limbo. I've been grieving the loss of my family as I knew it but I guess I just came to realise I'm lucky, really... that at least they're both still around. And I want them to be happy, to make the most of their lives, even if they're not together. Not live it through gritted teeth and become resentful and cold and... I don't know, there's so much beauty in the world, right? We can't go around with our eyes closed to that just because some things don't pan out how we expect them to.'

'You're right.' I smile in wonder at how this sixteen-year-old girl has more emotional intelligence than most adults I know.

'My sister, too. You know, I could be angry at her for carrying on like nothing's happened, but why should I resent her for trying to get on with her life? It's not like she can change anything by not going to uni. It's got way beyond that point, so I should just be happy for her. And I can still visit, so...' She smiles as her voice trails off and I'm lost in her eyes. I can still detect a melancholy – a hint of regret, maybe – but she seems so much freer than she was when we last spoke.

I look at my watch, conscious that staff might soon be arriving. It's still only 7.45am. I take a sip of my coffee and breathe out through my nose, gazing absently into the blackness of the liquid, my heartrate returning almost back to normal. I look up and catch Laura looking at me, intently. Her cheeks are pink and she smiles gently. 'And how are *you*?' she asks, tilting her head to one side as she sits back in her chair.

I blink and shake my head slightly, surprised at the question. 'Oh, I'm alright, you know. Doing the days.' I laugh, nervously, as I wonder whether I should say what's on the tip of my tongue. 'I'm glad you came to see me. I mean, I'm glad... that you're doing OK.'

'Thanks,' she smiles and starts to get up from her chair. 'I, er, I got you a gift, actually. I hope that's not weird?'

'Oh?' I ask, raising an eyebrow. 'What kind of gift?'

'You'll see.' She smirks as she looks up from under her fringe. 'But it's in another room. Can I show you?'

'OK?' I say cautiously, as I wonder where we're heading, my heart starting to beat faster again.

'Come with me,' she says as she takes my hand and I feel a jolt of electricity coursing through my body. This doesn't feel right.

I breathe deeply through my nose, trying to quell the nervous energy rising from the pit of my stomach as I follow her down the corridor and towards one of the classrooms.

'Where are we going, Laura?' I ask her firmly. I look around, hoping no one can see a student leading me down a deserted corridor in the early morning. This feels so wrong, yet I can't let go of her hand.

She opens the door to the empty classroom and a sudden flash of light makes me squint and cover my eyes. Her scent hits me and I blink my eyes open.

Laura moves in close and whispers in my ear, 'It'll be OK.' She takes both my hands in hers, looking deeply into my eyes.

Suddenly she turns, letting go of my hands and leaps from the doorway into a nothingness I can't make out.

'Laura, wait!' I cry, a pain roaring through my chest and, before I realise what's happening, I leap after her, reaching desperately for her hands. I'm falling for a split second then gasp for breath as I open my eyes into the darkness of my bedroom. I'm drenched in sweat and goosebumps prick my skin like tiny needles.

'*Paul*? What is it?' Lisa asks in alarm as I rub my eyes and prop myself up in bed.

CHAPTER NINE

My heart is still racing and sweat is running down between my shoulder blades. Why is my mouth so dry? I catch my breath and rub my hands down my face. It's still dark outside but I've no idea what time it is.

'Sorry love, I was dreaming... I think.' I swallow hard, trying to steady my voice.

'About Laura?' Lisa asks. 'You were shouting her name?'

'Yeah, sorry... I don't know, it was weird. It was like she'd come to tell me she was OK. But...' I breathe out through pursed lips, realising how ludicrous this all sounds. 'It was as if she wasn't dead.'

I make out the shape of Lisa's sympathetic frown across her face. She hasn't corrected me so Laura must still be dead. My eyes ache. What the hell was all that about? I suddenly feel like I need to explain myself to Lisa.

'I was trying to help her. She'd been having a tough time at home with her parents separating and, I don't know... I just felt for her, you know, I kind of saw some of my own teenage suffering in her. We'd had a chat, that night, the night she...

died.' I bite my lip as the reality of her death, the guilt of letting her go comes flooding back, all over again. 'I'd kept her behind after class... there'd been a ruckus between her and one of the lads and I needed to talk to her. I guess I blame myself for what happened.' I stammer between trembling lips, trying not to let my pain escape. 'If I hadn't kept her back she'd have walked home with Manny. And if I'd kept her back longer, she wouldn't have got in the car and none of this would have happened...' I cover my face as I feel tears rising behind my eyes. 'But I let her go at that *precise* moment. And now she's dead. She's *dead*. And it feels like it's all my fault.'

'It's not your fault, Paul.' Lisa moves closer and strokes my hair as I rest my head listlessly on her shoulder.

I squint through blurry tears at the alarm clock on the bedside table: it's 6.43. Almost time to get up. Not that I'd be able to get back to sleep anyway.

I wipe my nose on the back of my hand. I wonder if I should tell her about the pills and the doctor's note. I can't bring myself to say the word 'medication' but I feel like she has a right to know. And if I can't tell my own wife that I've been prescribed some medication for my anxiety then what is our marriage even based on? I take a deep breath and hold the words in my throat, ready to say them out loud.

'I should start getting ready for work.' Lisa puts on her bedside lamp as she gets up and heads towards the en-suite.

'I saw Dr Rowley yesterday,' I blurt out in a now-or-never sort of way. 'Martin covered my classes for a couple of hours yesterday morning and I made an appointment.'

'Right.' Lisa nods, a quizzical frown creeping across her brow. 'And... what did she say?'

'She's prescribed me some medication.' I look up to see Lisa's eyebrows gently raised. 'I've not been feeling in control of

my mind for a few weeks now, like, a lot worse than before, so...'
I examine my fingernails before biting down on the end of my
thumb. 'And, well, what with Laura and... I just thought I
should speak to someone before it gets really out of hand. So
she gave me a prescription and put me on the referral list for
some more therapy. I took the first one last night.'

'You've started taking them already?' Lisa asks, affronted.
'Don't you think you should have told me? We've got a child
together, Paul. I need to know if you're on mind-altering
medication.'

I bristle at her tone. 'I'm telling you now, aren't I? And it's
not *mind-altering*, Lisa. It's to balance the chemicals in my
brain, so I can start feeling better. Dr Rowley said it was the best
thing, to start with, until I can start with some counselling
again.'

'Well I just hope you don't have any mad side-effects or
anything.' She walks into the en-suite and takes her toothbrush
from the cabinet above the sink. 'You know what my dad thinks
about these *happy pills*. That's probably why you're having wild
dreams! Can you still drive, while you're taking them, I mean?'

'Yeah, it's fine. Although she has signed me off work for
three weeks.'

'Three weeks?!' she splutters between mouthfuls of tooth-
paste. 'Wow. So are you not going in today then?'

'I don't know, I feel like I'll be better just going in and
waiting 'til the Christmas break. I'll see how I feel then. Plus I
don't want to leave Martin in the lurch. Not on top of everything else.'

'Well, see how you get on today then I guess and take it
from there.'

It feels like she's talking about test-driving a new car, rather
than me trying to get a handle on my spiralling thoughts. Just

when I catch a glimmer of empathy, it slips through my fingers. Maybe I just feel things more deeply than other people. I've always erred on the side of melancholy.

I creep downstairs and make myself a coffee. By some miracle Emilia is still asleep. One more day to get through before the weekend, I think optimistically. Lisa's first meeting isn't until 9.30 so she's agreed to drop Emilia off at nursery this morning, so I can talk to Martin before class.

The coffee smacks me in the face and I have a rare and fleeting regret that I ever gave up smoking. I could really do with a cigarette right now.

At school, the mood remains sombre. It's another crisp, sunny day and, although it's the week before we break up for the winter holidays, it feels odd that there's a Christmas tree in the main foyer. I think of Laura's family and how Christmas will never be the same for them. The pills seem to have put me in a weird dream-like state where I can't really feel much but I'm still constantly on edge; my entire consciousness consumed by thoughts of Laura. I wouldn't have thought they'd have an effect already.

I head to Martin's office and knock gently on the door. I know he's in as I've seen his car in the car park. I'm glad I can leave my beaten-up old Astra around the corner and walk rather than parking it next to his gleaming, racing green Jaguar.

'Come in, come in,' he bellows and I hear him closing one of his filing cabinet drawers. 'Ah, Paul, good to see you.'

'Morning, Martin. You got a minute?' I ask, as I stand in the doorway. I've decided to tell Martin about the medication. I was vague about why I needed to see the doctor yesterday but I figure it's best to be open with him. Just maybe not about the doctor's note. There's no point telling him if I'm going to keep coming into work, I figure.

'Of course, come on in. Take a seat.' He gestures to the large swivel chair at the desk opposite his. His office is gloomy and I glance towards the venetian blinds which are almost completely closed. He notices and walks over to let some light in. A shaft of sunlight shows up the dust hovering in the air. I sit down in the chair and rest my satchel on my knees.

'How are you doing today?' he asks as he sits down and pours himself a coffee from the percolator on his desk. 'Do you want one?'

'Er... no, thanks.' I gesture with a shake of my hand. 'I, erm... yeah I'm feeling OK, I think, you know, all things considered.' I offer a knowing smile as I notice the darker-than-usual circles around his eyes. He looks like he hasn't shaved this morning.

'Well, good, I'm pleased to hear it. It's going to take a while for the... er, the dust to settle, with the students, I mean.'

'Of course.' I nod and shuffle awkwardly in my seat. 'So I... I managed to see the doctor, yesterday, when you took my lessons. Thanks, for that, by the way.'

'Not a problem. And what did he say, the doctor?'

'Er, *she*...' I take a breath, but lose my nerve at the last second. 'She said I should probably get some physio, for my shoulder. But I've got some painkillers for the meantime.' I realise I'm wringing my hands.

'I see. Well, that's a step in the right direction, isn't it?' I'm conscious he can see right through me but I can't bring myself to tell him the truth.

'Er, yeah, I started taking them yesterday, so, I... I think they'll do the trick.'

'Right you are. Well, you know where I am, Paul, if you need anything,' he says with a knowing look.

'Yep, thanks, Martin. I appreciate it.' I start to rise from my chair and he heads towards the door to open it.

'Not at all, not at all. Nearly the weekend, eh?' He winks as he gives me a firm-but-friendly pat on the back and I leave the room wondering whether I'm doing him a disservice by not mentioning my medication. And a fleeting doubt tangles in my stomach as I deliberate whether I should have told him about the sick note. I didn't think it would do my head of department chances much good. Martin is kind and understanding but he comes from a generation of men who are expected to 'soldier on', and I get the impression he might start questioning my fitness for the job if I spring three weeks off work on him. And anyway, once the pills start taking effect, I'll be back on form, I tell myself. This time it'll be different. If I tell him I've been signed off, he'll almost certainly insist I stay at home for fear of Ofsted finding out. And I don't know if kicking around on my own at home is so good for me at the minute.

The kids start to arrive and I check in with them all quietly to see how they're doing. Looking for clues that any of them might need referring to the school counsellors. It seems that they're all still in shock but I wonder what exactly it is I should be looking out for. Where's the textbook on this kind of stuff?

I take out the week's register from my satchel which is now looking pretty dogeared, and prop myself up against the desk at the front of the class, legs outstretched, gripping onto my coffee.

'James?'

'Yes.'

'Erin?'

'Yes.'

'Jo?'

'Yep.'

'Laura...' My voice trails as I realise I'm reading this on autopilot. I look up at the empty desk where Laura used to sit. Manny Dhindsa's chin begins to tremble as she fights back tears and Erin Robson leans over to console her.

'Sorry guys, I'm not really thinking straight.' I bring my hands up to my eyes and draw them slowly down my face. 'That was an awful mistake. I guess it's going to take a while before we all get used to the idea that Laura's not coming back.' I have a feeling that I am not dealing with this particularly well. I already can't wait for today to be over.

I see Julia in the staff room at morning break as I top up my bloodstream with more coffee. My head is banging, probably from too much caffeine and too much thinking. My eyes ache again. I wonder how long this feeling of grief will remain physically painful.

'How's it going, Ju?'

'Yeah, alright... I think. Didn't sleep much last night. How about you?'

'Yeah, same. You could say I'm ready for the weekend.' I want to tell her about the pills I've started taking but I just can't find the words. I try and straighten out my hair for something to do with my hands. I can't remember actually looking in the mirror yet this morning. I must look like shit.

'Yeah.' Julia squeezes my shoulder.

'Ju, can I tell you something?' My stomach churns.

'Course yer can.'

I clear my throat, ready to tell her about the prescription. I look her in the eye but it doesn't come. I improvise.

'I had a mad dream last night, that Laura wasn't dead. She came to see me; we were talking about her parents and that. Honestly it was as real as me and you here now. Which kinda makes me wonder if *this* is real.' I point at us both. Maybe if I set the scene, I can lead up to telling her. 'I'm just going round in circles.'

Julia sighs and smiles at me with sad eyes. 'You've had a massive shock, Paul.'

'Yeah, I know.' I decide to start with half of the story. 'Listen, between you and me, I went to see the doctor yesterday and she signed me off for three weeks with, er... stress. But I'm going to see how I am between now and the holidays. I've not told Martin. He thinks I was seeing someone about my shoulder yesterday.'

Julia takes a sip of her coffee and looks at me over her purple-rimmed glasses. I swear she has a different pair for every day of the week. 'Well, I knew he was covering your lessons but I didn't like to ask. You sure that's the right thing to do, not telling him?'

'I dunno, probably not, but he's got enough on his plate. And I'm better while I'm here, to be honest.'

'Fair enough, I won't say owt. Just keep me posted, yeah? And you know you can talk to me, don't you? Don't keep it bottled up.'

'Yeah, cheers Ju.' I'm about to tell her about the medication but she changes the subject.

'You might not be feeling up to it but Martin mentioned there's a special service on at St. Matthew's on Sunday morning. I might go along if you want to join me?'

My stomach starts to churn. The thought of having to deal

with this grief publicly, in front of Laura's friends and family, makes me panic. I exhale gently through my mouth to calm myself.

'Oh I don't know, Ju, I don't know if I'm...' I stop mid-sentence when I realise what I'm about to say appears cowardly and selfish. I don't feel up to it, but who does? Certainly not Laura's parents. I get the impression that I will be expected to go. 'I'm not really a churchgoer,' I protest weakly.

Julia reads me like a book. 'Well, no pressure, just let me know. I can pick you up if yer want.' She places her cup in the sink. 'Right, I'd better get to the studio, I'll catch yer later.'

I can't think of anything worse than going to church for prayers on Sunday. Prayers aren't going to bring Laura back. It all feels a bit, well, futile. But if it brings comfort for Laura's friends and family then I suppose it's worthwhile. I just hope I can hold it together.

CHAPTER TEN

Lisa's already home when I get back after picking Emilia up. We always have a takeaway on a Friday and I see a bottle of chardonnay has already been opened.

'Hey, y'alright?' she asks me, as she picks Emilia up. 'Shall we take your coat off, poppet?'

'Yeah, alright. Glad it's the weekend.' I sigh as I go to hang my coat in the hallway.

'What do you fancy tonight, Chinese or Indian?' She waves two takeaway menus and puts them down on the side. It feels weird carrying on as if this morning's conversation didn't happen. But we're doing our best, I guess.

'Erm... I don't mind, you choose,' I mumble absently. I don't really feel like eating. I just want to sleep so I can stop thinking.

'I think I fancy curry. You want some of this?' She picks up the bottle of wine and tops up her glass. I'm not a big drinker these days. Alcohol tends to amplify my anxiety rather than anaesthetise it. But I guess one can't hurt, maybe it'll even help me sleep.

'Yeah, go on then, just a small one,' I say as I head slowly into the kitchen with Emilia waddling in front of me, arms stretched up over her head for balance. I hold my hands just above hers, ready to catch her fingertips if she wobbles over. 'How was your day?' I ask as Lisa hands me a large glass of straw-coloured wine. 'I said a small one!' I remark, holding up the glass.

'Oh come on, it's Friday!' She frowns jokingly. 'And yeah, had a good day thanks. Met with the client on that new project I was telling you about. Rich and I took them to that new French place for lunch and we didn't get back to the office til half three!' she laughs, taking another sip of wine.

'Lovely,' I say, trying to sound enthusiastic. 'What was it like, the French place?'

'Yeah, food was amazing and the service was really good. They've done a great job of the décor too. I think Steve and Jeff were impressed, I guess they think we don't have places like that up here, but they're used to it in London. We had escargots for the table to start and Jeff said they were better than the ones he had in Paris a couple of weeks ago!' I search the depths of my O Level French to try and remember what *escargots* are. Snails, I think? I daren't ask for fear of looking like a philistine in comparison to these cosmopolitan new clients of hers.

'Cool,' I manage to say as she pauses for breath before continuing. I scoop Emilia up and feed her legs into her high-chair as she fights against me.

'So then we all had steak frites for main and it was... *amazing*.' She puts both hands out in front of her as if this steak was some kind of showstopper. Emilia is grizzling but Lisa doesn't seem to notice as she perches up on the breakfast bar stool to continue telling me all about her *amazing* lunch. I secure the bib around her neck before heading to the microwave to take out the batch of homemade casserole I've just defrosted for Emilia's tea. 'We'd already had a bottle of Chablis with the escargots and then Rich suggested we get a bottle of red to go with the steak so we were looking at the wine list and Jeff was like, 'Oh my God, they've got my *favourite* Chateauneuf du Pape!' so we *had* to get a bottle of that!' she laughs, shaking her head at the apparent hilarity of it all. I'm beginning to realise why it feels like Lisa's had a head start on the wine.

The casserole is still frozen in the middle and Emilia is getting hungrier by the second, banging her plastic spoon on the table and shouting with increasing volume.

'It's coming, poppet!' I sing in her direction while I frantically break up the icy mush with a fork before chucking it in the microwave for another two minutes. 'Won't be long now!' I search the cupboards for some kind of finger food I can give her in the meantime. Nothing too filling else she won't eat her casserole. I settle on a couple of breadsticks which I snap in half and place in front of her while I watch the timer dial slowly creep around to 'done'.

'So was it a good meeting then, with the client?' I chip in, trying to remain engaged in Lisa's story whilst appeasing Emilia. The microwave pings and I realise I've been holding my breath. My shoulders are tense. I open the door and take out the bowl, testing the temperature by cautiously lifting a spoon of casserole to my lips. 'Shit!' I gasp. 'That's hotter than the sun!'

'Yeah... I mean, we didn't really go into much about the actual project, it was more of a... business development exercise, I guess.' She shrugs with a nonchalant smirk. 'Rich was really pleased with how it went, though.'

'Oh, well that's good, then.' I'm not sure what else to say. I grab the milk from the fridge and stir some into the casserole to cool it down. Emilia has gummed the breadsticks down to a paste that's now smeared all over the table. I check the casserole again and it's a bit cooler so I sit down at the table, blowing a spoonful of it before testing it again on my top lip.

'Yeah, it's just good to get to know them a bit better, you know.' She swings her legs from the stool and takes another swig of wine. 'Do you want a top up?' she asks, as she pours some more into her glass. I offer Emilia some of the now-cooled casserole. She tentatively tastes it before pulling a face but eventually goes for the rest of the spoon.

'Oh, I've still got some I think, thanks,. I look over my shoulder, spotting my untouched glass on the worktop next to the hob. I offer Emilia another spoon but she turns her head away. I sigh. 'Come on poppet, this is your favourite,' I reassure her weakly. *For fuck's sake*, I seethe silently. There's a pain at the back of my head, right at the top of my neck, radiating down between my shoulder blades. Maybe I need that wine after all. 'Could you just pass it to me, actually?' I ask Lisa, nodding towards my wine glass.

'Hmm?' She looks up from her phone that she's picked up off the side.

'My wine, please?'

'Oh, yeah...' She reaches across for my glass and leans over to pass it to me. 'Here you go.'

I take a long gulp before resorting to the aeroplane method with Emilia's casserole.

I wake up to a searing pain down the left side of my neck and my tongue is stuck to the roof of my mouth. I sit up and realise I'm on the sofa in the front room and my head spins. I look at my watch, 4.37am. I'm still in my shirt and chinos; my leather belt has been digging into my hip. Everything hurts.

Lisa must have taken herself off to bed and I see she had draped a blanket over me, which is now on the floor. I search for a glass of water in the dark, the orange glow of the streetlamp outside the front window just illuminating the room through the venetian blinds enough for me to be able to make out shapes. There's no water. I notice two empty wine bottles on the coffee table and I've no idea how much of that was drunk by me. But from my headache I'm guessing it was more than I should have had. For fuck's sake. I knew the wine would be a mistake. I get up and walk into the kitchen. My back is on fire. I hate falling asleep on the sofa, it never ends well.

I flick the small light under the extractor hood on and open the cupboard to reach for a glass. A loud vibration on the worktop makes me jump and I notice the green light of Lisa's mobile phone illuminate the screen.

'*1 message received,*' it says.

Who the hell is messaging her at this time? My thumb instinctively hovers over the button to click 'read' but I hesitate. I can't read her messages, it's the ultimate invasion of privacy. I've never done it in the whole time we've been together. I stop and wonder what she would do in this situation. My curiosity gets the better of me and, before I know it, I've pressed the button and the screen flicks to her inbox. RICHARD, it says next to the little unopened envelope symbol. My stomach drops to the floor and I squint at the screen. Richard? From work? Why is he messaging Lisa at half four in the morning? On a Saturday? I feel like I'm in a scene of *Eastenders* but refuse to think the worst. Such a cliché. I'm desperate to know what his message says but if I read it, she'll know. And what's worse? Discovering my wife's having an affair by betraying her trust or it turning out to be nothing and her knowing that I don't trust her? I don't know the answer, right now. An emptiness rolls around inside me. I rationalise that it's probably some emergency at the office, the alarm going off or something. Anyway, she wouldn't leave her phone lying around if she was having an affair. Surely? I put her phone back where I found it and lock the screen.

I fill the glass from the tap and down the best part of a pint of icy water in one go. It sends a sharp ache into my back teeth. My eyes hurt. I'm knackered, I need to get to bed. I just hope I don't wake Emilia; I could really do with a good couple of hours.

You won't wake Emilia because she's dead. I shake my head. No. Not now, I plead with myself. I'm exhausted, I just need to sleep. I know the thoughts are only creeping in because I'm so tired. And the wine probably hasn't helped either, as predicted. *Emilia is dead. She's dead. Go and see for yourself.*

I creep into her room and look closely for the rise and fall of her chest. I panic and move closer, squinting in the darkness, holding my own breath, concentrating so hard on looking for hers. I exhale deeply as I see the light movement, up and down, up and down. My shoulders fall from around my ears. She's not dead, she's asleep, safe in her cot. I imagine what it would be like to find her dead in her cot. My eyes prick with acid tears. *Just pull yourself together, for fuck's sake.*

Then I think of Laura. Her parents getting the call. Seeing her in the hospital. Touching her cold skin. Having to leave her there. How could they leave her? My blood runs cold and I need to sit down. Goosebumps spread all over my body and I feel lightheaded. My heart is racing. Why is this happening to me? I wonder if anyone else has this constant internal battle. And how do they cope?

I wake up on Saturday morning – again – to a blinding headache. But this time it's light outside. I look over at the radio alarm clock and the blocky red numbers tell me it's 10.47am. At least I've managed to sleep, I think, although it hasn't made me feel much better. I can hear giggling downstairs and there's a smell of coffee wafting through the house. I get up and wrap myself in the thick grey towelling dressing gown that Lisa got me last Christmas, before I head downstairs.

'Daddddaaaaaaa,' Emilia chirps as I walk through to the lounge. I scoop her up and sleepily hold her close, taking in the scent of her hair.

'Morning,' Lisa says, smiling. 'I thought I'd let you have a lie in. Seems like you needed it.'

'Thanks. Yeah, I woke up at half four on the sofa. How much wine did I drink? I feel rough.' I rub the back of my head and wince.

'Well we finished that bottle that was open, and then had another, so we probably had about a bottle each,' she says, wrinkling her nose. 'Although I'd had a head start, so you probably only had three-quarters of a bottle.'

'Right.' I squint, wondering how on earth she seems so fresh on that much wine when I feel like death. Death. I wonder what it actually feels like.

'We were just getting ready to go out for a walk, you coming?'

'Yeah, I could do with some fresh air, I think.' I wonder whether I should ask her about Richard's late-night SMS. I have to. I clear my throat. 'Your phone was going off in here last night when I was getting a glass of water. Looks like someone was trying to get hold of you?' I look at her questioningly but trying not to appear accusatory.

'Oh yeah, it was Richard, I've spoken to him. The alarm was going off in the office; I'd locked up last night and he wondered if I was awake so he could pop by and get the keys but he sorted it in the end.'

There you go. A perfectly reasonable explanation. One less thing to worry about. But now I feel guilty about doubting her. I need to pull myself together.

———

We head out into the freezing cold late-morning sunshine and I start to feel a bit more normal. My headache is subsiding and the seasickness of my hangover is starting to fade. I breathe in the crisp air and enjoy the sun on my face. Emilia is asleep in the pushchair, all wrapped up in her snowsuit.

'So next Saturday, are you still OK to pick Mum and Dad up from the station?' My face must be blank as Lisa reminds me that her mum and dad are coming to stay for a few days over Christmas. 'It's just that it's my work's Christmas party on the Friday night so I probably won't be in a fit state to drive,' she laughs. 'And it'll be my turn for a lie in.'

I'd totally forgotten they were coming. Friday is the last day of term before the Christmas break and we don't know yet when Laura's funeral might be.

'Errr yeah that'll be fine, I'm sure. I reckon Laura's funeral will be early the week after so I'll have to leave you to it at some point. Thursday's Christmas Eve so I would have thought it'll be before then.'

'Christ, what a shit time for a funeral. I mean, there's never a good time to bury one of your kids but a few days before Christmas has to be the *worst*.'

'Yeah,' I agree, absent-mindedly. She's right.

'I might pop out tonight if that's alright?' Lisa asks airily. 'Emma and Gurpreet are having drinks at the wine bar and they asked if I wanted to join.'

'Yeah, fine.' I shrug. The thought of spending the evening alone doesn't fill me with joy but I'm never one to stop Lisa doing what she wants to do. And I don't suppose I'm particularly sparkling company at the minute anyway.

'Cool, I'll head out after Emilia's in bed, then. I think they're planning on having food so I won't want any tea.'

'Ready meal for one then,' I retort, sarcastically.

'Don't be like that, I won't go if it's a problem?' she barks.

'It's not a *problem*, Lisa. I'm just, well, you know I'm struggling at the minute that's all. I could do with a bit of company, moral support, you know?'

'Look I know it's awful and you've had a horrible shock, but she wasn't *family,* was she? You've got to be prepared for these things, statistically, I mean. You're going to be lucky if you get through your career without something like this happening, really. Life goes on, doesn't it?'

I look at her face. When did my wife become so cold hearted? After everything we spoke about yesterday, I can't quite believe she's behaving like this.

'Wow, Lis, that's... harsh?' I mutter, still processing what she just said.

'I'm just saying, we can't put our lives on hold just because someone you know died. I know it's tragic, it is, really. But we've got to get on with it, haven't we?'

'She was sixteen, Lisa. Sixteen years old. Someone's *daughter*. Imagine...' My voice trails as I can't actually bring myself to imagine. 'And anyway, it's not just what happened with Laura. I was struggling before all that.'

The silence walks alongside us. I'm too exhausted to convince her that I think my feelings are justified, in the circumstances. She barely seems to notice. *Maybe she should have died instead.* I shake my head and hope Lisa doesn't notice. Christ, what a thing to think?! She's your wife. The mother of your daughter. I know these thoughts aren't my own, but I wonder why my brain has to torment me like this. I could really do with the referral for the therapy coming through soon. I need to talk to someone before I get trapped inside my own head.

Lisa's always been the pragmatic, unsentimental half of our relationship. But then I wonder if I'm being unfair. Perhaps 'rational' would be kinder. She has an ability to cut through the emotion of a situation and see the wood for the trees. Not over-think, like me. But then I guess we complement each other. I guess that's why we're together.

CHAPTER ELEVEN

'So the service is at 10.30 on Tuesday morning, at St. Matthew's on Matlock Road. I suggest we all gather at 10.15 in the church-yard, so we're there in plenty of time to congregate together, as a team,' Martin announces at our staff meeting on the last day of term. It feels like we're meeting for a football match.

'Is there a wake afterwards, do you know?' Chris enquires from the back of the room.

'There is, I believe, but I think it's appropriate for us to simply attend the funeral service and leave the wake to the family and close friends. It'll no doubt be a massive turnout.'

Chris nods in agreement. I'm relieved. The last thing I want to be doing afterwards is exchanging pleasantries with Laura's aunts and uncles, as selfish as that might seem.

'What's the dress code? Families often ask for colourful clothing at kids' funerals, don't they?' asks Julia. *Kids' funerals*. Two words that should never have to be spoken together. I need to get my suit dry-cleaned.

'They haven't said, so I think we need to stick to the stan-dard black, to be on the safe side.'

'We've made a donation in the name of the school to the air ambulance fund, rather than sending flowers,' Martin continues. 'And I've been asked to give a short address about Laura. Unless you'd rather do it, Paul, as her tutor?' He looks up at me over his glasses.

'No!' I must look visibly alarmed as the thought of having to do that makes me feel sick. I try and soften my response. 'No, it's OK, thanks Martin. I think it'd be better coming from you.'

'Right you are.' He rises from his perch on the edge of the staff room table. 'I think that's it then. So 10.15 on Tuesday at St. Matthew's. And I don't think it would be inappropriate for us to have a very quiet drink together afterwards, somewhere out of town perhaps?'

There are some nods and mumbles of approval and we all disperse for the last two lessons of term.

I pick up some oranges from the bottom shelf and put them into my basket. Lisa's parents are coming tomorrow so I swing by the little Tesco to stock up on essentials before picking Emilia up from nursery. As I rise, I'm face-to-face with Lisa's friend, Emma.

'Ey up Paul, y'alright?' she asks cheerily. I've not seen her for ages. I wonder why it is that we don't really hang out with her and Pete anymore.

'Not bad ta, Emma, how you doing? Not seen you for a while.'

'Yeah, alright thanks. I know, time flies, dunt it?'

'Sure does. How was the wine bar the other night? Lisa was a bit hungover on Sunday!' I chuckle. But Emma's face is blank.

'You were out together on Saturday night weren't you, you and Lis and Gurpreet?' I try and fill in the gaps for her.

'Err, oh yeah, well no, actually, I couldn't make it in the end. Lewis was throwing up so I had to stay in with him.' I can't help but look at Emma with a hint of suspicion.

'Oh right, she didn't mention it. Is he alright now?'

'Oh yeah, right as rain now, these toddlers are always bringing summat home from nursery, aren't they?' she laughs nervously.

'Yeah, tell me about it. Speaking of which, I'd better get going to pick Emilia up. Nice to see you, Emma. Hope you have a good Christmas.'

'You too Paul, take care, won't you?' She squeezes my arm as she walks past. I don't know if I'm imagining her pitying eyes.

I try and shake off the sinking feeling she has left me with. Was she telling the truth about Lewis being ill? How come Lisa didn't mention it? I hate this merry-go-round of mistrust. Maybe I'm just exhausted from the constant battle with my own mind. Maybe Emma knows something is going on between Lisa and Richard? Or maybe she has no idea but didn't want to put her foot in it and get her mate into trouble. Or maybe, just maybe, she was telling the truth and I need to get a grip of myself.

———

My mind is elsewhere the next morning as I'm getting Emilia dressed and ready to pick Lisa's parents up from the train station. I let Lisa lie in as I know she didn't come home from her work's Christmas party until gone 3am. And from the smell of stale alcohol in our bedroom this morning it seems that she got her money's worth of the free wine. I can't help but replay the conversation with Emma over and over in my mind, looking for any clues I might have missed. Emma and Lisa have been friends since they were at school so they're thick as thieves and seem to instinctively have each other's backs covered.

I get up to fill the kettle and hear footsteps on the stairs. The kitchen door creaks open and Lisa walks in, looking decidedly worse for wear.

'Morning love, d'you want tea?'

'Urgh. No, not yet thanks.' She heads over to kiss Emilia on the forehead and slumps into the sofa in the corner.

'You OK? How was last night?' I examine her face as she replies.

'Yeah,' she says, looking away, 'It was brilliant, thanks. Venue was great and the food was nice, we had a really good time.'

'Who was there?' I try to ask as casually as possible which makes my voice inadvertently go up an octave.

'Err... me, Darren, Bhav, Sophie, Richard and Lucy. We ended up in the jazz bar til kicking out time.'

'All of you?'

'Nah, just me, Bhav and Rich I think in the end.'

'Oh right, lovely. Glad you had a nice time.' I pour myself a cup of tea and check my watch. Need to get off soon to pick the in-laws up. 'You sure you don't want one?'

'No I'm alright thanks. I feel a bit queasy to be honest.' She looks pale.

I can't wait another moment; I have to ask her. 'I, erm... I bumped into Emma last night, in Tesco.'

'Oh yeah, is she alright? Is Lewis better?' My heart skips. So she was telling the truth. Unless Emma has tipped her off already.

'Er, yeah, she said so. I didn't realise she didn't make it out last Saturday. You never mentioned?'

'Yeah, Lewis was throwing up so she had to bail,' she explains nonchalantly.

'You didn't mention it? I thought it was the three of you?' I press, a bit annoyed that she's so cool about it.

'Well yeah it was, until Emma bailed at the last minute. These things happen, don't they? Especially when you've got kids.' She seems a bit irritated but I can't let it drop.

'I just looked a bit of a tit, that's all, when I asked her if she'd had a nice time at the wine bar. She'll think we don't talk to each other!' I snort, sarcastically.

'For fuck's sake Paul, what do you want me to say?! Sorry I didn't mention it, but I didn't think it was particularly important! And why does it matter what anyone thinks anyway?'

'I'm just saying, it was a bit embarrassing.' I shrug but wonder how I've ended up as the one in the wrong. 'And, as it happens, we don't really speak to each other at the minute, anyway, do we?' I continue, immediately regretting getting into this now, the next four days with her parents looming. This will probably make it even more awkward than usual.

'Well it's been busy, hasn't it, since I started working full time? It's going to take a while until we get into a proper routine with it. I'm doing my best!' she shouts back, raising a hand to her forehead.

'I just can't help but wonder why you're being so distant with me at the minute? You took absolutely no interest in my head of department application and you've basically told me to pull myself together over Laura's death! And now your friends are filling in the gaps for me in Tesco?! What is it, Lis? Why are you pushing me away?'

'Oh God, I can't be arsed with this *now* Paul. Jesus!' She

throws her arms up in the air. 'I'm hungover and my parents are on their way. Can we just drop it?!'

'Fine, I'm going anyway.' I neck the last of my tea and put my cup down on the side, a little too firmly so it looks like I'm sulking. Which I probably am, to be fair. 'Shall I take Emilia with me then?'

'Yes. Please. And I can get a shower.' She stomps off upstairs and I head to the hallway to get our coats.

Well, that went well. Maybe this is just what married life evolves into when you've got kids? But what happened to 'for better or worse'?

CHAPTER TWELVE

I take my black suit from the built-in wardrobes and hang it on the back of our bedroom door. There was no time to get it dry-cleaned, what with picking Lisa's parents up, but I give it a brush and it looks alright. I feel inside the inner pocket and pull out the order of service from my grandma's funeral last year. It's my only black suit and it seems to be reserved for funerals these days.

My reflection takes me by surprise as I button up my shirt in front of the mirror. I look absolutely knackered, as if I've aged ten years in the last few months. Maybe I should shave, that might help. I grab my electric shaver and start to glide it across my chin and up along my jawline. That's slightly better.

The suit goes on and I start to feel emotional. *Not already*, I think. I take out the silver cufflinks that Mum bought me for my thirtieth and press them through the holes in the shirt cuffs. The navy polka dot handkerchief that Lisa bought me on our wedding day catches my eye from my drawer in the dressing table and I put it in my inner pocket. Just in case. Although if I get through today without shedding a tear it will be a miracle.

I head downstairs and take my black brogues from the cupboard under the stairs. Lisa comes into the kitchen just as I'm polishing them.

'You look smart.' She kisses me on the cheek with a sad smile.

'Thanks.' I smile back but don't feel anything. We haven't really had much chance to talk properly since our row on Saturday morning what with George and Miriam being here so it feels like we're just going through the motions.

'What time you setting off?' she asks, filling the kettle and taking three cups out of the cupboard.

'Oh Julia's picking me up at ten. I thought you guys might want to head out in the car somewhere today so I figured it'd be best to get a lift.'

'Ah OK, thanks. Yeah, we might pop out then, Mum and Dad said they'd like to go to Chatsworth at some point.' I've dodged a bullet there I think, the annual ritual of traipsing round some entitled aristocrat's fancy house not exactly being my idea of fun. Am I supposed to be impressed? Then I remember what it is I'm doing instead. 'I guess you'll be back after the wake, will you?'

'We're going to give the wake a miss. But we were thinking of having a quiet drink somewhere out of town afterwards so I'll probably be back mid-afternoonish.'

'How are you feeling?' she asks, with a kindness I've not seen of late.

She notices my jaw clenching, and puts her arms around me. 'I...' I breathe out through my nose and purse my lips. 'I just don't know how I'm going to get through it, Lis. Seeing her coffin, her parents, all the kids from school. It's going to be awful.'

'Yeah, it will.'

I notice Julia's car outside and give Lisa a kiss on the cheek. 'Right, Julia's here, I'll see you later on.'

'OK love, hope it all goes OK.'

The air is cold and damp, as if rain is suspended in the air, like tears waiting to fall. I climb into the passenger side of Julia's Ford Fiesta and close the door, except it doesn't catch properly. The upbeat Christmas song on the radio feels incongruous with our mood.

'Sorry, bit dodgy that one. Try again.'

I open the door and slam it shut. This time it works. I glance back at the house and see Miriam standing at the window, watching. She doesn't wave.

'There you go. You alright?'

'Think so. You?' I'm shivering, partly from cold and partly from nervous energy trying to escape.

'Yeah, I guess. Shit day for it, eh?' The wipers squeak as the rain starts to come down.

'Yeah.'

It's only a ten-minute drive to St. Matthew's so we should be there in plenty of time to meet the others.

'Where you gonna park?' I ask because details help me feel calm. A distraction gifted by the mundane.

'Behind Co-Op I think, then we can just walk through the jitty to the churchyard?'

'Good plan. It's free behind Co-Op int it?'

'Yeah, free for two hours then you have to pay. But we'll be done by then, won't we? Then Martin mentioned maybe going to the White Hart down on Carsington Lane?'

'Yeah, sounds good. I'm gonna need a drink.'

'Me too. I haven't worn this dress since my auntie's funeral in May.'

'Yeah, I found my grandma's order of service in my pocket from last year.'

We turn onto the high street and into the Co-Op car park. It's rammed – last minute Christmas shoppers are probably taking advantage of the two hours' free parking – but Julia skilfully manoeuvres into one of the last spaces. There are probably a few others going to the funeral parked in here too.

Julia pulls out a large black umbrella from the boot of her car and we walk under it together, through the jitty and up the tree-lined path of the churchyard. I see other mourners gathered in small groups and the vicar at the door ushering people through the porch. A large wooden-framed photo of Laura sits on an easel and my heart skips a beat. She must be seven or eight, smiling at the camera and wearing a pair of colourful sunglasses. There's a sharp pain in my stomach as I think of Emilia. *Laura's dead because of you.*

I breathe in sharply and hold my breath to stop myself crumbling. I spot Martin and nod to Julia over in his direction. His face looks ashen against his black suit. I don't ever remember seeing him wear a black suit. And I've still not seen him without a tie on.

A group of us take a pew towards the centre of the church; it's already starting to fill up despite us being early. I can't stop shivering. There's a playlist of what I assume were some of Laura's favourite songs playing softly in the background, a mixture of Spice Girls and Backstreet Boys blended with Fleetwood Mac and The Cure. A memory of her coming into school in a Def Leppard t-shirt on 'wear your favourite band t-shirt to school day' in Year 8 makes me catch my breath. None of the other kids knew who Def Leppard were but she chatted excitedly to me for ages about the merits of their long-awaited *Hysteria* album. My heart aches in my chest and try to regulate my breathing. I spot a few students accompanied by their parents. This will be the first funeral some of them have attended. It shouldn't be like this. I wonder what sort of an impact this will have on them as they grow up into adults. What will it do to them?

The church fills quickly and, as I look behind me, the sea of desperately sad faces gives me goosebumps. It feels like a bad dream.

'Please stand,' the vicar announces solemnly and gestures with both arms outstretched, palms raised to the sky.

I swallow hard and smooth down my tie as I rise. The first melancholy piano chords take my breath away, as I recognise the song to which Laura's white wooden coffin is being carried in. Tears burn my eyes as I try to contain them but I've got no chance. They spill over then stream down my cheeks as I anticipate the opening lines of Nick Cave and The Bad Seeds' *Into My Arms*. It's one of my favourite songs. It's as though I can feel my heart breaking.

It's more than I can bear. The tears won't stop. Seeing her coffin, knowing that she's in there, wishing I could turn back time and keep her behind longer so she didn't leave at that exact moment. The van would have been long gone. She'd still be here. My ears start ringing as I feel the blood rush to my head. *It's your fault.*

'I shouldn't have let her go.' I realise I'm thinking out loud as I try and catch my breath.

'Come on, mate.' Julia puts her hand on my shoulder. I wipe my eyes in an attempt to gather myself, breathing slowly through pursed lips. Every fibre of me is shaking.

I wonder if Laura's parents believe in God.

I take out the navy polka dot handkerchief from my pocket and pinch my nose. The sight of Laura's parents and sister walking, hand in hand, behind the coffin leaves a pain in my heart that I worry won't ever go away. I don't know how they can possibly do this. A vision of Lisa and me in their shoes, following an imaginary tiny white coffin flashes into my mind and I suddenly feel like I might throw up.

The service is a blur. People often talk about feeling 'numb' to the point that it feels like a cliché. Today is the closest I've ever been to feeling numb; this ethereal state where my mind feels detached from my body, almost as if I'm watching all of this happen from somewhere else. And still not quite able to believe or fully grasp that Laura is dead. A body in a box, with no signs of life, no words left to speak, no thoughts left to think, no blood coursing through veins. How did it come to this?

I think back to my first day of teaching at Melbury High, when I first met my tutor group. Monday 5th September 1994. They all looked so small. And so terrified. As was I, if I'm honest, but I had to pretend I had it all together. I'd been teaching for a couple of years at my first school but I'd never had my own tutor group before and the pressure seemed immense. I told myself it was normal to feel nervous, it was only because I cared so much, about these kids, about their futures. But now I'm surrounded by them, all of us cloaked in a grief so incomprehensible it makes me question what the point of it all is. And one of them is never coming back.

Laura was always such a high-spirited character to have around, to the point that some of my fellow teachers found her too loud and vivacious for the classroom. But I loved her energy, her curiosity and her appetite for learning new things. I guess that's why I'd become so worried about her recently, her mischievous spark having disappeared and her interest in lessons dwindling. I'm hit by a wave of sadness as I realise she spent what turned out to be her last few weeks on earth worrying about her parents' divorce. Her silent turmoil, I remember it well. If only we could all live each day as if it were our last.

'Anyone would think she can do no wrong, this *Laura*,' Lisa said to me one night as I was recounting a heated debate a handful of the class had got into in one of our PSE lessons about the Battle of Orgreave during the 1984 miners' strikes. 'Would you have let Andy Smithurst behave like that and get away with it?'

'Well,' I defended, although I realised she had a point. 'She just has a way of articulating her points that the others don't seem to be capable of just yet. But, yeah, I guess her rant about the police was a bit much, maybe.'

'You don't want to set yourself up for any accusations of favouritism, Paul,' she retorted, looking at me with those raised eyebrows, as she marched off to top her wine glass up. 'People will talk, you know.' I thought she must be joking but her snide remarks left me uneasy.

As we emerge from the church into the still-dismal late-December weather, I realise I was not an active participant in Laura's funeral but I'm so relieved it's over. I don't remember much that was said in the eulogy, the poems, Martin's address. I was there in body but my mind was elsewhere. Memories of Laura, trying desperately to fight thoughts from the darkest corners of my self-destructive imagination, blaming myself for her death. And batting away the creeping suspicion that my wife is having an affair with her boss. *It's only what you deserve. You've brought this on yourself.*

I shake my head and touch both cufflinks twice. It doesn't feel quite right so I touch them both again, twice, making sure this time I think of Emilia and Lisa safe and healthy and happy. I smooth down my tie twice then catch Julia watching me.

'Alright?' She squints at me cautiously. 'That was tough, hey?'

'Yeah, it was,' I agree, not really knowing what else to say. It was a front-row seat to a show I didn't want to be at. The usual mutterings of *nice send off* and *good turn out* just don't seem to work when you're talking about a sixteen-year-old's funeral.

———

There are only a handful of us having a drink in the White Hart afterwards. I'm glad it's a small crowd rather than the whole staff. I was in two minds about going at all but Julia seemed up for it and she's giving me a lift back. Plus I don't really feel like hanging out with Lisa's parents just yet. They'll be after all the gory details and I just don't have the energy for it.

Everyone comments on how well Martin delivered his speech. I don't know how he did it. I sometimes wish I was a bit more like him. Statesmanlike and steady, not emotional and overly sensitive like me. I've never been very good at supressing my feelings. But then I'm not particularly good at talking about them either. It takes all sorts, I tell myself. We can't all be like Martin.

There's some polite conversation about what everyone has planned over the Christmas holidays and it feels weird to me that the event of the year is about to take place just days after something so devastating. I've always had a complicated relationship with Christmas. It seems to bring out the melancholy in me, but often to the point of a profound sadness that I can't seem to shake. I don't really know why. My memories of Christmas as a kid are happy ones; Mum and Dad always making such an effort to make it special and magical and all the things Christmas should be for a little one. We did all the usual stuff families typically do together. There was never any real drama to speak of. Then when dad left it was just me and Mum on Christmas morning, but by that point I'd grown out of the mysterious Santa stuff anyway so it was more about getting together with the aunties and uncles, cousins and grandparents, games of Pictionary and seeing how quickly I could smash my way through a selection box before anyone noticed and made me eat some vegetables.

But there was always an underlying sense of guilt. Shame, maybe, around the excess of it all, the mountains of food, piles of presents. It wasn't as if we were extravagant, especially after dad left, but we never went without. And the house was always so warm and full of love, I couldn't help but feel desperately sad that some people just don't have that. I remember telling Lisa once about my difficulties with Christmas, wondering if it's something other people experience too. 'Just try and *enjoy* yourself, Paul!' she'd said. 'It's not like it's *your* fault some people can't afford a decent Christmas.' She was right, I guess. But then whose fault was it? Is it so bad to empathise, to try and put yourself in someone else's shoes?

I try to focus on the positives for this year. Emilia will be more excited now that she's walking and starting to chatter. And it's a good two weeks off work, at a time when I need it the most. Hopefully it will give Lisa and me a chance to hang out a bit. It occurs to me that today is the winter solstice. A day to celebrate the light returning.

'You're into music, Paul, help me out!' Chris shouts from across the table and I'm shaken back to reality at the sound of my name.

'Sorry Chris, what was that?' I ask, pretending not to have heard to try and buy myself some time to figure out what they've all been talking about.

'This song!' He points up to an imagined speaker in the ceiling above him. I struggle over the background noise to focus on what it is. Generic, sad Christmas song. Then I recognise the vocals. 'It's Elvis, int it, this one?' He starts to sing along to *Lonely This Christmas* in an exaggerated Elvis impersonation.

'Erm, no, I think this is Mud, actually.' I wrinkle my nose and squint to feign uncertainty. No one likes a know-it-all.

'See – I told you it wa'n't Elvis!' Ju pipes up.

'No way, I won't believe it!' Chris laughs. 'I've *always* thought this was Elvis! Every day's a school day, hey?'

I know for a fact it's Mud as I remember creeping downstairs one night to find my mum lying on the sofa, crying as she watched them performing it on *Top of the Pops* the Christmas after my dad left. But if I tell them that I'll look as much of a sad sack as I feel. The mood has been gradually, cautiously, picking up as we've all started to slowly decompress from the devastation of this morning. I don't want to bring it back down again. I just laugh along with Chris. 'Yeah,' I say.

'One more for the road, shall we? Same again?' Martin asks the table. We all look to each other and nod tentatively in approval.

'Thanks Martin. I'll come and give you a hand.' Ju gets up from her seat next to me and puts a hand on my shoulder. 'That alright, pal?' she asks me quietly, probably noticing my absence. I smile and nod at her, words not quite making it out of my mouth.

I remember what the vicar said about Laura and her dad learning how to play *Into My Arms* on the piano together. It breaks my heart that I'll never be able to tell her that it's one of my favourite songs. So much I didn't know about her. So much left unsaid. I could have helped her through all the struggles with her mum and dad. But I don't suppose any of that matters now. I wonder what sort of effect the death of a child has on a relationship that is already struggling. In some ways such a profound loss must surely bring you closer together but, if the cracks are already chasmic, is it possible to heal the rifts?

Julia returns to the table with some of the drinks and someone passes a pint of lager in my direction. I smile in acknowledgement and take a sip, to fill the space left by my loss of vocabulary. I can't wait to get home. It's paradoxical – all I want to do is escape my mind but at the same time I have an urge to retreat and connect with the pain I've been carefully avoiding these past couple of weeks. But I'm so scared of where it might take me, how it will look to everyone on the outside if it all floods out of me. Scared of the damage it might do to my marriage. It seems like the only way I'll be able to get through it, though; by actually letting myself feel the enormity of grief that I appear to have parked in a holding bay while I wait for a more convenient slot.

I think back to my dream of Laura, just after she died. It felt so real, more of a vision than a dream. The feeling I had when she took my hand, the electricity, how alive I felt – it makes me question again whether I had feelings for her that I've been refusing to acknowledge. I can't shake off that we seemed to have made a connection, that night, before she died. More of a connection than I've felt with anyone else just lately.

CHAPTER THIRTEEN

'Is it time for another cup of tea?' Miriam says to Emilia in a singsong voice which I take as my cue to put the kettle on, again. I finish unloading the shopping I've just brought in from the car and open the tap to fill the kettle.

'Another tea, Miriam?' I call over to her, breathing slowly through my nose as I unpack the vegetables into the fridge. I notice my shoulders are tight.

'Oh yes, please, if you're putting the kettle on,' she answers, as if the question has taken her by complete surprise.

'George?' I prompt Lisa's dad to join in with the drinks orders. 'Tea? *Coffee?*'

He lowers his newspaper and looks up over his reading glasses. 'Coffee please, Paul, thanks,' he mutters as he returns his gaze to *The Times*.

Emilia is chatting away to herself happily as she clatters the cupboard doors of her play kitchen open and closed repetitively. I wonder what she's thinking. Miriam is reading the literary supplement from George's paper. I'd love to sit down with Emilia and join in with whatever imaginary scenario it is she's conjured up. The kettle clicks off the boil as steam fills the corner of the kitchen. I pour water over the teabag before noticing the cup is chipped and have to start again. Miriam won't like that and I can't be arsed with a snidey comment about standards slipping while 'Mummy isn't here'. I spoon coffee into the cafetiere and use the rest of the water to fill it up before stirring and resting the plunger on top while it brews. I could have just made him an instant Gold Blend but that seems a bit petty. And I may as well have a coffee myself if I'm going to the effort for everyone else.

'I bet you're glad to have the funeral over and done with, aren't you, Paul?' Miriam asks as she puts the magazine down next to her. 'Awful business, wasn't it?'

I bristle at '*wasn't it*', the implication that, now the funeral's over, we can all just go back to normal. As if I don't have the prospect of returning to school after Christmas, still one student down. Still having to see her empty desk, every day I go to work. As if Laura doesn't consume all my thoughts, and I've no idea when that's supposed to end. Will it ever? Is there something wrong with me, that I'm still so broken by her loss?

As I plunge the cafetiere the bitterness of the coffee aroma fills the air, alongside my silent resentment. I wonder if they've noticed. Probably not. 'Yeah, dreadful,' I agree. I take the milk from the fridge and pour some into Miriam's cup, stirring as I take out the teabag.

'Here you go.' I make my way over to the sofa and place the tea down on the bookshelves next to where Miriam is sitting.

'Lovely, thank you,' she says as I crouch down next to Emilia to see what she's up to. She hands me a plastic biscuit and I pretend to eat it. 'Mm-mmm, yummy,' I smile at her before kissing her rosy cheek. 'Have you got one for Granny?' I ask her, hoping that Miriam might take an interest in what she's doing while I carry on trying to unpack the shopping. Watching her for an hour while I was at Sainsbury's picking up the Christmas food shopping was obviously enough for them.

I remember George's coffee and hand it to him as he continues to flick through the paper. 'Oh, do you not have cream, Paul?' he asks, crestfallen.

'Errr, no, sorry... it's full fat milk though, is that alright?' I reassure him as a compromise, wondering if I should be offering to nip out and fetch cream for his coffee.

He nods slowly, pursing his bottom lip as he examines his coffee and takes a tentative sip, as if I've tried to poison him. 'Righto, not to worry,' he concedes.

My nostrils flare and I breathe out silently. I need some fresh air. 'I was thinking of taking Emilia to the playpark after lunch, if you fancy that?' I ask chirpily, changing the subject.

I'm met with silence as I catch them stealing glances at one another. They appear visibly alarmed at the prospect of a kids' playpark. Either that or having to spend another minute with only me for adult company. I look up at the clock. It's only 11.30.

'Yes, maybe, dear. What time will Lisa be back?' Miriam asks weakly.

'About half four I think, she's finishing early today.'

'You call that *early*?! It's Christmas Eve tomorrow!' She turns to address Emilia although the comment is clearly aimed at me. 'She does work so hard, doesn't she, your mummy?'

'Must be nice for you to get all that time off at Christmas, eh, Paul?' George pipes up. *Here we go*, I think. As if I'm here with my feet up, sherry in hand.

'Yeah, it's great.' My face automatically moves into a shape vaguely resembling a smile, probably unconvincingly. 'I'm very lucky.'

I'm busy chopping onions when Lisa strolls through the door at 4.55. Everyone appears to let out a silent sigh of relief, the tension of the afternoon having built to a crescendo of reticence. Even Emilia seems to have picked up on the awkwardness of strained conversation and passive-aggressive remarks murmured within overly polite tones.

'Mama!' Emilia jumps to her feet at the sound of the door closing behind Lisa and wobbles out into the hallway to greet her.

'Hello, baby!' she squeaks as she scoops her up and carries her back into the kitchen where we're all congregated, me at the hob, Miriam and George still on the sofa although now sipping glasses of wine and watching the *Fifteen-to-One* celebrity Christmas special on the portable in the corner.

'Mummy's home!' Miriam chimes, looking comforted. 'How was your day, darling? Come and get a glass of wine!'

'Yeah, it was good thanks, glad to be finished for a few days now!' She comes over to the hob and kisses me on the cheek, asking with her eyes if I'm OK. I reply with a weak smile and a look of *I'm glad you're home* as I set the chopped onions aside. It feels like all I do is chop fucking onions. She takes a wine glass from the cupboard and pours herself a small merlot.

'So how was everyone's day?' she asks brightly, looking to us all. 'What have you been up to?' She crouches down next to Emilia who is now trying unsuccessfully to put a giant floor puzzle together.

'Oh just pottering, really,' Miriam replies. 'It's been very relaxed. Hasn't it George?'

My eyes widen as I wonder what part of my day has been relaxing.

'Lovely, yes, very nice,' Lisa's dad agrees, on cue. 'When are you back at work then sweetheart? You've got a few days off now, have you?'

'Yeah, well Monday's a bank holiday so I'm back in on Tuesday for three days and then it's a long weekend for New Year, isn't it?' She gets up off the floor and pulls up a stool at the breakfast bar whilst I quarter the tomatoes. 'So, we'll run you back to the station on Boxing Day before we pick Paul's mum up to come here if that's alright?'

Christ, we've got another two whole days of this, I think. Still, at least Lisa is around to make conversation now and I can just hide away in the kitchen prepping for Christmas dinner.

'I'm meeting the uni girls the following day for lunch and drinks in Leeds. It was the only day we could all do what with work and family stuff,' Lisa announces, which appears to be more of a reminder for my benefit.

'Oh that'll be nice, darling. Good that you can have a bit of time to yourself before rushing back to work.'

Now that Lisa's home, I feel my defences drop against the intrusive thoughts that have been threatening all day to simmer over from the back of my mind. Trying to silently neutralise them while maintaining an outwardly calm and normal façade is exhausting. There's an ache in my lower back that's starting to burn. But then some of them are just too disturbing to be ignored, locking me out of my rationale and throwing away the key. *Imagine what you could do with this knife*. My blood runs cold. I instinctively let go of the knife I'm using to slice a clove of garlic but it clatters noisily onto the kitchen floor, causing them all to turn around and look at me.

'You OK, love?' Lisa asks with a quizzical frown.

'Yeah, sorry,' I answer absently, a dizziness descending on me and causing my ears to ring. I bend down to retrieve the knife from the floor. The length and severity of the blade terrify me. How can I be sure I'd never hurt my own family?

'What do you fancy watching?' Lisa asks me, as the credits start to roll on whatever was just on the TV. She's flicking through the pages of the Christmas TV guide and reading out various options, none of which I could really give a shit about. 'Oooh, there's a *Gladiators* Christmas special on channel three in a minute?'

George has started lightly snoring and Miriam is engrossed in her book in the armchair by the window.

'I'm pretty tired actually, I think I'll just get off to bed.'

'Oh.' Lisa looks a bit annoyed but it's beneath her to convince me to stay up. 'Fair enough, more Quality Street for me then.' She goes back to the TV guide and mutters goodnight.

I offer a half-smile and close the door to the front room behind me as I head into the kitchen for a glass of water to take up to bed. *No wonder her parents think you're a waste of space.* Here we go again. I roll with the punches as the school bully of my mind springs back to life. *Won't be long before Lisa comes to her senses and leaves you. And she'll take Emilia with her. She can't be left with a nutjob like you.*

I fill my glass from the tap and catch sight of the five gleaming kitchen knives attached to the wall by a magnetic bracket. My heart rate quickens. What if I sleepwalk in the night and stab them all to death? You hear of that happening, sometimes. I can't let this be the last thought I have while looking at the knives, in case my subconscious takes over when I have no control. Don't be ridiculous, I reassure myself. You'd never hurt them. *Would you*? My head is spinning. I don't know which voice is real now. I only came in for a glass of water. I just want to go to bed. *You'll have to hide the knives, just in case*. For fuck's sake. Don't give in to this nonsense. You're not going to kill your family in your sleep. *Nonsense? But you're the one thinking it.*

There's a clamminess creeping across my forehead and a nausea in the depths of my stomach. I give in and take all five knives off the bracket and place them carefully at the back of the cutlery drawer. Just in case.

'I just feel so guilty. It's not fair on Emilia, or Paul. I don't know what to do for the best, really.' I overhear Lisa speaking in hushed tones and my stomach drops. They think I'm already upstairs. I feel guilty eavesdropping but I'm desperate for any clues as to what's going on with her at the moment so I pause outside the door to the front room as I pass to head upstairs. I hold my breath to try and focus on what they're saying. Why does she feel guilty?

'Well, dear, you've got to do what's right for you,' Miriam soothes. I can hear George snoring heavily now so they're obviously having a heart to heart now I'm out of the way.

'I think I need to talk to him,' Lisa says, sighing. 'It's just so hard, getting any time to ourselves. Having a conversation while Emilia's around is impossible. We're both so busy with work and stuff. And now all this going on at school, it's hit him really hard.' There's a softness to her voice that I've missed.

'Yes, he's taken it rather badly, hasn't he? He wasn't very chatty today. Even less so than usual.'

'He's really struggling, Mum. You know what he's like, he overthinks things. He said something the other week about it being his fault, the accident, that he'd held her back after school and if he hadn't then it wouldn't have happened. But I don't think I've been particularly sympathetic, really. I've been that busy with work and, I don't know, I just see things differently to him, I guess. He's grieving as if she's family and I just can't help but wonder why that is...' Lisa's voice trails.

My heart starts to race. I shift my weight and wince as the floorboard creaks, but they don't seem to notice.

'What? You're not...? You don't think he had *feelings* for her, do you?' Miriam's whisper becomes more audible and I can imagine the look on her face.

'No! God, of course not, I'm not saying *that*.' Lisa pauses. 'He's my husband, he's not that kind of person. But we've not been right for a long time and... I don't know, I just wonder what's happened to us. I miss him. I didn't know you could miss someone you see every day but we're just not how we used to be. Something's changed.'

My heart aches and I want to rush in and take her into my arms, tell her I'm still here. It can be how it was, again.

I hear Miriam muttering something about how life changes when you've got kids but Lisa jumps in.

'I know that, Mum! We never thought it was going to be easy! But it just makes me so sad, he's a good man, he's always so thoughtful and such a brilliant dad... I just wish we didn't have to lose ourselves in the process. It feels like a light has gone out.'

George splutters and starts to cough. 'You alright, dad?' Lisa asks and my shoulders drop as I realise the conversation is over.

'Sorry, dear, must have nodded off,' I hear him mumble as I creep away and up the stairs, the heaviness sitting on my chest even more so than before.

CHAPTER FOURTEEN

I glance up at the clock in the kitchen again as I get Emilia's bedtime bottle ready. Six forty-five. I've already kept her up later than usual, Lisa was supposed to be back straight after work. It's New Year's Eve and we're meant to be getting a takeaway.

I suddenly feel hot and a sickness rises up in my stomach. She should have been back over an hour ago. I pick up my phone again. No new messages. I wonder if I should have called her sooner but I've been so preoccupied trying to keep Emilia happy I hadn't really thought about it. And I never want to appear as one of those overbearing husbands that are always checking up on their wife's whereabouts. But she'd normally call if she was going to be late. It's very rare that she'd miss bedtime. There's a familiarity to my dread and I begin to panic. I reassure myself that it's perfectly acceptable to call her now, in the circumstances, so I dial her number but it rings out to her answerphone.

I sigh, shoving my phone into my back pocket, as I scoop Emilia up in my arms and wipe the warm dribble from her chin. Her cheeks are bright red and she's making a constant whining sound that tells me she's teething. Which would explain the awful mood she's been in all day. I remember the agony I was in with my wisdom tooth a few months ago and suddenly feel guilty that I haven't been as patient with her today as I perhaps ought to have been. But three days at home trying to entertain her while Lisa's been back at work have tested my tolerance. I cradle her head into my shoulder as I carry her upstairs.

'Daddy's here baby, it's OK,' I whisper as I kiss her gently on her hot, red cheeks.

'Shall we get you some Calpol?' I ask, not expecting an answer, as I carry her into the bathroom and open up the cabinet. I rest her on my hip, holding her with one arm around her waist as I reach for the bottle of medicine on the top shelf. I realise I can't do this one-handed so I sit her down on the closed toilet seat while I fumble with the child-safety cap. It finally clicks and I twist it open, before spilling half the bottle of sticky pink liquid into the sink as I over-zealously pour it into the tiny plastic spoon.

'Fuck's sake,' I sigh under my breath as Emilia's whimpering gets louder and my irritation moves up through the gears. I shouldn't be doing this on my own, I think.

I spoon the medicine carefully into Emilia's mouth, scooping up the excess dribbling down her chin with the spoon and back into her mouth. 'Let's get you into bed,' I say as I bundle her into my arms. I want to do this forever but I'm exhausted by the monotony of it all. I take my phone from my back pocket to see if Lisa's been in touch. She hasn't.

I close Emilia's bedroom door behind me once she's settled and check my phone again. Still nothing. It's now seven-fifteen, I see from the numbers in the top right-hand corner of the greeny-yellow screen. I feel my stomach flip as I start to imagine all the possible scenarios and the blood rushes to my head,

making me dizzy. What if she's been hit by a car? I imagine the local paper headlines 'Grieving teacher loses wife in identical New Year's Eve hit-and-run'. Lightning doesn't strike in the same place twice though, right? Maybe she's been attacked by some drunk who's been in the pub all day? She could have been left for dead in the jitty off the High Street as she left the office. I imagine her lifeless body, lying in the cold. My heart flipping as I see the blue lights silently approach the house. Opening the door to two police officers who have come to break the news. Me breaking down as soon as I see their faces; the man my age with the sad eyes (it could have been his wife) and the slightly older female officer with the comforting scent that reminds me of my mum (they always send a woman when they're bearing bad news). I imagine explaining to an oblivious Emilia that Mummy isn't coming home. A pointless conversation but one I have to keep repeating every time she asks for Lisa. Tears prick my eyes at the thought of this loss of my own invention. I sit down on the top step of the staircase and lean against the banister as I dial her number again.

The line rings several times before a man's voice answers and I frown, glancing at the screen, wondering if I've dialled the wrong number.

'Oh hey, I'm trying to get hold of Lisa?' my voice shaking as I wonder what the hell's going on.

'Hi, is it... Paul?' a man shouts over background noise.

'Yes. Who's this? Is Lisa there?' I can feel myself getting irate but I try to keep my tone amiable. Why is it so difficult to track my wife down?

'It's Richard, she's, er...' he stammers, letting out a little laugh, 'she's just in the bathroom. Shall I get her to call you?' His voice is cocky and annoying. There's laughter in the bac| ground. They're obviously in a bar somewhere and he sound

bit pissed. What sort of a twat calls the toilets the 'bathroom' anyway? My heart sinks as I realise she's chosen to sneak out for drinks with her work pals with apparently no concern for me or our daughter. But at least she's alive.

'Yeah, if you could please mate, cheers,' I reply.

'No worries ... *mate*. Speak soon!' He sings before hanging up. I want to throw the phone down the stairs but instead I sink my head into my hands and run my fingers through my hair, clutching at handfuls. Why is she doing this to us? I clench both hands into a fist with my hair still between my fingers, the stinging sensation of pulling on the roots keeping me from bursting into tears. I feel like screaming but I don't want to wake Emilia up, now she's finally settled.

Rising up from my seat on the top step, I take a deep breath through my nose and close my eyes. What would she do if I threw myself down the stairs? How would she cope? *Don't flatter yourself.* I head down the stairs and make a start on tidying up the carnage left behind after another whole day at home with a toddler. My body feels heavy.

Is it Lisa's company I miss? Or just *someone's* company? I can't decide whether I miss what we had, what we were – Lisa and Paul – or if I'm just tired of feeling so lonely. I can't help but think this isn't what I signed up for.

My phone vibrates in my pocket as I finally finish packing away Emilia's Duplo. I answer quietly, trying to keep my tone neutral until I hear her side of the story.

'Hey, did you ring me?' she shouts over background noise which fades as she walks outside. I hear her footsteps on the pavement and then a car door opening.

'Yeah, a few times. Are you OK?' I ask, incredulously.

'Yeah fine, just jumping in a cab,' she replies airily and I

wonder if it's me that has the problem. I hear her give our address to the taxi driver. 'I'll be home in ten minutes.'

'Where have you been? I was worried sick.' I ask, my temper threatening to escape.

'Oh we just went for a quick one after work. Sorry I thought I'd messaged you, did you not get it?' she says nonchalantly, ignoring my concern.

'No, I *didn't* get it. And it's gone half seven, that's hardly a quick one is it?! Emilia's in bed. I thought we were getting takeaway?'

'Yes, we still can! I'll be back in ten, OK?'

'OK,' I hang up, so angry and disappointed I don't know what to do with myself. My head is swimming.

I finish throwing Emilia's toys into the basket and head to the kitchen to pour myself a glass of red wine, in the hope that it might calm me down a little before Lisa gets home. I put *OK Computer* into the CD player and lie back on the sofa in the corner of the kitchen. Does anyone else put up with this kind of bullshit? When does it get too much for someone to cope with? At what point am I allowed to be pissed off? The scenarios that were just taunting me now feel ridiculous. It feels like we're falling apart and I'm angry that she can't see that.

Lisa eventually comes tumbling in through the door and I sit myself up, waiting for her to come into the kitchen.

'Sorry love, I honestly thought I'd messaged you, the guys were just having a quick drink after work so I thought I'd join them, it's been a bit of a day,' her speech is slurred and she's obviously trying really hard to focus on my face. *A bit of a fucking day?!* I think, but swallow it down before I say it out loud.

'Lisa, it's nearly 8 o'clock. I thought we were supposed to be having a quiet night in?! You and me, some time on our own, *finally*? And I was worried about you, I had no idea where you were. Anything could have happened!' I can feel my insides trembling but if I'm going to get through to her, I need to stay calm.

'Well it didn't, did it, I'm fine, look!' she giggles and tries to put her arms round my neck but the smell of booze is repulsive to me. 'Come on, it's New Year's Eve. It was just a little drink, I'm home now. What do you fancy to eat?'

'A *little drink*? You reek of wine, Lisa! Fuck's sake! How much have you had?!'

'I don't know, maybe two bottles between three of us, I think,' she's answering my questions as if we're just casually chatting about our day, which makes me even more angry.

'Three of you? So who was there then?' I raise my eyebrows, whilst waiting for her response.

'Well it was me, Richard and Bhav to start with but then Bhav had to get back for the kids so it was just me and Rich in the end.' I can feel my blood boiling. I try and tell myself I'm not a jealous person but this gets the better of me.

'So just you and Richard, having a cosy drink on New Year's Eve, when you're supposed to be at home helping me put our daughter to bed?! It's out of order!'

'*Cosy drink*?' her eyes narrow. 'What's *that* supposed to mean?'

'Well, how come he answered your phone while you were in the toilet? What the fuck is all that about?' I'm shouting then I stop myself, not wanting to wake Emilia. 'I've had a really, really tough day, Lisa. Emilia's been struggling with her teeth, it's been hard work. She was asking for you at bedtime.'

'I know, I said I'm sorry didn't I? Christ, Paul, it was just a drink to celebrate the end of the year! We don't all want to sit around listening to *fucking Radiohead* you know! On New Year's Eve?! It's *depressing*.' She throws her arms up in the air and pulls an appalled face. I feel sick as the words I want to scream back at her clog up in my constricting throat. I splutter and put my palm to my forehead before taking a breath in.

'Of course it's depressing! Do you think I wanted to be stuck here on my own, worrying myself to death about where you are, *who you're with*?!' I instantly regret those last words as I realise they're loaded with implication, but she doesn't seem to notice. 'And maybe I *am* depressed! It's been a bit of a shit few weeks, don't you think?!'

'Well you do it to yourself, listening to this rubbish! You're turning into a fucking cliché, Paul! Why don't you just put something a bit more *uplifting* on?!'

I'm stunned. I laugh out loud as it becomes clear she has no ability to empathise with me. And I'm not sure where that leaves us. I slam down my wine glass and grab my keys from the kitchen side.

'Where are you going?' she asks, following me into the hallway as I snatch my coat from the coat hooks.

'I don't know. I need to get out. This is not how I'd hoped tonight would go.' I feel tears of frustration rising again and I try desperately not to let them flood out. 'I was looking forward to us spending some time together. I really need it right now. I'm desperate, Lis,' my voice cracks. 'I'm just so... lonely.'

She looks up at me with uncharacteristically remorseful eyes. In fact, she looks a little scared. I don't like the idea of leaving her with Emilia when she's had so much to drink but I need to remove myself from the situation.

'I'll see you later,' I mutter as a wall of cold air hits me through the open front door.

CHAPTER FIFTEEN

I've not really thought about where I'm going to go. I've had a fairly large glass of wine so I don't want to risk driving. I march into the fresh evening air, my hands thrust into the pockets of my navy wool overcoat. I pull up the collar around my neck, wishing I'd grabbed my hat.

I walk for about half an hour and, without realising, have ended up in the direction of my mum's house. I saw her last week, on Boxing Day, but didn't have much chance to speak to her properly in all the excitement of Emilia's presents and preparing the buffet tea I'd put together at ours.

You can't disturb her on New Year's Eve, I think, before realising that, if it were Emilia in my shoes, wanting to knock on my door for a chat, of course I'd want her to disturb me. I walk past the off-licence just before the corner of her road then turn back and impulsively step inside. A bottle of port catches my eye, Mum likes port. I ask the shop assistant for a bottle, with ten Marlboro Lights and a lighter, then turn the corner into her road. As I stand at the bottom of the steps leading up to the door of her mid-terrace house, I take a deep breath and close my eyes. All the pain of the last few weeks is knotted in the pit of my stomach and I need to release it. I need to talk to my mum.

I walk up the steps and, through the open curtains in the bay window, I can see her sitting in her armchair next to the record player, reading a book by lamplight. I feel a pang of guilt that she's sitting here alone but I know she enjoys her own company. She probably turned down several invitations in favour of a quiet night in. I knock on the door gently so as not to startle her.

As I knock, I see her lift her round, dark-rimmed glasses onto the top of her head, looking at her watch as she gets up and wanders over to the hallway. She opens the door and greets me with a wide smile which quickly turns to concern.

'Paul? Is everything alright, love?' she searches my face and ushers me in before closing the door and taking me gently by the shoulders. 'What is it?'

I've had plenty of practice of holding it together in front of my mum.

'I come bearing gifts,' I smile, holding up the port and cigarettes.

'Come on, let's go through,' she says, taking my coat and hanging it on the coat hooks in the hallway. I trip up over her yoga mat which is propped up against the wall. 'Sorry,' I mumble as I clumsily try and prop it back up.

I walk in through to the warmth of the lounge and the soft jazz coming from the record player. *The Complete Poems and Plays of T.S. Eliot* is resting upturned on the arm of her chair. She's always had good taste.

'Sorry Mum, I don't mean to barge in. Especially on New Year's Eve,' I shuffle and look down at my feet.

'Oh don't be soft, you know my door's always open for

you,' she smiles, holding up the bottle of port. 'Shall we have a glass of this, then?'

I nod, so relieved I can feel my shoulders drop as I sink into the sofa facing the bay window. Groups of people walk past, presumably off out into town to bring the new year in. Mum comes back from the kitchen with two glasses and sets them down on the coffee table. She sits down on the sofa next to me before easing the cork out of the port bottle with a squeak, followed by a satisfying pop. She pours us both a generous measure and we toast before each taking a long sip.

'So, I'm delighted to see you, but what are you doing here at nine o'clock on New Year's Eve?' she places her glass down and sits back into the sofa, tucking her legs underneath her. I relay the events of the evening to her but also open up about the ongoing saga over Lisa and our marriage, and my suspicions of Richard.

'Well, yes, it sounds like she was out of order tonight, darling,' she concludes, as she takes another sip of port. 'And I'm afraid I don't like the sound of this *Richard* character.'

'I just don't know what to do to get through to her, Mum. It's like she doesn't *want* to be reached. She seems to be happy to let us drift apart.' I look down into my glass, not entirely sure how I ended up here tonight. It all escalated so quickly. I think back to the conversation I overheard between Lisa and her mum, but I push it out of my mind. I suddenly realise I'm ravenous.

'Well, I'm sorry to say that's how it ended up with your dad and me, I'm afraid.' She looks away, as she often does when she's talking about my dad. 'We were distant with one another for a good few months, possibly years, before he left me for Michelle. I'd tried everything; I'd booked us weekends away – you used to stay at your grandma's – we started dance classes together, bridge, we even tried couples' counselling which was a pretty new concept back then, believe me. But in the end, nothing worked because he belonged to someone else.'

Her last sentence hits me like a tonne of bricks. I can't help but feel that Lisa belongs to someone else now too. Her heart isn't mine anymore. A fear about where we go from here grips me. I'm not sure what I've done to deserve this.

'And how long was it before you found out? I just can't bear that we could drag on and on like this for years and then I find out she's been seeing someone else all that time. I'd rather just know now and get it over with.'

'It wasn't that long, really, in the scheme of things. Probably about eighteen months of being in a really rocky patch, but things had been going downhill for a bit before that. I guess you just think you'll get through it one way or another but that time we didn't.'

'We just seem … I don't know … we seem to be on completely different pages at the minute. She's really focused on work, which is great, I want to support her. But I just don't get that same support back from her.' I sigh. 'It's really made me look at her in a different light.'

'I'm sorry, love,' Mum says gently as she pats me on the knee. 'It's awful when there's an emotional imbalance within a couple. Someone always feels like they're losing out. Either one isn't getting the support they want or the other thinks they're being too needy. But as a couple you have to be able to take the rough with the smooth. Has the school been supporting you, after what happened?'

'Yeah, they've been great, but it's been tough these past couple of weeks being off work. I thought it would be good to get away and clear my head a bit, especially with Laura's funeral out the way. But it's actually been harder not having my colleagues around to share the grief with. We all kind of get it, look out for each other, you know?'

'Come here, love,' she pulls me into her arms. Her warmth and familiar scent make me feel safe. The knot that was lodged in my stomach starts to melt away.

I wonder if I should tell her about the medication, but I can't bring myself to admit it. I sit up and dab my nose on my sleeve before reaching for my glass and taking a long sip.

I close my eyes and rest my head on the velvety cushion of the sofa. 'Mum, I'm starving, have you eaten?'

'Oh I met Penny for a late lunch in town, but I can put a cheese board together if you like? I'm a bit peckish too, now you mention it.'

'Yes, please,' I take her hand in mine and kiss it. 'Thank you. For listening.'

'That's what I'm here for, darling. You know that.' She rises from the sofa and heads down the hall into the kitchen. I follow and bang my head on the low-hanging light fitting as I take a seat at the table. Maybe I don't visit her at home as much as I ought to.

CHAPTER SIXTEEN

On the way to school on the first day of term I think about what Mum said to me that night. It's never going to be sunshine and Calippos all of the time, we need to be able to ride the storms along the way too. I make my way into the staff room and Julia is there, already making coffee.

'Ay up Paul!' she seems her usual chirpy self. 'Happy new year! Did you have a good 'un?'

'Yeah, not bad, thanks. How about you? Get up to much?'

'It was lovely thanks, lots of fun with the kids and we did a bit of travelling around to visit the family. Then just chilled out really, was *so* nice to have a couple of weeks off! Back to reality though, hey?'

Back to reality. I wish I knew what that meant. 'Yeah, I guess.' Julia looks into my face and sits down at the table next to me. It's still early so it's just me and her in at the minute.

'How you feeling?'

'I'm alright, just, er... struggling a bit, still, you know,' I fill Julia in on the events of New Year's Eve.

'So what happened after the row, did you clear the air?' Julia asks sympathetically.

'Not really, it's been pretty frosty at home ever since. She went to bed early the following night then she locked herself away and said she'd got work to do the next day and here we are. She just doesn't seem interested in talking things through. I feel like I've lost her already,' I rub my fingers across my eyes. 'Anyway, we've got a night away on our own this weekend, my mum's going to have Emilia at hers overnight while we head off to the Peak District.' I want to tell her about my first therapist's appointment, which is on Wednesday afternoon, but the words stick in my throat.

Julia squeezes my arm. 'I'm sure a bit of time on your own will do you good. And how are you feeling, you know, about Laura an' that?'

I shake my head and shrug, words escaping me. 'But at least my failing marriage is giving me a bit of a distraction,' I laugh. If I don't laugh, I'll probably cry.

I head to the classroom a little earlier than usual to see if any of the kids have arrived yet. Manny is at her desk, chatting to Robyn and Erin. A few of the boys are milling around outside.

'Morning guys,' I say gently, as I enter the classroom. 'Happy new year.'

'Same to you, sir,' Robyn replies with a soft smile.

'How was Christmas?' I ask them, cautiously. I guess it was far from normal.

'Yeah it was alright, sir, thanks,' Erin volunteers. 'How about you?'

'Well, it was nice to be at home for a bit,' I nod, clearing my throat as I wonder how to casually ask them how they're dealing with their friend's death. 'But, you know, Laura was in my thoughts. How are you all feeling, since the funeral?' Manny is quiet, I notice.

A few others start to filter in and it feels a little like the moment for any deep conversation is lost.

'Well, it wasn't easy, that's for sure,' Robyn looks down at her feet. 'I still can't believe she's not coming back, you know?'

'Yeah, I know,' I agree. It's almost as if her energy is still in this room. 'Manny, you OK?' I ask her, moving in closer to see if she'll open up.

'I'm alright, I guess,' she shrugs, her eyes tired. 'Like Robyn says, it's hard to believe she's not here anymore. Like, maybe she's just been on a long holiday and she'll be back any day now. I miss her...' her voice trails and her nostrils flare as she tries to stem the tears.

'Oh Manny,' I sigh as I put a protective arm around her shoulder. 'I'm not sure what to say, just that it's completely understandable that you feel that way. Have you spoken to the school counsellors?'

She nods, biting her lip. 'Yeah, they were really good at the end of term, just before the funeral. And I'm going to see Miss Hughes at lunchtime today, to check in.'

'OK, that's good,' I breathe out, relieved that someone more qualified than me is around. 'But you know where I am, OK?'

'Thanks sir,' she says with a half-smile. 'I appreciate it.'

We're reading Shakespeare's *Romeo & Juliet* in my Year 11 English class and the last lesson today is with my tutor group.

Alongside reading the play, we've been watching the Baz Luhrmann film that came out a couple of years ago. At least it means the kids are actually interested in it now.

We're watching the famous love-at-first-sight scene, Act 1 Scene 5. There's a bit of nudging and giggling and some of them have started to squirm around awkwardly like when you're watching TV with your parents and a sex scene comes on. I pause the video at the end of the scene, after Juliet has realised that the man she just fell in love with is a Montague.

'So what do we think Juliet means, here, with the line: "*My grave is like to be my wedding bed*"?' I ask the class, turning back to the text as they start to shuffle back to life in their seats. I draw up the blinds which I'd lowered to keep the late afternoon sun off the television screen.

There's an awkward silence as I look out towards the class. Erin tentatively puts up her hand.

'Does she mean she'd rather die than get married?' she suggests.

'Well, yes, sort of, Erin... that's good, thank you. She's saying if she can't have Romeo – because he might already be married or betrothed to another – then she would never want to marry another man, as her heart already belongs to Romeo. So she resigns to the idea that she might die unmarried.'

'And this line is also an example of foreshadowing; can anyone tell me why? What is Shakespeare foreshadowing with this line at this point in the play?' I'm optimistic that some of them might have been paying attention when we read the play.

James puts up his hand. 'Yes, James?'

'Is it that actually she will die, not unmarried technically, but only just after she marries Romeo?'

'Great, well done James, thank you. I'm sure that's not a

spoiler for anyone, right?' I laugh and a few of them chuckle politely along with me. I look at my watch.

'OK, guys, I think that's about it for today. Homework is to continue with the reading of Act 5, Scene 3 and write a 250-word summary of what happens. I'll need that in for Monday's lesson please.' The bell rings. 'Right, go on, get outta here. See you in the morning!'

I gather my papers and the dog-eared old copy of *Romeo & Juliet* and put them into my satchel while the kids make their way out of the classroom. My appointment with the therapist is at five so I need to get the bus across town in the rush hour traffic. Lisa's picking Emilia up from nursery so I make my way to the staff room to collect my coat before heading out into the damp evening air.

CHAPTER SEVENTEEN

When I reach the old Stucco-fronted Georgian terraced building that the therapist's office is in, I realise I've been counting my steps all the way from the bus stop.

I feel a churn in my stomach as I approach the heavy front door to the building and press the buzzer. A voice crackles over the intercom and I announce my arrival.

'Oh, hi, it's er, Paul Johnson, I've got an appointment at five o' clock.'

There's another muffled voice which says something I can't make out but there's a click and the door moves in its frame slightly. I push it open tentatively and step inside.

It's boiling. *Why are these places always so hot?* I think as I take off my coat and undo the top button of my shirt from underneath my cotton pullover, loosening the collar. I approach the reception desk and repeat my name to the woman sat behind it.

'Thank you, Mr Johnson. Is this your first appointment?'

'Er, yeah, this time around,' I give a nervous laugh and she smiles kindly.

'Well, you might remember the drill then. I just need you to complete this questionnaire before we send you in for your appointment, if you want to take a seat over there?' she hands me a brown clipboard with a heavy metal clasp holding down a sheet of A4 paper. I take a blue biro from the pot on the desk and head to the seating area against the back wall. I'm still roasting, so I pull my jumper off over my head and drape it over my satchel on the floor. I run my fingers through my hair to try and neaten it back up.

I look down at the questions and remember some of them from last time. My name has already been written across the top of the page in large, rounded letters. I start to circle some of the answers, which are mostly 'on a scale of one to ten...' questions.

Question 7: How do your symptoms affect your close relationships?

I take my phone from out of my pocket and see I've had no message from Lisa. From the available answers of: slightly, mildly, moderately, highly or extremely, I hover over 'highly' before reconsidering and circling 'extremely'. I run my fingers across my eyes and realise I have to be honest with myself if this is going to work.

I hand the clipboard back to the receptionist and she tells me to wait for the therapist to call me in. There's no one else here and a loneliness settles beside me. Why has Lisa not messaged me?

I close my eyes and rest the back of my head on the wall behind me.

Footsteps coming down the stairwell are followed by a creaking of the door to my right. A gentle, male voice with a hint of a Liverpool accent calls my name and I turn around to see the familiar face of the same therapist I saw for a few sessions last year.

'Hello,' I say warmly, as I offer my hand to shake.

'Hi, Paul,' he smiles as he accepts my handshake. 'Jeremy. We've met before, haven't we?' He holds the door open for me as he gestures towards the staircase. 'We're just up here.'

'Yes, I saw you last year, briefly. You keeping well?' I ask out of habit, as we climb a second flight of stairs.

He nods and smiles more with his eyes than with his mouth, but doesn't reply. I don't suppose they're meant to talk much about themselves.

'Just in here,' he steps to the side as we reach the doorway. It's a different room to last time. I hear someone else leaving a room on the floor below, blowing their nose. They do a great job of making sure you never see anyone else, although I know I can't possibly be the only patient in the building.

The room is massive and there's an orange glow from the streetlamp outside streaming in through the huge sash windows. It's a different room to last time. A large, up-lighting lamp sits in the space behind the door and, by the windows, there's a high-backed armchair on which Jeremy's glasses, a spiral-bound notebook and a pen are resting. So that's his seat, I realise.

Opposite Jeremy's chair is a small, two-seater grey sofa with a couple of mustard coloured down-filled cushions that you can really sink into. I take a seat on the sofa and place my coat and satchel on the space beside me. There's a large jug of water on a low teak coffee table in front of me and I pour myself a glass. I notice a small basket of Lego – a mixture of random coloured bricks and generic characters with varying expressions – and a box of tissues. I take a deep breath in through my nose.

I don't usually find silence awkward but I notice the long pause between Jeremy showing me into the room and him examining what I assume are my questionnaire responses. He takes his glasses back off and places them on top of his head before he looks over at me and smiles gently. I realise there's about seven or eight feet of space between our seats.

'Do you want to talk me through how you've been feeling just lately?' he asks in a such a soft voice I struggle to hear him.

I clear my throat and feel my stomach start to churn. I'm not sure where to start.

'Erm, well, it's been a bit up and down just lately,' I laugh, trying to put myself at ease before I pour my heart out to this relative stranger. 'I, er, I started having some quite intense intrusive thoughts a few months ago and it was at a time when I was pretty run down – we've got a toddler – and I guess I found it hard to control my compulsions so my OCD started to take over again...' I take a sip of water from the glass on the table. 'And then, I er, I...' I clear my throat again as my eyes start to sting. 'Sorry.'

'Take your time Paul, there's no rush.'

I'm suddenly overwhelmed by his kindness and the tears spill over. How am I here again? I start to wonder if this is just a cycle I will need to continue for the rest of my life. Maybe I'll never get truly better. I bring my hands up to my face then reach for a tissue. As I surface, I take a long, gasping breath in through my mouth as if I've been under water. I breathe out purposefully through my mouth to regain control. 'Sorry,' I say again.

'No need to apologise.'

'I'm a teacher and I lost a student in a hit and run just before Christmas.' I surprise myself by stringing a full sentence together without stumbling over my words. OK, *keep this up*, I think. Jeremy is nodding encouragingly but doesn't say anything while I'm in flow. 'And so just when I was feeling really overwhelmed with my OCD flaring up again, I had this horrible shock and it was Christmas and my wife and I aren't in a particularly good place at the minute...' I pause to check I've mentioned everything that is currently causing me pain. 'Plus, you know, sleep deprivation with a toddler.'

Jeremy looks down at his notebook and makes a quick note before looking back up at me. He's probably mid-fifties, with long grey hair that he has tied back in a ponytail, a hint of stubble across his jawline. 'I'm sorry for your loss, Paul. So you've had a lot on your plate just lately, then?'

'Yeah, you could say that. It feels like I'm trapped in a Kafka novel.' I laugh because that's what I do in these situations. He smiles politely.

'And what seems to be causing you the most trouble at the moment? Is it the symptoms of the OCD or the bereavement?'

'A bit of both I guess,' I start to feel a little calmer, knowing I've got the worst bit over with. For now, at least. 'I mean, obviously Laura's death has had a big impact but then the OCD was already starting to show up again before... you know. And then afterwards it just became more, I don't know, omnipresent, I guess. It just never leaves me at the minute. It's exhausting.' I take another sip of water.

'Yes. And you mentioned things aren't great at home. Do you think that's a result of the struggles you're facing at the minute, or contributing to them?'

'Well, if I'm honest, the cracks were starting to show before the intrusive thoughts returned, so I guess it's been a contributing factor. But I suppose my mood just lately hasn't exactly given us space to work things out. I can't imagine I'm much fun to live with at the minute.'

He nods as if he understands every word I've said. It's so comforting to be listened to so intently, without judgement or preconception.

I elaborate on my fears around Lisa and Richard and the fact that we have drifted further apart than I ever thought possible. Her apparent abandon and lack of empathy or understanding of my grief over Laura.

'It seems there's a lot to unpack in terms of the current state of your relationship with your wife,' he makes another brief note in his notebook. 'But I think the most pressing issue at the moment is getting you back up to fitness, Paul. Would you agree?'

I think about how air stewards advise you to fit your own oxygen mask before helping others, and it seems to make sense. I can't very well work on my marriage until I'm feeling better myself. 'Yeah, I guess so,' I agree weakly.

'Here's a leaflet which goes into a bit more detail about the different kinds of obsessions that people with OCD tend to experience,' he hands me a bi-fold leaflet with lots of bullet-pointed information. 'There's a bit in there about managing compulsions too, and we can talk more about that next time. My first thoughts are that some cognitive behavioural therapy might be a good idea to start with, followed by some counselling. Have you tried CBT before?'

'I'm not sure, I don't think so.'

'It's essentially a technique which helps us to understand the way we think, whilst challenging the beliefs we attach to those thoughts and how these make us act. In the meantime, try to remember that these thoughts *are just thoughts*. If we attach meaning to them, or try to push them away, that can give the intrusions more space to develop. Some people find it helpful to think of the intrusions like leaves in the wind, or passing clouds. They can come and go. What we need to address is how we respond to those thoughts.'

'OK, let's give it a go.' At this point, I'm willing to try anything.

———

After the appointment I head back to the bus stop wondering if I'm doing the right thing, dragging all these feelings out to be pored over by a relative stranger. Perhaps it's just easier to try and figure it out in my own head, save the awkwardness of saying it all out loud. But I'm desperate to try and unravel my thoughts so I can see the way forward with Lisa. She deserves that at least.

I lean my head against the cold window and close my tired eyes. I'm tired of the constant sting in my eyes. Always trying to conceal the threat of tears. I wonder if deep down I always knew we wouldn't last. We just seem to operate on different levels; she vivacious and full of optimism, me melancholy and measured. The night we met she described me as 'the strong and silent type', which made me laugh. I took it as a compliment, but later wondered if it was a thinly veiled way of saying I was boring.

She was in her first year at Sheffield Hallam, studying English, while I was doing my post-graduate teacher training. Adam, one of the guys on my course who I'd got to know, had a sister on the same course as Lisa and he invited me along to a house party one Saturday night in mid-October, 1988. I was reluctant to go but he talked me into it and I figured I could just stay for a bit and sneak out quietly when it got too much.

'Mind if I grab one of those?' a girl with bouncing curls of blonde hair resting just above her shoulders brushed past me in the kitchen, pointing over at a box of Babycham bottles on the worktop I was leaning on, awkwardly. Her bright pink lipstick was smudged slightly on her lower lip.

'Sure, go for it,' I smiled, making way as she reached for a bottle. She scanned the littered worktop for something, lifting up empty crisp packets before trying all the kitchen drawers.

'Here, is this what you're after?' I handed a bottle opener to her, noticing the warmth of her hazel eyes.

'My *hero*!' she exclaimed as she cracked open the bottle with a sharp fizz, before taking a sip.

'You can just call me Paul,' I said with a shy smile, hoping she wouldn't notice the thumping in my chest.

'Well, *Paul*,' she smirked, with a raise of her eyebrows, 'I'm Lisa.' She took another sip of her drink and leaned back on the worktop. Someone else came along and reached past us for a bottle before wandering out again. Lisa straightened out her shoulders and I noticed her slender waist in a black leotard, tucked into skintight black jeans. 'Are you at Sheffield Hallam then?' she asked, having to lean in to make herself heard over the Pet Shop Boys pumping out of the stereo in the other room.

'Er, yeah, I'm doing my teacher training at the minute... I, er, graduated in the summer,' I managed to stammer as she locked her eyes on mine.

She nodded coolly. 'A *teacher*. And what did you study?'

'English,' at this point I was reduced to one-word answers, my heart stuck in my throat.

'Oooh, snap!' she declared excitedly. I smiled but nothing came out. 'Well, it was nice to meet you, Paul.'

'You too,' I watched her disappear into the other room and caught a glimpse of her raising her arms to join her friends dancing.

I spent the next hour or so oscillating between propping myself up in the kitchen and wandering between the rooms, trying to look purposeful. I watched Lisa's every move over shoulders of people I was pretending to listen to, wondering if

I'd be brave enough to try and talk to her again before the night was over. My mind was swimming with things I could say, ways to catch her attention.

I watched as she headed for the front door and decided to take my opportunity, telling Adam I was going to the loo. I took a long swig of my warm can of lager to try and muster up some courage.

She was fumbling in her handbag for her packet of cigarettes as she sat on the steps leading up to the porch. 'Hey,' I said as I brushed past her on my way down the steps. I figured I could just pretend I was leaving if she wasn't interested in talking to me.

'Oh hey!' she said, taking out a cigarette and clumsily flicking at her lighter. 'You're not *leaving* are you?!'

I took this as encouraging. 'No, I've just come out for some air.'

'Yeah, me too,' she said holding up the cigarette. 'Kim says I'm not allowed to smoke in there,' she nodded backwards towards the house, rolling her eyes. 'Do you want one?'

'Yeah, why not,' I said, taking a seat next to her on the steps. 'Thanks.'

We sat in silence as I lit my cigarette just as awkwardly as she did. *Come on, Paul, now's your chance. Say something.*

'So, you don't live here then?' I asked, blowing out the smoke from my first drag. The nicotine gave me a massive rush, together with the adrenaline of actually plucking up the courage to talk to her.

'Nah, this is just my mate's place. I'm still at home, actually,' she admitted, looking a bit crestfallen. 'I'm from Sheffield so my parents only live just the other side of town. Seems extravagant to pay rent when I can save it and have my washing done too.'

I nodded, before taking another drag to give me time to

think of something else to say. She beat me to it. 'What about you?'

'Yeah I'm at my mum's at the minute, too. I was in a flat share with my uni mates last year but they all headed home after graduation so I figured I may as well save the cash and head home for a bit. I'm from round here too. You didn't fancy getting out of Sheffield then?' I ventured, curious as to why this lively, confident girl wouldn't want to leave her hometown and explore the world.

'My mum's not well, so…' she shrugged and dropped her gaze. 'Didn't really want to be too far away while she was getting her treatment and stuff.'

'Shit, sorry,' I kicked myself for putting my foot in it.

'It's OK, she's alright… I mean, it's been awful, but she's getting better,' she smiled, noticing my regret. 'I just felt like a bad daughter disappearing off to uni when she needed me. So I turned down a place at UCL. And anyway, Sheffield's a good uni, right? It could be worse.'

'Yeah, yeah it's good, I had fun here.'

'*Had*? Don't write yourself off yet, Paul,' she locked her eyes on mine as she took another drag and blew it out slowly, flicking the ash away. 'Still lots more fun to be had, I'm sure.'

Fuck. I'm way out of my depth. I could feel my heart racing as I noticed the muffled chorus of Tiffany's *I Think We're Alone Now* playing from inside. 'I'm sure there is,' I somehow managed to sound way cooler than I was feeling.

She looked at me curiously, as if trying to sum me up. I laughed and kicked at the step beneath me before catching her gaze again. I could feel the energy trembling between us like a magnetic field and, before I realised what I was doing, I was drawn to her, uncontrollably, my head leaning in slowly to kiss her bright pink lips, half expecting her to pull away. She didn't.

'Wow,' she said with a smile, 'and I thought you were shy.'

I laughed and closed my eyes, wondering where that sudden confidence came from.

Lisa's eyes widened as we heard the beginning of *The Only Way Is Up* by Yazz followed by excited whoops from inside. 'I *love* this song! Do you like dancing?' she asked, rising from her seat on the steps.

'Er... I don't know,' I stumbled, not really wanting to dance but not wanting the night to end, either.

'Come on!' she insists, taking me by the hand. 'There's still lots more fun to be had.'

The bus jolts to a halt. I wonder if there is still some fun to be had.

CHAPTER EIGHTEEN

I've often wondered what it is that Lisa saw in me that night at the house party. I could barely string a sentence together and was hardly sparkling company, but apparently that didn't put her off. She took my phone number, making me write it on her arm with a biro we found on the kitchen worktop. And by some miracle, it hadn't rubbed off by the time she made it home to her parents' house to transfer it into her phone book. I was secretly pleased she took my number rather than the other way around, the pressure on her to make the first move. I never expected her to, to be honest, but my heart leapt that Wednesday evening when the phone rang and my mum called me down from my room to say there was a 'young lady' on the phone for me. There was something reminiscent of high school about those early conversations, me speaking in hushed tones out in the hallway as Mum went back to *Coronation Street* in the lounge.

'Who was that, darling?' Mum asked as I put my head round the door to offer her a cup of tea.

'Oh, erm, just someone I met the other night, at that party I went to with Adam. She's studying English at Sheffield, we got chatting...' I answered, gazing at my feet like a sheepish teenager.

'Oh, lovely,' Mum's eyebrows raised, as her voice went up an octave, a hopeful half-smile creeping across her face. 'Are you planning on... seeing her again?'

'*Well*, I am actually, tomorrow night,' I said, unable to keep a straight face. 'We're going to have a drink in the student union, so...'

'Very nice, dear.'

The drink at the student union led to cheap dinner dates, gigs at The Leadmill and walks in the Peak District until, before long, we were introducing each other to our respective families and eventually looking for our first home together. And although it felt like we were still so young when we settled down, there had been plenty of fun together on the way. We had quite different tastes – she was a big trip-hop and electronica fan, whilst I was always more into the indie and art rock scene – but these differences seemed to give us plenty to talk about, plenty to explore, both individually and together.

I remember surprising her with tickets for Massive Attack at The Leadmill a few years ago, just before Christmas. It was my gift to her for our first wedding anniversary – paper being the traditional theme. I'll never forget her squeals of excitement as she flung her arms around my neck, planting kisses all over my face.

'Oh my God!' she cried as she examined the tickets that had fallen from out of the card. 'This is amazing, Paul! Thank you.'

As I turn the key in the front door, I realise I need to show Lisa we can get back to how we were.

CHAPTER NINETEEN

I'm busy marking Year 10's essays on *Of Mice and Men* in my tutor group classroom when I hear a gentle knock on the glass window of the door.

'Come in,' I say, without looking up. I put down my pen as the door opens. I raise my eyes to see Laura standing there.

'Morning, sir,' she smiles and closes the door carefully behind her, bringing in a kind of spectral light I've not experienced before.

'Laura?' I start to feel agitated, a strange sensation as if someone or something is physically pinning me down, and this time I realise I'm dreaming. At least I think I am.

'You don't mind me coming to see you, do you?' she asks, as she perches on one of the long rows of tables facing my desk at the front of the classroom.

'I don't know what's going on, here, Laura. But I know this isn't real,' my voice shakes slightly as I try to be firm. How do I make myself wake up?

'Well, that's for you to decide,' she grins and tilts her head to one side as she folds her arms and stretches her legs out in front of her.

'You gave me quite a fright, last time, when you left.'

'Yeah, sorry about that,' she laughs. 'I just wanted to let you know that I was doing alright, considering.'

'Thank you. It was nice... if a bit weird,' I laugh as I lock eyes with her and sit back in my chair. 'So what brings you here this time?' I wonder how long we've got until I wake up. I've never been one of those people that knows when they're dreaming, so I'm not sure how this all works.

'Just thought I'd pop by. I really liked your last lesson on *Romeo & Juliet*. Found it very... relatable.'

'Oh? In what way?' I reason that if this is a dream, there's no danger of anyone finding me having an intimate conversation with a student. Especially one that's dead.

'Well, you know the forbidden love and all that. I always used to think of you as the Romeo I couldn't have.'

I laugh nervously, with a frown. 'Laura, stop it. This isn't right.' I feel my face flush and I run my hand through my hair, stopping to rub the nape of my neck.

'Come on, sir,' she jumps herself up to sit on the desk, swinging her legs as she leans back on her hands. 'You must know *all* the girls fancy you. Especially Erin Robson.'

'Laura, don't. I don't want to hear this.'

'She'd kill me if she knew I'd told you that.'

I can't help but smirk at her attempt at a joke. 'Good one,' my eyes narrow as I look closely at her face. 'I could always tell you had an appetite for mischief.'

'Well, sir, this is *your* dream. So is it me who's mischievous? Or you?'

'Fair enough,' I snigger, realising she has a point. Unless she is genuinely visiting me from another realm. I never believed in any of that before. But sitting here with her now, the early morning sun streaming in, her scent catching the breeze through the open window, telling me things I don't want to hear, stirring feelings I don't want to feel; I start to question my previously unshakeable belief in science and reason. This must be why some people put so much faith into religion and the promise of an afterlife, in the face of grief. I've always had a certain respect – envy, even – for those who can truly believe that they might one day reach their lost loved ones, or meet them again on the other side. And who's to say we won't, anyway?

'So are these visits going to become a regular thing?' I sense a change in the light and I wonder if this means I'm about to wake up.

'Do you want them to be?' she asks, raising her eyebrows.

'Well it's always nice to see you,' I admit as I walk over to the window and look out from the third floor over the school grounds. Everything looks so real, as if I could touch it.

'Did you ever think of me... you know, in *that* way?' she looks up at me provocatively from under her fringe.

An uneasy feeling rises within me as I allow myself to consider the question. 'Laura, I'm married. And I'm nearly twice your age. Not to mention that I'm your teacher. And you're barely sixteen,' I close my eyes and sigh as I wonder if I ever really trusted myself. 'It's not right. I'm just not that kind of person, I'm sorry. I always cared a lot about you,' I realise I've switched to referring to her in the past tense. 'I'd be lying if I didn't admit you were my favourite. But I'd never abuse my position like that, Laura. I was always, I don't know, in awe of you, I guess. You were such a promising student, so talented and articulate and, well... clearly very mature for your age. You stood apart from the rest. It just makes me so sad,' I shake my head slowly as reality sinks back in. I feel a sudden urgency, as if time is running out.

Laura looks up at me with tears in her eyes. She stops them with the heels of both hands then wipes carefully under her eyelashes with her forefinger. 'Me too,' she smiles sadly. 'I like our chats,' she inhales and breathes out sharply through pursed lips. 'You were always so kind to me. That's what I liked about you. That and your dazzlingly blue eyes,' she winks as a playful smile crosses her lips.

'I just wanted to help you.'

'I know. Maybe I can come back, another time. If you'll have me? It can be like that Gorky's Zygotic Mynci song, *Let's Get Together In Our Minds*,' she laughs through tears now spilling over and running down her cheeks. 'Have you heard their new album?'

'Yes. I love it.'

'We wouldn't be doing anything wrong.'

I think of Lisa. And Emilia. This feels wrong even though I know it's not real. 'I think it's time to say goodbye, Laura.'

She nods slowly and looks down at her feet. 'You're right,' she whispers as she walks over and kisses me gently on the cheek. 'Take care, sir.'

Laura turns and walks towards the door, looks back to give a little wave and is gone.

A sudden noise wakes me up with a start and I realise the breeze from the open window has blown the en-suite door shut. I prop myself up onto my side and squint at the alarm clock. It's still early and I have to concentrate for a moment to remember what day it is. Saturday, I realise. Today's the day Lisa and I head to the Peak District for our night away.

I hear Emilia's gentle breathing through the baby monitor on my bedside table and glance over at Lisa but she has her back to me. I can tell from the deep and steady rhythm of her breathing that she's fast asleep. I roll onto my back and rest my head on my arm underneath me, staring into the darkness as my eyes adjust. I have an uneasiness sitting in my chest as I recall my dream of Laura; a mixture of guilt and sadness.

I'm appalled by the fact that I clearly imagined all of what happened in my own subconscious and wonder what that says about me. I feel like I'm betraying Lisa with these thoughts of Laura but what troubles me most is that I don't know where they're coming from. Why do I keep imagining us in these scenarios? Is it a yearning, or a recollection of events that I've somehow blocked out, in denial? But that doesn't make sense in the context of what I know to be true – that Laura is dead. Then again, nothing much of my life seems to be making sense to me at the moment.

I need to try and connect the dots. I pull on my pinstriped pyjama bottoms and a white t-shirt from the chair next to the bed and creep downstairs. The dawn light fills the hallway through the front door. I pick my grey hoodie from where it hangs off the banister at the bottom of the stairs and slide on my slippers which are sitting in the hallway.

I head to the kitchen and take my personal stereo from out of my satchel which is lying on the breakfast bar. Running my index finger down the CD rack next to the hi-fi, I find my *Gorky 5* album and put the CD into my personal stereo. Can I get away with making a coffee without waking Lisa and Emilia? I decide to risk it and make myself a strong one, then remember that I'd stashed the remainder of the cigarettes from New Year's

Eve in the top drawer. I take a sip of my coffee, pull out a cigarette and go to sit on the backdoor step. Holding the cigarette between my lips, I untangle the wires to my headphones and put them in my ears before skipping to track three, *Let's Get Together In Our Minds*. As the CD whirrs in the player, I light the cigarette and take a long drag just as the wistful opening guitar riff kicks in, backed with the romantic piano melody and slow drumbeat. I close my eyes and sink into the song, lightheaded from the cocktail of nicotine, caffeine and forbidden thoughts. By the time the chorus kicks in with its rising violin section and the tension of the now-urgent percussion, there's a deep ache of guilt settling in my chest.

CHAPTER TWENTY

'See you tomorrow then poppet,' I kiss Emilia's caramel curls on the top of her head as I hand her over to my mum on the steps leading up to her front door. My mum gives Lisa, who's stayed in the car, a wave and she waves back with a hint of a smile.

'So, she usually naps just after lunch, but no longer than an hour else she won't settle at bedtime,' I hand my mum the ruck-sack that we usually use for nursery as Emilia toddles along the Minton tiles of Mum's hallway. 'I've put her favourite pyjamas in there and she will not go to sleep without this guy,' I hold up a rugged brown bunny rabbit and waggle his ears before handing him over. 'Oh and she'll have some warm milk before bed, maybe about six thirty.'

'We'll be fine, darling. Go on! I hope you have.... a good time,' she strokes my stubbly cheek as she remembers that this is more of a crisis summit than a dirty weekend away. 'I hope it goes well,' she smiles.

'Thanks Mum,' I kiss her on the cheek. 'We'll probably be

back about teatime; we were thinking of popping for a Sunday roast on the way back if that's alright?'

'That's fine love, take your time. I'll see you tomorrow.'

'See you, then.'

'Oh, and Paul...' she calls as I turn to head down the steps. 'Stop smoking, dear. It's not good for you. A cheeky cig on New Year's Eve is one thing, but don't make a habit of it, eh?'

I laugh that I'm being told off for smoking at thirty-one years old. 'Alright, Mum.' I laugh as I wave behind me, blowing her a kiss as I reach the bottom of the steps and head towards the car. I suddenly feel nervous about being alone with Lisa.

It's only a short drive to the Derbyshire village where we're staying but it involves driving past the spot where Laura was killed. I realise I'm distant as we drive along the A57, my mind elsewhere. Lisa is quiet and it feels like we're struggling to get off the mark of even making small talk. We need to reconnect, before this chasm appearing between us becomes impossible to bridge. But I can't get the melody of the Gorky's song out of my head and it brings back thoughts of Laura.

'Feels weird, doesn't it, not having Emilia in the back?' I nod towards where her car seat would ordinarily be strapped in, breaking the silence.

'Yeah, quite a milestone this, our first night away since she was born,' Lisa agrees. 'Maybe we should have done it sooner?'

I nod quietly as it dawns on me that we haven't exactly made an effort to make time for each other over the last 18 months or so. But that's just early parenthood, I figure. It's hard work. Time runs away and before you know it, it's weeks since you've had a proper conversation, let alone time for anything else.

'So, how's the new project coming on at work?' I ask.

'Yeah, it's alright, we're just brainstorming at the minute but Richard's pleased with some of the ideas I've come up with so...'

'Ah, good.'

'We're going to be meeting with the client again at some point over the next few weeks, I'm just waiting for Rich to get back to me with some dates. It'll mean a couple of nights in London this time so we're just trying to get things organised,' she says all of this without looking up from the text message I can see she's punching out on her mobile phone, through the corner of my eye.

'Right,' I nod slowly. I don't know why this pisses me off but it doesn't seem like a great time for her to be heading off to London for a few days. I wonder if I'm being unfair. 'What do you need to be in London for, exactly?' I'm genuinely interested but it instantly feels like an interrogation as soon as the words tumble out of my mouth.

'Well, it's easier to get honest feedback from the client face-to-face, rather than on a conference call where you can't see their reactions. We're just sharing ideas for the marketing campaign at this stage but it's always good to have some time getting to know them better too, you know, drinks and stuff.'

'Yeah, I guess.' Her job is in a different world to mine.

'How was your session the other night with the therapist? Not had much chance to speak to you properly since then. You found it helpful, did you?' she asks, looking up at me.

'Er, yeah, I think it went well. It was with Jeremy, the same guy I saw last year. He's really nice.'

'Oh that's good then.'

'Yeah, he seems to know his stuff.'

'And what did you talk about?'

I'm a bit taken aback as I'm not sure I want to go into any real detail right now, but don't want to make it weird by seeming closed off when we're meant to be opening up to one another. 'Er, well, it was just a kind of initial assessment really, just telling him what's been going on and stuff.'

'And what has been going on?' her tone is quite measured, almost as if she's trying to catch me out rather than show concern.

'Well, I told him about my OCD flaring up before Laura died and then that was obviously a shock. And I said that I didn't feel like we were... I don't know, it's been hard, just lately, hasn't it?'

'Yeah, you could say that,' she sends me a sad smile.

I indicate and pull into the long driveway of the spa hotel I've booked us into. 'This is us.'

'Looks nice,' Lisa says as she opens her door and steps out onto the gravel. Her footsteps crunch as she walks around to the boot and takes out our weekend bag. 'Did you pack your cossie?'

'Yeah, I'm looking forward to a sauna later after our walk. We're booked in for dinner at eight tonight.'

'Lovely,' she looks up at the Edwardian mansion house and heads towards the entrance doors.

We lace up our walking boots in the reception area of the hotel before heading out into the hazy afternoon sunshine. The January sun is trying its hardest to burn through the low cloud and it casts a gentle, creamy glow across the Derbyshire hills.

Perfect walking conditions, I think to myself. And it feels like spring is not too far away, now that Christmas is a distant memory and some early snowdrops are peeping through the verges by the roadside. I reach cautiously for Lisa's hand and she interlocks her fingers around mine.

'This is nice,' I say as I pull my sunglasses down from the top of my head. We used to do this sort of thing often, before Emilia, but she's at a funny age now where she can't walk very far but is getting too heavy to be carried for any real distance. It'll be easier in a couple of years, I tell myself. But then I wonder if we might try for another baby in the next year or so, maybe once Emilia's out of nappies. Being an only child myself, I hate the idea of Emilia growing up without a sibling.

'Yeah, lovely day for it,' she swings my arm playfully. 'That hotel is amazing. I'm looking forward to the spa. And dinner!'

'Me too,' I beam as I feel we might just be able to make something special of this weekend. 'We're this way,' I point to the fingerpost which leads through a gap in the hedgerow to a footpath over some undulating farmland.

Our honeymoon was a week spent hiking in the Lake District in the late-August sunshine. It was wonderful – not the villa in an Italian vineyard or trip of a lifetime to South America that some of friends were organising for their honeymoons, but we weren't exactly flush with money after buying the house and, anyway, it was perfect for us. All we need is each other, we said. A nice, quiet break after the chaos of the wedding, before I had to head back to school. And a love of the outdoors was the biggest thing we had in common.

'So, do you think these tablets you're on are working?' Lisa asks as she joins beside me again after we squeeze through a stile in single file.

'It's hard to say but, I guess so,' I actually engage with the question which I don't feel like I've given much thought until she asked. 'I suppose I feel a bit... I dunno, lighter I guess.' I feel the gentle sun on my face and take a lungful of the cool air. It feels so much cleaner out here, despite being only a 40-minute drive out of town. I recall how good it feels to move my body, to have my heart rate raised by exercise rather than chronic terror. I look around at the glorious countryside and remember what Laura said in my dream, about there being so much beauty in the world.

'You seem a little less agitated by things than you were a few weeks ago.'

'Yeah, I guess,' I don't really know what to say. 'I have this kind of fogginess around my head sometimes, like I'm in a bit of a dream, which is a bit unsettling. But the intrusions have become less frequent, I think.'

'And these... intrusions, I mean, what do they actually *involve*? What sort of things do you think about?'

'Well it's not really like I'm *thinking* them,' I pause. 'It's hard to explain... but it's not like the thoughts are coming from my conscious brain, it's more like another voice that's plaguing me, taunting me almost. It's exhausting to be honest. Like a constant battle. The devil on my shoulder.'

'Right,' she frowns and looks a little alarmed at the realisation of just how fucked up my mind actually is. 'And what does the voice say?'

'All sorts of stuff really, but it's usually pretty dark, like something terrible will happen if I don't do things in a particular way, or follow a certain ritual,' I wonder whether I should give her specifics but decide to wait and see if she asks. 'And that's where the compulsions come into play. To try and neutralise the awfulness of whatever just popped into my mind.'

137

'Sounds mental,' she laughs sympathetically.

'It is,' I laugh with her. 'And, well, it's been like this in my head for... I dunno, the best part of twenty years, now.'

'How do you get anything done?! I thought it was just that you got stressed if things weren't, like, neat and orderly and stuff,' she laughs incredulously. Then her face changes. 'Why have you never said anything before?' she asks, showing a compassion in her eyes that I've not seen for so long.

'Well, it's just hard, really, saying it out loud. I've never properly gone into detail about it with anyone,' I think about my chat with Laura, the night she died. 'Like you said, it sounds mental. I guess I was worried whoever I told would think I needed locking up. I think that's quite common for people that suffer from it, this need to try and hide what you're doing. The rational part of your brain knows that none of these compulsive rituals will change anything but then there's a niggling doubt, just hiding at the back, that if you don't step on that crack again then the horrible thing you just imagined *will* happen. That's why the therapy helps – it's nothing Jeremy hasn't heard before. And it helps to be told that what you're going through is actually something that lots of people suffer from and there's a name for it.'

'But we're *married*, Paul,' I'm taken aback as her eyes start to fill with tears. 'You must know you can tell me anything?'

'Yeah, I know, I... I guess we've just got more important things to worry about now, haven't we?'

'Yeah, but doesn't that make it worse for you? You know with the anxiety?'

'I suppose in some ways, the intrusions can be more disturbing, I guess. But day-to-day when we're so busy seeing to Emilia and rushing to and from work and stuff, I guess there's just not as much room in my head for it. But it tends to pounce when I'm knackered or overwhelmed with things. And that's when it becomes all-consuming.' I realise this is the most openly we've talked about things for ages. 'That's why I had to see the doctor this time last year, you know when she was newborn and we were totally exhausted, on top of the sheer terror of being responsible for this tiny new person, well it just all got a bit much and the thoughts started creeping back in. But I knew you were finding it hard too, you know with the pressure of the breastfeeding and me being back at work and that. So I didn't want to burden you with what was going on in my head.'

She squeezes my hand and looks remorseful. 'It's been a tough year, I guess. I'm sorry. That I never really stopped to ask how you were doing. A new baby just becomes the centre of attention I suppose and we tend to fade into insignificance.'

'Maybe we need to do this more often? Just me and you?'

'Yeah, maybe,' she smiles sadly.

I step out of the shower and grab one of the fluffy white towels from the heated towel rail in the bathroom. *I could get used to this*, I think. I run the towel through my hair and over my face before wrapping it around my waist and sliding my feet into the complimentary slippers. I glance in the mirror but it's misted up from the steam of the shower so I head into the bedroom and see Lisa sitting at the dressing table, applying her mascara. The sight of her golden curls scooped up away from her slender shoulders sends a shiver up my legs.

'You look nice,' I whisper into her ear as I kiss the nape of her neck and take in her scent. 'Shall we...?' I raise an eyebrow and nod over to the king-size bed on the other side of the room.

'Later,' she giggles, as she strokes the side of my cheek. 'Dinner's in fifteen minutes. We're going to need longer than that, aren't we?' she lifts her eyebrows.

'Yep, definitely,' I nod, feigning confidence. She laughs.

'Anyway, I can't take you seriously when you've got that white fluff all over your face,' she laughs as she takes hold of my jaw.

I glance in the mirror. 'Oh yeah,' I wrinkle my nose as I examine my face in the mirror and see that the fluff from the towels has stuck to my stubble. 'Maybe I should have shaved?'

'No, you look good with a bit of stubble,' she winks. 'Go and get dressed and we can get a cocktail before dinner!'

I do as I'm told. I pull on a light grey fine-knit sweater with my smartest dark blue jeans. I stand in front of the full-length mirror in the corner of the room and notice a colour to my cheeks and a depth to the blue of my eyes that I've not seen for a while.

CHAPTER TWENTY-ONE

'That was... delicious,' Lisa murmurs then lets out a sigh as she rolls onto her side to face me, our bodies tangled up together with the crisp white sheets on the bed. Her cheeks are flushed and I reach over to tuck some stray curls behind her ear, running my fingers across her shoulders and down her back. Her skin is so soft and warm. I didn't realise how much I needed this.

'We really *should* do this more often,' she says sleepily as I look into her hazel eyes and catch a glimpse of the woman I fell in love with all those years ago. I'm relieved she's still there. 'You still know how to look after me, don't you?'

I shift onto my back and she runs her fingers across my chest. 'We're good together,' I whisper, as I kiss her forehead. I wonder how much we had to drink last night, as I feel an ache creeping across my eyes and into my forehead. My mouth is dry.

'I need some water,' I say, sitting up and reaching for the glass on my bedside table. I take several gulps and close my eyes. I open them slowly to see Laura sitting in the chair in the corner of the room, a coy smile across her lips. I take a sharp breath in and Lisa looks at me with a frown.

'You OK?' she asks, stroking my arm gently.

'Er, yeah... sorry,' I lie back and exhale through my mouth as I rub my eyes with my fingertips.

'Do you want coffee?' she laughs.

'Ugh,' I groan. 'Yes, please. How much did we drink last night?' She seems pretty fresh, compared to me.

'A couple of cocktails to start, then I think we had a bottle of red between us and you were on the whisky after that,' she recalls as she puts a pod into the swanky coffee machine and presses the button. 'I had a couple of G&Ts to finish off.'

'Christ. My head's banging.' I run my fingers across my eyes, pinching the bridge of my nose. I'm almost worried to open them in case I see Laura again.

Lisa brings my coffee over and gets back into bed beside me, cradling her cup.

'I love these espresso machines, they're like magic! Maybe we could treat ourselves and get one for home?' she says, raising her eyebrows playfully.

'Ha! Maybe a bit extravagant, don't you think?' I laugh as I take a sip and place my cup back down on the bedside table.

She shrugs and puts down her cup. 'You know we don't need to check out til twelve...' she says suggestively as she runs her fingers slowly up my inner thigh. I flinch as I think of the vision of Laura sitting in the corner of the room. Lisa senses my reluctance and backs away. 'Sorry, I thought... well, earlier... it was nice, wasn't it?'

'Nice? It was... amazing. Sorry... I just... I'm not feeling too great.' I take a sip of the coffee and lean back slowly against the headboard of the bed.

'I've missed us being... together, like that. How had we

managed to leave it so long?' she's propped herself up on her elbow and rests her head on her hand, looking at me intently. 'Do you remember our first holiday to Madrid? We barely left the hotel room! We may as well have stayed at home.'

'Yeah,' I laugh. 'I remember. I guess it was just easier then, to make time for... it.' I find talking about our sex life so incredibly awkward. 'Fewer... interruptions, you know?'

'It's not that you don't want me?'

'No, of course not! It's just... it's hard, don't you think? When we're knackered and busy with work and Emilia and stuff.'

'Yeah, I know,' she sighs. 'Well, anyway, it's nice not to have to get up,' she mumbles as she nestles beneath my arm and closes her eyes. I finish my coffee and sink back down into the bed, trying to shake the image of Laura from my mind.

I wake to the sound of a door gently closing in the corridor outside of our room and blink my eyes open. It's now light outside and I realise we must have been asleep for another couple of hours since we drifted off again this morning. I squeeze my shoulder blades together to feel the stretch across my chest. My head's still fuzzy.

As I roll over my heart stops at the sight of Laura lying next to me in the hotel bed. I'm arrested by a regret I can't quite place. 'Morning, sir,' she murmurs gently as she smiles, her hazel eyes gazing at me from under her chestnut fringe.

I bolt upright, gasping as I rub my eyes.

'Paul!' Lisa cries, sitting up. 'What the fuck?'

I breathe out through my mouth to calm myself and a cold dampness runs across my forehead. My head's spinning.

Lisa throws off the duvet and pulls on a pair of grey jogging bottoms from the chair in the corner of our hotel room.

'You were saying 'Laura' in your sleep, Paul! What the hell is that all about?' her eyes widen as she throws her arms out, exasperated. 'And it's not the first time that's happened, is it?!'

She sits down in the chair and puts her head in her hands, then looks up at me, her hands in prayer position to her mouth, eyebrows raised, poised to ask me something. 'I don't know how to say this, but... was something going on between you?' she asks, her voice trembling as she locks her eyes on mine.

'No! Christ, Lisa, of course not. She's sixteen!' I realise I'm talking about her in the present tense, forgetting. I close my aching eyes, questioning what it means seeing Laura lying next to me in bed. Did something happen between us and I've just blocked it out, like a defence mechanism against my conscience? No, I would never. I just wanted to help her. That's not who I am. *It was just a dream*, I reassure myself. I feel like the bed might disintegrate underneath me, everything about to collapse and swallow me whole. I swing my legs over the edge of the bed, and rest my head in my hands. I don't know what's real anymore. I wait for more words but none arrive. Is silence worse?

She gets up from the chair and walks over to the window. I can hear her stifling tears as she looks out across the hotel courtyard.

'Things just haven't been right between us... for a while now, have they?' she turns to face me. I'm relieved by the sadness etched across her face.

'No, they haven't,' I say, jumping up to comfort her. 'But I swear, Lisa, I would never do that. I love you. You and Emilia, you're all that matters to me.' I move towards her to put my arms around her waist but she backs away, tears streaming down her face. 'You do believe me, don't you?' I look at her, searching for a glimpse of the trust we promised one another with our vows. 'I don't know what's going on with my mind, Lis. I'm so scared.'

'Lisa?' I raise my voice now. 'Lisa, talk to me. Please. You don't really think I was having an affair with one of my students?' my voice breaks. Saying it out loud makes me feel nauseous.

Her face turns to stone. 'Well I had wondered if you've been getting it elsewhere. But I never really thought you'd go *that* far.'

'*Getting it elsewhere*?' my eyes widen and my stomach churns, but I don't know whether it's repulsion or guilt.

'It just went through my mind, that's all. You've been pretty distant with me lately. And you *never* make the first move!' She's shouting now. 'Even when I try you hardly seem interested!'

'Lisa, what do you take me for, seriously? For fuck's sake.' I'm incensed. 'I love you! You're my *wife*. Do you remember, what we promised each other? I meant *every word*. I just... Christ, I don't know... do you not *trust* me?!' My temperature rises and I start to raise my voice.

'Alright, I'm sorry,' she offers a reluctant apology. 'But it's hardly *unheard of*, is it? *Man gets bored of wife after five years of marriage and a baby, tries his luck somewhere else*,' she reads like a gossip magazine headline. 'Plus teenagers are always lusting after their young, attractive teachers, I can see how it happens,' she raises her eyebrows as if to say she knows my secret. It almost feels like she wants me to have been unfaithful, to give her a clean getaway. 'Men don't just *completely* lose their sex drive for no reason, Paul. And I mean, after your dad's track record, you can't blame me for wondering whether it runs in the family.'

My jaw falls away from the rest of my face, my eyes widening. 'How could you say that?' She gets like this when she knows she's in the wrong but can't admit it. 'You really know how to cut me to the core, don't you?! Jesus!'

I have a sudden urge to leave the room, I can't be around her when she's like this. There's an ache in my chest again and I don't know what to do with my hands. It dawns on me that we might have crossed a point of no return. I head for the door then stop and turn around. 'Don't you think what my dad did might make me a more faithful husband? I saw, *first hand*, how what he did tore my mum apart. Do you think I'd do that to you? To Emilia?'

She doesn't answer but looks at me, unmoved, and shrugs her shoulders. 'I just, I don't know, Paul. Like I said, it just felt like you stopped wanting me, all of a sudden, and I didn't know what to think. Plus it's like you've been living in your own head for the last few months, it's felt like there's been no room for me.'

'Then why didn't you *talk* to me, instead of just jumping to these horrible conclusions? Maybe I have been trapped in my own head just lately but I've not been well! *For fuck's sake*. You've hardly stopped to ask me how I'm feeling, you've been so absorbed with work!' It feels like I've loosened a thread that's unravelling in front of me. 'And we never do anything together, just the two of us! How many times have our plans been cancelled recently because you're busy off down the wine bar after work?! Have you ever stopped to think how that might make *me* feel, as your husband? For me, intimacy comes from a real connection, like it used to do. Where did that go?! I want to feel *close* to you, Lisa, not just go through the motions because it's what we're supposed to do. I can't be something I'm not!' My voice cracks and I run both hands through my hair, taking a deep breath in as I tug on the roots.

Lisa sits on the bed, reticent. The words dissipate into the room, hanging in the air with my heartbreak and the smell of stale booze.

CHAPTER TWENTY-TWO

The night I arrived at Mum's, three months before our wedding, was the first time I allowed myself to wonder if I was doing the right thing. It's hard to admit, when you catch a glimpse of something ugly in the person you're planning to spend the rest of your life with. It's just a blip, I told myself, head buried, trying not to look.

'Listen, love,' Mum ventured, as she handed me a cup of tea, still in her pyjamas from me waking her just before midnight. 'I know you love her, but it's not too late to change your mind. I just want to make sure you know that.'

'We're getting married in *August*, Mum. The invites have gone out! I'm hardly going to call it off because of one big row, am I?'

'It's not the first time though, is it? Her flying off the handle and sending you packing for the night seems to be a bit of a common theme,' Mum said, eyebrows raised, taking a sip of her tea. 'Who's with her now? I don't suppose she's in any fit state to be at home on her own?'

'Emma took her back to ours in a cab. And yeah, she's had a

few drinks. But, look, it's not like this all the time, she just needs to... let off some steam sometimes. It's not like we don't get on, on the whole.'

'Well, yes, maybe she'll grow out of it,' Mum waved a hand in the air. 'I just don't want you to feel like you've got to put up with this behaviour. I must admit I was a little surprised when you got engaged so soon after you moved in together. You're both quite... *different*,' Mum put her hand on mine and looked straight into my eyes. 'It's a big commitment, if you're not certain.'

'I am certain! Mum, I love her. And of course we're different, everyone's *different*. But we're good together!' I insisted, throwing my hands up in the air. 'Opposites attract, don't they?!'

'I'm just saying, you don't need to settle, Paul. Let's face it, it's not as if you had many long-term relationships, before you met,' which was Mum's polite way of saying 'any'. 'You don't need to rush into it, is all. You could just leave it another year and see how things go.'

I want to say OK, that sounds sensible. But I know I can't. And anyway, we're good together. Opposites attract, don't they?

I sink into the sofa in Jeremy's office and notice I'm picking at the skin around my thumb, as he looks over the notes he made from our last session. It feels like I've had to wait an age for this appointment but it's actually only been a couple of weeks. Needless to say, the atmosphere has been tense at home, but Lisa is in London for a couple of days for work so Emilia is at my mum's whilst I'm here to pour my heart out to Jeremy.

He looks up at me, his square rimless reading glasses perched on his nose. He's wearing a navy blue and brown checked flannel shirt, open at the collar slightly so I can see the grey t-shirt underneath. His tan leather desert boots are scuffed around the toes. 'So how have you been feeling since our last session?'

Where to start?

I'd been wanting to tell Jeremy about the dreams of Laura but now I have the opportunity, I'm hesitant. But I need to know what it all means. I inhale before opening up the floodgates, barely pausing for breath.

Jeremy nods as he scribbles away in his notebook, before looking up at me. 'A classic symptom of OCD is becoming obsessed that we might have done something without realising, perhaps to damage our relationship, or to hurt somebody, and we might start to worry that we'll get "found out",' he uses air quotes to emphasise there's no danger of being *found out* for something that hasn't actually happened. 'It's important to remember these obsessions are not a reflection of our personality. Just because these intrusions come into our mind, it doesn't mean we will act on them.' I start to feel more relaxed as I realise this is exactly what is happening to me with the thoughts of Laura.

'Well, this is the thing because I know – *I know* – I'm not the sort of man who would ever do anything like that. I would never cheat on my wife or risk losing my daughter. And the idea of being involved with a student physically repulses me. But I can't help but go over and over these scenarios that play out in my dreams, searching desperately for clues as to whether it's all in my imagination or a recollection of something that actually happened. And, if I am imagining it, what does that say about me? Did I *want* it to happen?!'

Jeremy nods, waiting for me to continue.

'So the next one I had, I knew I was dreaming, which was a pretty weird sensation in itself. But we were becoming... close, I guess. And I seemed to be enjoying it. It was nothing physical, really, it was just a suggestion of what could happen if we allowed it to. But I knew she was dead, so I knew it would never happen and I knew I was dreaming, and it felt almost like we could do whatever we liked because it was just in our minds. *My* mind, I suppose.' I remember the Gorky's song we talked about and how that made me feel so close to her. It's the betrayal of being emotionally, rather than physically, close to someone else that I feel guiltiest about. 'In fact, that was part of our conversation, she suggested that some of the girls in my class find me attractive,' I wince at the awkwardness of saying it out loud. 'And I told her she was being mischievous. But she pointed out that this was all in *my* mind so it was, in fact, me being mischievous. I think that stayed with me, the guilt, that this is all going on in *my* head, so it must be something wrong with *me*.'

'You must find this internal battle exhausting. Do you notice that these intrusions make you behave differently, when they're at their worst? Say, after you've had one of these dreams?' A relief washes over me as it feels like Jeremy knows exactly what's happening in my mind.

'Yeah, so, I had one of these dreams whilst my wife and I were away. Although this one was more of a vision than a dream, I think, sometimes it's hard to tell whether I'm asleep or in a waking dream. Or even if it's real, to be honest.'

'Do you want to tell me what happened?' Jeremy asks casually, taking a sip of his herbal tea. He has a way of making me want to tell him everything without feeling like I'm being interrogated. I can see from the glass mug he's drinking from that it's probably peppermint, or maybe green.

I recount, awkwardly, what happened that morning in the hotel room with Lisa, and my vision of Laura in bed with me. 'That was when she asked if I'd been unfaithful. But it really disturbed me, not just that she thought I would be unfaithful, but that she thought I was capable of allowing something to happen with one of my students.'

'That must have been upsetting for you, after the progress you were making while you were away?'

'Yeah, it was,' I recall Lisa's comments about me taking after my dad. 'She basically argued that, if I *wasn't* sleeping with someone else, there must be something wrong with me because men don't just lose their sex drive. As if it's an indication of my masculinity, or lack of, so she seems to think.'

'Well, we all have different libidos, whether we're male or female. And of course it's likely to fluctuate over time, depending on our stress levels, physical and mental wellness, etcetera.'

'That's exactly what I said. We've got a toddler and we both work and I've not exactly been on top form recently so, I mean, to my mind, it's hardly surprising. Plus, I don't know, I guess I find different things about her attractive now, it's not just the pure lust of when we were first together. We were talking so openly with each other whilst we were away, I felt a real connection and that's when I'm most attracted to her. It just feels like we're on completely different pages these days. There's a part of the circuit that's just not firing up, I guess.'

I try and settle into the silence as Jeremy takes in what I've said and considers his reply.

'And have you spoken with her about this? About how her accusations have made you feel?'

'Not really, not since the heat of the moment. She's been busy with work and now she's away for a few days so we've just been kind of skirting around it, I guess. I can't make up my mind whether I feel more betrayed that she's not supportive of my struggles or guilty for making her life a misery,' with that my voice breaks and I start to feel my shoulders tremble. 'Sorry.'

'You don't need to apologise.'

'I just don't think I make her happy anymore. She seems to want something from me that I can't give, at the minute, anyway. And maybe vice versa, if I'm honest.' There's liberation in being able to talk about what I want without danger of it turning into yet another argument.

'And what is it that you want, from her?' Jeremy shifts in his chair and crosses one leg over the other.

'I want a connection. I want to be able to talk to her, properly, I mean. Not just about what Emilia's had for lunch or who's picking her up on Wednesday. A proper conversation, about things that get us thinking, things that help us examine our ideas. How else do we grow as people? As a couple? It feels like there should be more than this.' I think back to when we first got together.

'Is that what brought you together in the first place?' Jeremy asks, reading my mind.

'Yeah, I guess. She just stood out, you know, we understood each other. She seemed to share a love of the arts and how our beliefs and experiences of the world can be challenged through... I don't know, hearing a new song or reading something interesting. We used to share so much. Now she just seems closed off and I can't break down the barrier.'

'It seems to me that this is something you can get back, with some work, if that's what you both want.' Jeremy suggests as he looks at his watch. 'I'm afraid that's our time up for today, Paul.

I hope you've found it helpful, to begin untangling some of that?'

'Yes, thank you.' I smile weakly as I'm suddenly anxious about facing the actual world outside. I feel like I've been through the wringer.

Jeremy heads for the door and holds it open for me. He's taller than he appears when he's sitting down.

'See you next time,' I hold out my hand to shake Jeremy's as we reach the bottom of the stairs. I don't know if I'm supposed to but it seems like a solid, manly way to end an encounter in which I've been mostly crying.

He smiles as he shakes my hand gently. 'Bye, Paul.'

CHAPTER TWENTY-THREE

'So she's in London again this week, is she?' Julia asks as we walk around the park across the road from school. The decay of winter is starting to give way to thoughts of spring as crocuses peep through the grass.

I nod, then relay Lisa's itinerary to Julia as if I'm her personal assistant, I'm so used to this new regime.

'And how does that leave things for you with Emilia, you know with work an' that?' she asks, between mouthfuls of her salt and vinegar crisps.

'Well, it's usually me doing drop off and pick up anyway, but, yeah I guess it's been a tiring few weeks, it just being me to get up if she wakes in the night or whatever. And she misses her, you know.' I wonder if I miss her, too.

'Must be pretty lonely, just kicking around at home when the little un's in bed?'

'Yeah, I guess so,' I thrust my hands in my coat pocket. There's still a bite in the early-February air, despite the sun warming my face.

'Listen, why don't I come over tonight? I'll bring a bottle. We can shout at the contestants on *Who Wants To Be A Millionaire*?'

I remember my appointment with Jeremy this evening and that I'm having dinner at my mum's afterwards, as she's picking Emilia up from nursery. 'I, er, I can't tonight, my mum's getting Emilia so I'm going to hers for tea.' I think how it would be nice to have some adult company though. 'You free tomorrow though?'

'Yeah, it's a date. I'll bring some of my mum's jerk chicken round if yer want? Anthony usually teks the girls to t' chippy after swimming on a Friday so they'll be alright.'

'Yeah that'd be nice, Ju,' I flash her a grateful smile. 'Thank you.'

'Anytime, pal. No one ever wants to watch *Millionaire* wi' me,' she laughs as she checks her watch and scrunches up her empty crisp packet. 'Right, we'd better be gettin' back, ha'n't we?'

'Yeah, I've got the Year 11s for a double lesson this afternoon,' I roll my eyes.

It's noticeably lighter than it was this time two weeks ago, as I head back to my mum's after my appointment with Jeremy.

I run up the steps to my mum's front door and give the faded brass knocker a sharp but cheerful tap. I hear a happy squeal from inside and see my mum's silhouette approach the front door.

'Hello darling,' she kisses me on the cheek and gestures to the kitchen. 'We're just in here.'

I follow her down the hallway and through to the kitchen where Emilia sits in her highchair by the island as my mum stirs something on the hob. 'Daddy!' Emilia chirps as she lifts both arms towards me.

'Hello, sweetheart,' I lift her out of the highchair and give her a kiss on the forehead. 'Something smells yummy, doesn't it?'

'Spaghetti carbonara for us,' Mum declares, taking a taste from the wooden spoon she's holding. 'Emilia's had some scrambled egg and vegetables. They said she'd had pasta at nursery and I thought this might be a bit rich for her.' She wrinkles her nose.

'Yeah that's fine,' I stand Emilia on my knees as I sit down on the battered old leather sofa in the corner of the kitchen. 'You love scrambled egg don't you, poppet?'

She leans into me as she grabs a handful of my hair. 'Has she been alright?' I ask my mum.

'You've been good as gold, haven't you my little love?' she says to Emilia as she drains the pasta in the kitchen sink and spoons it into shallow bowls. 'They said she'd had a lovely day, at nursery.'

'Oh good,' I head over to the dining table and pop Emilia back into her highchair. 'You sit back down there while Daddy and Nanna have their tea.' I put some crayons and a piece of paper in front of her before she gets annoyed about being back in the chair. 'Have you got a yoghurt or something she can have?'

'Yes, in the fridge, love,' she waves over to the fridge along the back wall of the kitchen, as if I don't know where it is.

'Thanks for getting her,' I say, popping an olive from the fridge into my mouth.

'It's a pleasure, darling. Anytime,' I sit down and she places a huge bowl of steaming pasta drenched in a silky cream sauce in front of me. 'There's parmesan there, if you want it.'

'Thank you. God, this looks delicious!' I pick up the grater and start shaving curls of parmesan onto my plate before holding it out to my mum sitting opposite me.

'Goddd,' Emilia experiments. 'GOD, GOD, GOD,' she shouts.

My eyes widen and I give my mum a sideways glance as I turn to Emilia and say 'Good! Good, good, good.'

'You've got to be careful what you say around her now, you know,' my mum laughs, raising her eyebrows. 'She's like a sponge at the minute.'

'Yeah,' my heart sinks a little as I realise she's probably been picking up some pretty negative vibes from Lisa and me at home.

'So how did it go, this evening?' Mum asks as she twists some spaghetti into a spoon with her fork. 'Your... appointment?'

'Yeah, it was, good, I think,' I pour some water for us both from the jug she's placed on the table. I'm not sure I want to go into specifics, but I had to tell her about the sessions with Jeremy when I first needed her to collect Emilia from nursery. 'I think it's helping me... figure some things out, you know?'

'Well that's good,' she says, pouring herself a glass of white wine. 'Do you want some?' she asks, holding up her glass.

'No I'd better not, I'm driving.'

'And how are things... at home?' she lowers her voice as she looks over at Emilia who is busy scribbling clumsily.

'Yeah, not great to be honest,' I look down into my bowl and move some spaghetti around with my fork.

'Lisa asked me while we were away if there was something going on between me and Laura,' I confess, wondering what my mum will make of it all.

'Oh,' she says calmly, placing her glass down and turning to face me square-on. 'And... how did that make you feel?' It feels a little like a diplomatic way of asking if there's any truth in it.

'Well, horrified, I guess. That my own wife could not only think I might be unfaithful but, also... with one of my students?! The more I think about it, the more it hurts.'

'And what prompted her asking, do you think?'

I sigh as I wonder whether I should tell my mum about the dream. It feels a bit weird, disclosing the intimacy of it. And then she might start to wonder herself. 'I said her name in my sleep... Laura's I mean, I was... dreaming and, well... Lisa jumped to conclusions, I guess. But she said she feels like we've drifted apart and things haven't been right for a while. So, I suppose she's put two and two together and made up this story in her head. And she thinks I'm taking her death harder than I ought to be so I'm not convinced that she believes me, to be honest.'

'Well, we all deal with grief differently and I think it's fair to say you've always been a sensitive soul, darling. So you're bound to be feeling it. And as for the dream, you've had a huge shock. The mind does extraordinary things to try and help us make sense of stuff.'

'Exactly! Do you think she's pointing the finger at me because she's guilty herself? Or is that just a trope?' I venture, as I reach over to help Emilia with the last of her yoghurt.

'Well, perhaps it is a bit of a trope. But your father used to accuse me of having eyes for other men and he became quite controlling... in the end. Didn't like me going out to my yoga classes, always asking if there would be any men there. Which, of course, there weren't, not in those days. The audacity of it, after what he was doing!' she laughs through her nose.

'Sorry Mum, I don't mean to bring all this up,' I say apologetically, wiping some stray yoghurt from Emilia's chin.

She waves a nonchalant hand in the air. 'It's all water under the bridge now, darling. Anyway, it's good to talk about these things now, as adults. I couldn't talk to you about it when it was happening as I didn't want to burden you. Or make you think badly of your father. You were only a boy, despite your maturity.'

I take another mouthful of spaghetti, contemplating whether to ask her something I've always wondered. 'Mum, can I ask you something?' I swallow and decide to go for it.

She smiles as she places her spoon and fork down gently on the bowl. 'Of course.'

'Why do you still wear your wedding ring? You know, after how it ended with you and dad?' I glance down at her hand, which is starting to reveal her age, despite her otherwise youthful appearance.

She twists the thin yellow gold band on her ring finger, as if she'd otherwise forgotten it was there. 'Well, I never wanted a divorce, Paul. I just wanted our family to stay how I'd imagined it to be when I made my vows. It might sound silly, but this ring holds a lasting symbolism in my mind. Your father clearly had different ideas. But I made a promise and I always intended to keep it. I still love your father, in some way, despite what happened. He gave me you,' she reaches over the table and ruffles my hair and I realise that she and I are much more alike than I've ever noticed before. I always worried that I'd end up taking after my dad. 'Plus it's a good way of deterring any unwanted attention at the tennis club,' she winks.

I laugh. 'But don't you think it might be nice to meet someone, you know... a companion?'

'A *lover*, you mean?' she laughs loudly, throwing her head backwards, knowing the thought would make me feel uncomfortable. 'I've got lots of companions, Paul. Male *and* female. But I don't need a relationship to make me happy.' She makes air quotes around *relationship* for extra emphasis. 'I was happy with your father, until he wasn't. So I came to realise, through all of what happened, that my happiness is my responsibility and I've got to do whatever it takes to maintain it, not rely on someone else.'

I nod and smile as I finish off my pasta, before scooping Emilia up out of her highchair and sitting her on my knee.

'I think you need to have a proper discussion with Lisa about your future,' she urges, looking me straight in the eye. 'We've only got one life, Paul. And, whilst I would have happily stayed married to your father, if we could have worked through things, it's not a failure if you have to walk away and take your happiness into your own hands. Quite the opposite, really. It's bravery.'

I bundle Emilia into the car seat as Mum puts the door on the latch and comes down the steps to see us off.

'Thanks for tonight, Mum,' I kiss her on the cheek. 'I really appreciate it. And dinner was lovely, thank you.'

'Anytime, darling,' she strokes Emilia on the cheek. 'Bye, bye, sweetheart.'

Emilia's eyes are already starting to droop and it'll be a miracle if she stays awake on the way home. We can skip her bath tonight, I think.

'When's Lisa back?' Mum asks as she hands me Emilia's rucksack.

'Saturday,' I calculate. 'At some point.'

'Well, I'm here, if you need anything.'

'Thank you,' I wave out of the window before making our way back home.

CHAPTER TWENTY-FOUR

I laugh as I top Julia's wine glass up with the merlot she's brought round.

'It wasn't Chaucer, it was Milton! Did you actually go to your English lessons at school?' I tease, as we debate the answer to the £250,000 question on *Who Wants To Be A Millionaire*.

'Really?!' she giggles. 'I always thought *Paradise Lost* was Chaucer! Bloody 'ell, I dunno. I was probably smoking somethin' round the back of the bike sheds.'

'Remind me not to put you down as my "Phone a Friend",' I laugh, the irony not lost on me that she's actually my only friend. 'It was definitely Milton.'

'Well I knew it wa'n't Shakespeare – I'm not a complete idiot – and I've never heard of *that* guy,' she points to another answer displayed in the corner of the screen. 'So I might have got through on a 50-50, maybe. Unless it was between Chaucer and Milton!'

We both crack up and I spill a few drops of red wine onto my navy chinos. 'Whoops,' I chuckle, attempting to wipe them off with my hand.

'I think it's C: Chaucer,' the contestant declares nervously.

'Noooooo!' we both shout at the TV and fall about laughing.

'I can't watch,' I announce, getting to my feet. 'Shall I warm this up? It smells amazing!' I hold up the bag containing stacked Tupperware full of food that Julia has brought round.

'Yeah, I'm getting hungry.'

'Me too. OK, I'll be back in a sec.' I creep up the stairs to do my habitual hourly check on Emilia.

'And is it helping?' Julia asks as she curls up on the sofa beside me. I've had a little too much wine and decided to tell her about the therapy.

'Yeah, I think so,' I say, resting my head on the back of the couch and turning to face her. 'It's good to talk things through with someone who's totally unconnected to my life. I'm trying to get to the bottom of some stuff so Lisa and I can move forward, you know?'

'And what if you can't? Get back on track, I mean,' she shuffles around in her seat so she's facing me square-on and rests her elbow on the cushions.

I look at her questioningly. 'Sorry,' she shakes her head. 'I'm playing devil's advocate, I suppose. You don't have to answer that.'

'No it's alright, I just, I suppose I haven't really thought that far ahead... properly, I mean. Maybe that's a bit arrogant. You know, assuming we can make things work just because I want to. It's a two-way thing, isn't it?' I raise my eyebrows, wondering if I've been burying my head in the sand. 'I do wonder if I've been a bit hypocritical, at times. You know, I was so upset when she accused me of being unfaithful but then I've had my doubts about her, too. With this Richard guy. But I think it's one thing to have a fleeting suspicion and another to actually ask the question out loud.'

'Yeah, totally,' Ju agrees. 'And from what you've told me, it sounds like she wasn't particularly... sensitive about it? Plus, I think your suspicions are much more reasonable, based on how she's been behaving lately.'

'I don't know, I think a lot of it is just me being paranoid. I just hope we can turn this corner and move on.'

'Well, she'd be mad not to,' she finishes what's left of her wine and places the empty glass on the bookshelves next to the sofa. 'You're a right catch, you know.'

'You reckon?' I titter and put my own glass down on the coffee table in front of us.

'Yeah, look at you, you're a brilliant dad, fun to be around, devastatingly handsome...' she looks deeply into my eyes.

'Now I know you're taking the piss!' I laugh, blushing, but am secretly pleased that someone remembers I do have a fun side, despite all this angst.

'I mean it,' she puts her hand on my knee and moves in close to whisper in my ear. 'And you'd *definitely* win at *Who Wants To Be A Millionaire*.'

'Fuck off!' I slap her playfully on the arm.

She laughs and shoots me a wink. 'Seriously though mate, I'm sure you'll sort things out. It's just a blip. Me and Anthony had a similar thing when the girls were small, you know. It's hard work all this!' she throws her arms around, gesturing wildly into the air. 'But we got through it. And it can make you stronger, as a couple.'

'Yeah,' I breathe in deeply and sigh out through my nose, closing my eyes. 'I'm just not sure who I am anymore. I feel so lost.' I'm not sure where that came from. *Try not to bring the mood down, for fuck's sake.* But the words tumble out of my mouth. 'I sometimes wonder if she'd be better off without me. I just feel like I'm standing in her way, in the way of what she really wants. And I don't want to stifle her, that would just break my heart. To look back on a life together and realise I held her back, made her miserable. What sort of an existence is that? I know I don't make her happy, I'm hardly sparkling company. She'll just grow to hate me, eventually.'

'Hey, that's not true, you know that don't you?' she looks at me sternly but puts her hand on mine and gives it a squeeze. Her face softens. 'You're wonderful company, you're just going through a tough time, that's all. You're allowed to *feel* things, you know. You shouldn't have to pretend that everything's alright when it's not. That's not how life works. But you'll find your way back, Paul, I promise. You're not lost, you're *here*. And those worth having around you need to meet you where you are, wherever that is. Come here!' she pulls me towards her and I feel safe.

'Thanks for coming over tonight, Ju. I appreciate it, really.' I rest my head on her shoulder.

'Anytime pal, it's been nice,' she ruffles my hair.

'Shall I call you a cab?' I ask as I get up off the sofa and stretch my back.

'Nah, yer alright, I just messaged Anthony,' she says putting her phone down on the coffee table. 'He's going to swing round and pick me up. He'll be here in a minute. The girls are in bed and he's only had a pint.'

'Righto,' I head into the hallway to get Julia's coat.

'So has Martin said any more about the Head of English job?' she asks as I help her into her coat.

'I spoke to him about it at the start of term actually, he said he'd put reading the applications on hold, what with... you know.'

'Yeah,' Julia nods.

'So he was going to go through all of the external applications and let me have a date for interview. It's for a September start anyway so I don't suppose there's any rush.'

'No I guess not. And I think all the external application stuff is just following protocol, anyway.'

'Yeah, maybe.' I smile. 'I don't know if I'm doing the right thing, really, putting extra pressure on myself, at the minute,' I breathe out a heavy sigh.

Ju pulls a face. 'Nah, it'll be good for you mate, you're made for the job! And it's the natural next step, int it? The kids love you, you've got a good few years' experience behind you now,' she starts to list all the reasons I already know but struggle to believe in.

'I guess so, it's just... well it's a lot, isn't it? A lot of responsibility, I mean. I don't mind putting the extra hours in, although it's going to be tricky with Lisa's work and stuff... but I just don't want to let the kids down, you know?'

'I know, mate. But in a way that's why you're perfect for it. You care about the kids, and that's the most important thing.'

I nod a half-smile and give her a squeeze on the arm. 'Cheers, Ju.'

'You're brill, you are. Don't forget it!' We hear a car pull up outside and head for the door. 'I'll see you Monday then. Hope you manage to have a good chat with Lisa tomorrow.'

'Thanks,' I kiss her on the cheek and close the door, back to silence.

CHAPTER TWENTY-FIVE

'5-5-3-5-2-8,' my mum answers. She's of the generation of people who answer their phone by singing their phone number.

'Hey Mum, it's me,' I say, cradling the cordless phone between my shoulder and ear as I secure a bib around Emilia's neck. She flinches as I catch her hair. 'Ooh, sorry poppet,' I whisper as I hand her a spoon.

'Oh hello, darling, you OK?'

'Yeah, all good. Just wondered if you're busy today?'

'Well I'm just heading out to the tennis club, but I'll be back for lunchtime, why?' she asks.

'I was wondering if you wouldn't mind having Emilia for a bit this afternoon? Lisa's on her way back and I thought it might be good for us to have a bit of time to catch up, on our own.'

'Of course, love, no problem. Why don't you bring her over in the pram, about 1ish? I can take her out to the museum or something?'

'Ah she'd love that, they've got that new model railway in the upstairs gallery, haven't they?'

'Ooh yes, lovely. OK, darling, well I'd better dash, I've got a doubles game at 10 and I was going to walk down, seeing as it's such a nice morning.'

'Yeah, it looks nice out. Right, well, enjoy the doubles and I'll see you a bit later,' I feel like a plan is coming together.

'See you later, love. Bye.'

I press the button to hang up then put the phone back on its stand. The sun is streaming in through the kitchen and showing up all the dust that you wouldn't otherwise know is there. I look over at Emilia and she's somehow got porridge in her hair.

I decide we need to have a bit of a tidy up before Lisa gets back so I put the TV in the kitchen on for Emilia whilst I set to work.

I carry Emilia upstairs and put her down on our bedroom floor as I pull my black tracksuit bottoms from out of the chest of drawers and rummage in the basket of clean laundry for a grey t-shirt. I've decided to try and run back from my mum's seeing as it's such a nice day. A bit of exercise should put me in the right mindset for a good chat with Lisa. I pull the t-shirt over my head and examine my face in the mirrored surface of the sliding wardrobe doors. I feel slightly less dishevelled than I have done in recent weeks.

I sit on the bed and pull on my tracksuit bottoms then grab the matching jacket from out of the wardrobe. It's been a while since I've worn it.

'Come on then, little one,' I say as I scoop Emilia up and carry her downstairs into the hallway. 'We need to get you into this,' I coo, pulling Emilia's snowsuit off the coathooks. 'We're going for a walk to Nanna's!'

'Nanna's! Nanna's!' she shouts happily, toddling over to me. I pick her up and sit her on my knee as I feed her reluctant legs into the suit, followed by her arms, before zipping her in and pulling the hood playfully over her eyes. She giggles and puts her hands on my face. It's hard to believe that this little person still lived in her mummy's tummy less than 18 months ago.

'Right, you're ready!' It might be good for her to have a nap in the pushchair, I think.

I pull the front door closed and fold out the pushchair waiting in the porch, before strapping Emilia in and setting off for Mum's.

My heart thuds in my chest as I jog through the park back home. I start off slow and steady but it feels good to work up a sweat and have the coolness of the late-winter air on my skin. I rehearse what I'm going to say to Lisa when she's back this afternoon.

Exercise frees my mind. And gives me clarity to realise that I'm not completely innocent in the troubles that Lisa and I are having. She had to give up a lot when we had Emilia; the physical changes her body went through, the emotional strain of being at home with a new baby when I was out at work for much of the day, the identity crisis she faced when her career came to a halt. I tried to support her as best I could but I couldn't possibly understand the full extent of the effect new motherhood had on her. And we naturally became a little distant with one another, this new life we were suddenly responsible for both filling our hearts in ways we could never imagine, but at the same time creating a huge void within our relationship with each other.

It's hard to admit but I guess it felt to me like Lisa was focussing so much on work that she had no room for anything else. Emilia and I seemed like an inconvenience that was getting in the way of what she wanted to achieve and I suppose I started to feel scared. And that's when the intrusive thoughts crept back in, taunting me with images of what my life would be like without her.

It occurs to me that I've not had so many dreams of Laura just lately, that is to say she's not overwhelming my entire consciousness in the same way as in the weeks after she first died. Is that the healing effect of time passing? Of life at school carrying on, despite her ever-present absence, or just the constant demands of life at home with a toddler? I don't doubt that my conversations with Jeremy have helped me untangle some of the unspeakable thoughts swimming around in my head. Maybe that's why she doesn't visit so often, these days.

I head out of the park gates and the pedestrian crossing is on green so I run straight across the road, turning the corner into our estate. Not bad, for my first run in ages, I think. Our house comes into view and I slow to a jog as I approach the front door, panting. I use the sleeve of my t-shirt to wipe the sweat from my brow and untie the tracksuit top that I'd tied around my waist when I got too hot. The front door key is zipped in one of the pockets and I fumble trying to find it to let myself in.

Water, I think. Kicking off my running shoes, I head to the kitchen and fill a large glass from the tap in the kitchen. Maybe we should get one of those new fridges that has a built-in water cooler? Treat ourselves. Or even one of the fancy coffee machines Lisa had her eye on in the hotel room.

The clock in the kitchen says 1.45pm. Time for a quick shower before Lisa gets back, I think. Heading upstairs, I put my running kit in the laundry basket in our bedroom and step into the shower cubicle in the en-suite. I turn the tap on full and the cold water takes my breath away. I shiver violently and gasp before the water starts to warm up, soothing my muscles as it gets hotter.

CHAPTER TWENTY-SIX

The front door creaks open and I hear the clicking of the latch as it closes. 'Hello?' Lisa calls from the hallway.

'I'm just up here, love,' I call as I turn off the tap, slide the door open and reach for a towel. I take the squeegee off its hanger on the tiled cubicle wall and wipe the shower screen clean. Lisa's footsteps are on the stairs.

'Hey,' she greets me, then looks around the room. 'Where's Emilia?'

'Oh she's at my mum's this afternoon. I dropped her off just after lunch and ran back through the park. I only just got back,' I run the towel over my hair and lean into her for a kiss. 'You OK?'

'Yeah, I'm... good,' she says with a half-smile. 'You?'

'Good,' I examine her face. She looks different, I think. 'It's nice to have you back.'

She squeezes my arm and heads over to the dressing table, where she unzips her overnight bag and starts to unpack some things.

'So how was it, London?' I ask as I pull on a pair of black trunks.

'Yeah, it was... good. The meetings went well, so...'

'That's good,' my stomach churns as I wonder whether it's too early to launch into my heart-to-heart. 'Have you eaten?'

She bunches her hair up on top of her head and secures it with a hairband from around her wrist. 'Yeah, I had a sandwich... on the train,' she nods and smiles gently as she empties some clothes into the laundry basket.

I clear my throat, almost as a warning but the words roll around in my head.

Lisa sits down on the edge of the bed. 'Paul, there's something we need to talk about.' I panic, noticing the seriousness of her expression.

'Yeah, well, that's kind of what I was going to say...'

'I'm pregnant,' she interrupts me mid-sentence and I take a second to process what she just said.

'Pregnant?!' I splutter, my eyes widening. 'Lis, that's... amazing! Oh my God!' I laugh and take her face in my hands. But there's contrition in her eyes.

'No, Paul,' her face cracks and she takes a long breath in through her nose. 'It's not. I can't.'

'What? What do you mean?' my excitement fades.

'I'm sorry, Paul. I'm so sorry.'

'Sorry? Sorry, what for?' my head is spinning and my stomach flips with panic. I feel sick. Why is she saying sorry? 'Lisa, talk to me. What is it?'

She's slumped forward with her head in her hands, her elbows resting on her knees. I'm on my knees in front of her, searching. It feels like an age before she lifts her head and puts her hand to my face, tears streaming down her cheeks. Her silence is loaded and I brace myself for the bullet.

'I don't want another baby, Paul,' she says quietly, her eyes desperate. The shot is fired and her words hit me before ricocheting around the room. 'I'm sorry.'

'No, no… you *do*, we *can*… we'll figure it out, *please*,' I plead with her, realising this is my only chance to make my case. 'It's just a shock, that's all, we can do this. I promise.' My eyes are filling with tears. She's never been one to be talked around to anything, once her mind is made up.

She shakes her head slowly. 'I'm sorry, I just can't.'

'What about me? What about Emilia? Don't we get a say in this? Come on, Lis. Let's talk about it. Properly. When did you… when did you find out?' I need to go back to the beginning.

'I took a test last night. I was about a week late and that's not like me and, I don't know, I just felt… weird. So I thought it'd be worth taking a test.'

'Why didn't you tell me?!' I think back to when we took the test for Emilia's pregnancy. We waited, together, in the bathroom, full of anticipation before watching those two blue lines emerge.

'I'm telling you now, aren't I?' she seems agitated and gets up from the bed, pushing past me, still kneeling at her feet, to go to the bathroom. I follow her as she blows her nose and checks her face in the mirror.

'I know but, I mean, why didn't you call me, before you did the test? Remember when we did the test for Emilia?'

It was Christmas Eve, 1996. Lisa had a feeling, she said. We'd been trying, but not for long so I wasn't really expecting anything, which is to say I did want my half-baked dream of a family to sink before it had even risen. She sent me out first thing that morning, in the dirty slush that remained from snowfall earlier that week, to pick up a test from the pharmacy, which would close early that day for Christmas. As I rushed back, I dared to imagine what our life might look like if Lisa's 'feeling' was right. Maybe we could look at one of those houses on the new estate? I remember Lisa's eyes wide, me open-mouthed, as we saw the second line appear. Then the laughter of incredulous joy.

'That was a bit different, Paul, don't you think? We *wanted* a baby then.' Her words puncture my reverie.

'Well I want that again, don't you?' I regret asking, already knowing her answer.

'No! I've already said I don't want another baby. Not now, probably not ever. I'm sorry, but I can't pretend to want something I don't. Especially not a fucking baby!'

'And what about us? What if we want another baby?!' I realise I'm clutching at straws by speaking for myself and our infant daughter, in an attempt to outnumber her.

'There is no 'we', Paul. It's my body.'

'What if I were to take paternity leave? You could go back to work, I'll stay at home!' I'm yet to meet a single man that has taken a year off work to look after a baby but I'm willing to try anything.

'I'd still have to carry the thing! And deliver it! Remember that? *Do you?* Do you remember the state I was in, after Emilia? I was a fucking mess, Paul! A *mess*! The maternity leave was the easy bit, in comparison. Although that was hardly a walk in the park. And I've had to work twice as hard as any of the men at work to get back to where I am now. It's like snakes and *fucking ladders* once you've had a baby! And how are we going to afford that, anyway? On the two weeks' pay you'd get from school?! I don't think so. So no, that's not an option. OK?' She's shouting now, her face contorted as she throws her arms up and heads downstairs.

How can things fall apart so quickly?

I head downstairs after her and try to calm myself down before I say anything else, in fear of spooking her even more. She's standing at the kitchen sink and filling a glass with water.

'Look, Lis, I'm sorry if I've been... insensitive. I... it just seems, well this could be our fresh start, don't you think? That's what I was going to say, before... I've been thinking about us and things and... I think we can get back on track if we just sit down and talk about things, properly? We don't need to make any decisions yet, do we? About the baby, I mean?' I do a quick calculation in my mind, counting back to our weekend away and realise she must only be five, maybe six weeks pregnant. 'It's still early days, right?'

'Yeah, well, you must have some pretty strong swimmers, I'll give you that,' she laughs and I see a softening in her face.

'Please, let's just... let's just see how we get on, hey? I was thinking while we were away how nice it would be for Emilia to have a sibling. I was thinking maybe we could start trying in a few months but... this could be a new chapter for us, for our family?'

'And what about what *I* want? Hmmm? Where do I feature in this grand plan of yours? Am I just the conduit, the machine to produce what *you* want? Let's face it, we've hardly been playing happy families, have we?!'

I'm not articulating myself particularly well. 'That's not what I meant, Lis. I mean, can we just think about things for a little while?'

'I think maybe you should go to your mum's tonight. Emilia's there already so, maybe go and stay there for a few days and we can have some time apart, to think,' she says coolly, looking at me straight in the eye.

'We've just had two whole days apart! I was looking forward

to you coming back, so we could talk!' I protest. Why is she being like this?

'Please, Paul. I just need some space, OK?' She looks exhausted.

'Fine, if that's what you want! I'll go!' I head for the stairs to pack a bag. 'You're only back five minutes and you're kicking me out?! What is going on with us, Lisa?' I'm raising my voice now, as if that will help to get through to her.

'I'm not *kicking you out* Paul, don't be so dramatic. I just need some time to think, for fuck's sake!'

There's a pain in my chest and I notice the familiar dread rising up through my throat. My fingers start tingling and I feel myself on the brink of something about to take hold of me. My vision starts to blur and there's a ringing in my ears that's getting louder and louder. I sit on the floor with my back against the bedroom wall and close my eyes, counting my breaths. *Not now, Paul, snap out of it*!

I need to pack a bag, I think. If I'm busy it can't drag me under. I pull out some clothes from the wardrobe and stuff them into my weekend bag, the backs of my eyes aching as I hold in the tears that are threatening to flood out. I close my eyes as I try to think about what I'll need. My toothbrush. And Emilia's. Her bunny and her sleeping bag, some clothes for her, nappies. Christ, how did this happen?

Lisa's sitting at the kitchen table with a coffee when I get downstairs. She turns around as I grab my satchel from the breakfast bar.

'I'll go then,' I splutter through tears that refuse to be contained any longer. She looks at me with empty eyes. 'How can you be so *calm*? Don't you care?'

'Of course I do,' she scowls. 'But maybe I've already shed my tears. I just need to be on my own.'

'What about Emilia? Don't you want to see her?'

'Yes, just, not right now. It's not good for her to be around us when we're like this.'

'Right,' I nod slowly. 'So when can I come back?'

'I'll call you.'

I fight the urge to try and hold her and turn and head to the hallway, picking up my bag on the way out of the door.

I wipe my eyes on my sleeve and try to compose myself as I walk up the steps to my mum's front door. Breathing out through my mouth, I take the cold brass knocker in my hand and knock sharply three times. I've got a splitting headache.

Mum announces my arrival to Emilia as she opens the door and welcomes me in. She takes one look at my face and her eyes widen as she looks down at the bag in my right hand. My lips start to tremble and I know she knows what this means, without us saying a word.

'Oh love,' she puts her arms out and I fall into her. 'What happened?!'

'It's a long story,' I shake my head and wonder where to begin. 'Can we stay here tonight?'

'Of course, darling, of course,' she pulls me towards her again and holds onto me tightly. I hear Emilia running down the hallway and I quickly pull away, wipe my eyes again and put on my familiar mask.

'Hello poppet!' I rearrange my face, wondering if I'm convincing enough.

'Dadddda!' she shouts. 'Where Mamma?'

'Oh Mummy's still at work,' I figure she doesn't realise it's Saturday afternoon so won't question my lie. 'We're going to have a sleepover at Nanna's!' I say with over-excitement. If I make it as fun as possible for her maybe she won't notice the shroud of sadness draped over me.

I settle Emilia in the travel cot in Mum's guest room and she's out like a light. I unzip my bag which I'd left on the bed when I arrived and take out some jogging bottoms and a hoodie to change into. My eyes sting as I emerge from the darkness of the bedroom. I pull the door to and cross the hall to put my toothbrush in the bathroom before heading downstairs. I wonder how long I'll be staying.

Mum is standing at the hob and sliding some diced onion off the chopping board and into a pan. They let out a hiss as they meet the hot oil and the smell is comforting.

'Can I do anything, Mum?' I ask, conscious that she's been busy with Emilia all day and now she's cooking for me when she was probably looking forward to putting her feet up.

'No, love,' she smiles. 'Thank you. Come and take a seat and tell me what's been going on. It's chilli con carne, is that OK?'

'Yeah, amazing,' I blink, thinking how lucky I am to have my mum so close by. 'Thank you.' My nostrils flare and the muscles in my jaw clench tightly as I try and hold it together.

'Come on,' Mum nods to the stools by the table.

I take a deep breath and pull myself up onto the stool.

'Lisa's pregnant,' I blurt out.

Mum swings around to look at me. 'Oh?!'

'Yeah,' I nod slowly. 'She did a test last night and, well... there it is.'

'And how do *you* feel about that?' Mum asks, looking at me

cautiously. I get the impression she wants to ask if the baby's mine.

'Well, I'd be thrilled,' I pause, my stomach tensing up. 'Except she doesn't want the baby.'

Mum's eyebrows lift. 'I see.'

'I've tried to point out that there's no rush, you know, to do... anything,' the thought of what that actually involves makes me go cold. 'I said she should think about it for a bit. I really want a sibling for Emilia and I told her I'd take paternity leave so she could go back to work. I'll do anything.'

Mum's face is etched with sadness. She knows as well as I do that Lisa can be stubborn. Selfish, perhaps. But when it comes to one person wanting a baby and the other not, which one is being selfish? No one is going to win.

'Well, there's a bit more to it than that, isn't there, darling?' she says softly, knowing that I already understand.

'I know,' I close my eyes. 'And that's what she said. That it's her body and she can't pretend to want something she doesn't. I get that. I do, really. I have so much respect for what she had to go through with Emilia. But it just breaks my heart that I don't get a say in it, *at all*. We're meant to be a team.'

'It's a tough one, love. It really is. But you've both got to be fully committed to it, if you're going to make it work. And the damage it could do to your family, if you're not on the same page, well... it'd be catastrophic.'

I know my mum's right. We're hardly in the right place to weather the storm of new parenthood all over again.

CHAPTER TWENTY-SEVEN

I feel the vibration of my phone ringing through my pocket. I take it out and squint at the screen as the sunlight streams through the trees and into my eyes. LISA CALLING, it says.

Emilia is asleep in the pushchair so I take a seat on a nearby bench.

'Hey,' I answer. 'You OK?'

'Yeah,' Lisa says softly, 'I'm OK. You?'

'I'm alright,' I lie. 'I'm just walking Emilia through the park. She's asleep.'

'Ah OK. I was thinking, maybe we could meet later, to talk? Do you think your mum would have Emilia again for a bit?'

'Er, yeah, I'm sure she will. Shall I come over?' I find it unsettling to be asking if I should go to my own house.

'Yeah, OK. Just come over when you're ready. I'll be here.'

'OK, I'll see you in a bit then.' I'm listening for clues as to what sort of conversation we're going to have but get nothing.

'See you in a bit.'

I head back towards my mum's with an urgency in my step,

desperate to know what Lisa has to say about what happened yesterday. About our future.

By the time I reach my mum's Emilia is awake and I scoop her out of the pushchair to carry her up the steps to the front door. I take out the key from my pocket to open the door and put her down before running back down to fold up the pushchair. Mum's coming down the stairs and greets Emilia, taking off her coat and shoes.

'Mum, can you have Emilia for a bit? Lisa called to say she wants me to go over to talk. Is that alright?'

'Yes, darling. That's fine. How did she sound?' Mum asks. I wish I knew.

'I don't know, I... I just need to see her.'

'Of course. Go and take your time, we'll be fine. Just let me know how you get on.'

'Thanks, Mum,' I kiss her on the cheek and crouch down to kiss Emilia goodbye. 'See you later, poppet.'

My hands are clammy when I reach our front door and, for a moment, I wonder whether I should knock or use my key. *This is your house*, I think, and decide to enter. I never asked for this.

'Hey,' I call as I close the door behind me and start kicking off my shoes. I put my keys on the side in the hallway and head into the kitchen. Lisa is sitting cross-legged on the sofa with a pile of paperwork next to her.

'Hey,' she replies, putting down what she's been reading. 'I just made coffee, do you want some?'

'Yeah, go on then,' I say heading to the cupboard to take out a cup. There's another used mug by the sink. I look over to Lisa and see she has a cup in her hand. My stomach drops but I decide not to say anything, to avoid a row before we've even begun. I find the cafetière on the kitchen worktop and pour myself a cup.

'So, how… are you feeling?' I ask, softening my face.

'A bit shit, to be honest.' She looks pale and there are shadows under her eyes.

'Did you sleep?'

'Not really,' she looks up, cradling her cup in both hands. 'Did you?'

'Not really,' I can't dance around any longer. 'So, have you had a chance to think about… things?' I try and conceal my impatience.

'I've been offered another contract. Based in London, full time.'

My heart stops. She's never been one to mince her words but the abruptness of what she's just said, on top of yesterday's bombshell, hits me like a tonne of bricks.

'What?!' I ask, letting out an incredulous laugh. I can see from her face that she's thinking of accepting it.

'This project I'm working on, I need to be in London full time. So… there it is,' she raises her eyebrows and takes another sip of her coffee.

'And what about us? What about Emilia? What…' my vocabulary fails me as I try and process what she's telling me. 'It sounds to me like you've already decided that you're going take it?' my voice cracks with surprise.

'I'm sorry, Paul. I just… I really want this. I've been giving it a lot of thought, whilst I've been away. They've offered to pay for my accommodation during the week and then I can… come back at the weekend… to see Emilia.'

'And me? Where do I feature in all of this?' I raise my voice as the reality of what she's trying to say starts to sink in.

'I don't know what to say. I think we're heading in different directions. I'm sorry,' her face crumbles as she looks me in the eye. 'I need to do this. I'll regret it if I don't and that's no way to live, is it?'

'So, are you *leaving* me? Or... what's happening here, Lisa? Just fucking tell me will you?!' I'm shouting now.

'I guess so, yes,' she looks down at her feet.

'What the *fuck*?! How can you do this?' My heart is pounding. 'How can you leave us?'

'Look, I'm not...' she sighs in exasperation. 'I'm not happy, Paul. There, I said it. *I'm not happy*. I'm not happy and I know you're not either. We're not... right.'

'That doesn't mean you have to move to London! For fuck's sake, Lis. Can't we just... *try*? I mean, Jesus! I wanted to try and make this better, for us. I was starting to feel so much better. I thought we could get through it. Won't you at least try?' I realise that the possibility of her wanting to keep our baby is now out of the question but I ask anyway. 'What about the baby?'

'There's no *baby*, Paul. It's just a collection of cells that might turn into a baby, *if* I let it. But I can't, OK? I thought I made that clear yesterday.'

'I thought you were going to think about it? Let the dust settle a bit?'

'No. No, it's not going to happen. I'm sorry. I probably shouldn't have mentioned it, considering...'

My blood runs cold as I process the fact that my wife thinks it would have been morally acceptable not to tell me about a new life we'd created together. But then perhaps it would have been easier if she hadn't. The tingling returns to my hands and my ears are ringing. I take a deep breath in and hold it in my chest. I feel like I'm drowning.

'I need some air,' I splutter as I start to choke on the breath that I'm holding. I open the top drawer in the kitchen and find the packet of cigarettes, taking one out with a shaking hand before I step out of the back door and slam it behind me. I bring the tip to my lips and light the other end, the long drag I take helping me to recalibrate.

Tears sting my eyes as I exhale and my whole body is shaking violently. I'm aware that this is a moment I probably won't forget. The sun on the back doorstep is warming me but my blood is still chilling me to the core.

I finish my cigarette and go back inside. It feels like there's nothing to lose now, so I ask Lisa about the other coffee cup next to the sink.

'Richard was here, this morning,' she explains as if it's the most normal thing in the world. 'He came over to drop the draft contract off so I could have a proper look at it. He stayed for a coffee.'

My face turns hot.

'And where does *Richard* fit into all this then? Is he going to be moving to London with you?' I realise I'm sneering but I can't help it.

'No, he's still going to be based here. But he'll come down for meetings I guess, occasionally. And anyway, I'm not *moving* to London. I'll be staying there during the week and then I'll come back on Friday afternoons to be with Emilia for the weekend before I head back again on Sunday nights.'

'We can do that, and still be... together. As a family. As a couple, you and me. We can make it work!' I'm clutching at straws but I'll do anything to stop her leaving me.

'I think we need a clean break, Paul.'

The enormity of it comes crashing down on me and I fall to

my knees. 'Please, Lis, *please*. I love you, I can't... I don't know how I can do this without you.'

'I'm sorry,' her eyes start to fill with tears but she wipes them away quickly. 'I think you should maybe stay with your mum tonight. I don't want things to get... difficult, between us. I'm going to take this week off work so I can have Emilia and get to the doctors. Maybe you should have a couple of days off, too? You know, just to get your head around things?'

There's nothing left to say. It strikes me that the roots of our family tree are dead and this storm will bring it crashing down. I take one more look at her face, just to check for any hint that this might be a dark and elaborate prank. Her stony expression says it all so I head to the hallway, lace up my trainers and grab my coat before leaving our home behind.

CHAPTER TWENTY-EIGHT

The walk back to Mum's takes me almost twice as long as I dodge a constant stream of intrusive thoughts. *You deserve this,* my mind tells me. *You've only got yourself to blame. Did you expect her to just stick around waiting for you to stop fantasising about one of your students? You're disgusting. If anyone finds out you'll be locked up. And where will that leave your precious daughter?*

'No, no,' I mutter under my breath before smiling at a passing elderly couple. 'Afternoon,' I nod to them as they look up in my direction. Just try and act normal on the outside, at least.

I count my steps in an attempt to barge out the intrusions but still they flood my mind. I can't let Emilia see me like this. Suddenly the reality of what's about to unfold hits me. How is this going to work, on a practical level? Let alone the upheaval on Emilia, not having her mum around for most of the week. Most of her life. How *could* she? Mothers can't just leave their kids. What is she playing at?

That's right, don't worry about her and what she might want

*from life. Force the patriarchy's ideas about what's 'normal' upon
her, why don't you? No one would bat an eyelid if the shoe was on
the other foot. Dads are allowed to put their careers first, aren't
they? You're a hypocrite.*

I realise that the tormentor in my head has a point and this
just serves to fan the flames. Rationale escapes me but I try to
remember what Jeremy said about letting the thoughts come
and go. Leaves in the wind, passing clouds. That's easy for him
to say. I take a deep breath and continue counting my steps as I
turn the corner into Mum's road. My next appointment with
Jeremy isn't until Tuesday. I don't know how I'm going to get
through the next two days without talking to him. I just want
to shut down, give my brain a hard reset.

I'm relieved to find Mum and Emilia are out when I get
back. A note on the kitchen table tells me they're at the park. I
open Mum's drinks cabinet to find a bottle of single malt
whisky and pour myself a glass. I need something to calm my
nerves, I think. I take a sip and the heat of the alcohol stings my
tongue before warming the back of my throat. I sink into the
sofa before downing the rest of the whisky in one mouthful,
instantly regretting it as the dryness makes me cough. It goes
straight to my head and I put the glass on the floor next to me,
resting my head back and closing my aching eyes.

My phone vibrates in my pocket and a message from Lisa
illuminates the screen:

'Can I come & pick Emilia up in an hour or so?'

I don't like the thought of her staying at home without me
but I figure I need some time to sort my head out before I can
do any sort of parenting. Plus if Lisa's taking the week off work
it makes sense for her to be doing the nursery run. And I've no
idea how I'm going to be able to drag myself into school
tomorrow.

I tap a reply into my phone telling Lisa that I'll call her when they're back from the park so she can come and collect her. So this is what our marriage has reduced to, messages about passing a toddler around to the next convenient holding bay. I think about the profound effect my own parents' divorce had on me and wonder if it's better or worse that this is happening to her at an age that she's unlikely to remember, rather than the impressionable 12-year-old I was.

More whisky, I think. I need to numb this pain in my head and try to pause the cinema reel of mine and Lisa's conversation playing on a loop. I get up and pour myself another glass, slightly larger than before. Don't neck it this time, I think. I sit back down and swing my legs around so I'm lying on my back, my head propped up against the arm of the sofa. Taking another long sip, I close my eyes and suddenly I'm overwhelmingly tired. I let my body relax and hope that my mind will follow.

'I think perhaps you should give work a miss tomorrow, love,' Mum suggests as I stare into the risotto I've been pushing around my plate for the last twenty minutes. I can't stomach anything at the minute, and the beginning of an early hangover from my whisky binge this afternoon isn't helping. 'Do you want me to call someone? Let them know?'

I look up at Mum but my eyes can't handle it and I close them again. 'No it's alright, thanks Mum,' I mumble, resting my head in my hand. 'I'll give Martin a call later.'

'Are you sure you're up to it though, love?' Mum's sad eyes look watery. 'I could speak to them?'

'It's fine, I'm a big boy, you know!' I snap, suddenly feeling suffocated with all this concern. 'Sorry, Mum. I'm sorry.' I reach for her hand.

She smiles and squeezes my hand, knowingly. There's such power in her silent acceptance.

'It might not seem like it now, but perhaps this is where you need to be to move forward with your own life,' she hints, cautiously. I ignore her as it's not what I want to hear, but I have no reply.

'We're all dangling by a thread, aren't we? First Laura, now my marriage has fallen apart. How can things go downhill so quickly?' This familiar contemplation makes me panic and I think of Emilia. I've always been prone to thinking the worst and dwelling on imagined catastrophe. But it takes a firm hold of me when things really start tumbling out of control. Are things ever *in* control? It's a pretty precarious existence we humans inhabit, even with the relative safety net of being a white, heterosexual man living in a supposedly prosperous democracy. Anything can happen. And it does. People have to deal with horrible things. Illness, grief, abject poverty, oppression. Why do I deserve any better than that?

'Well, we have to be grateful for what's good in our lives, don't we? You've got a beautiful daughter who adores you. And I'm always here for you. You've got a good job and a roof over your head. But that's not to say you're not allowed to feel the rawness of the emotion that comes with grief and the breakdown of a relationship. It's normal to feel a sense of despair when things take a turn. But we can get through it, love. I promise.' Mum pours me a glass of water from the jug on the table. 'Are you eating that?' she nods towards my plate which I've pushed to one side.

'Sorry, I'm just not hungry at the minute.'

'It's alright, darling. Just try and keep your fluids up and eat something when you're ready.' She gets up and clears our plates into the dishwasher.

'How did you manage, when you and dad split up?' It's not lost on me that she had to deal with their separation mostly alone, whilst my grandparents lived a hundred miles away on the North Yorkshire coast. As well as having to deal with me as a teenager whilst trying to hold down her job at the council. Not to mention the instability of the late 1970s. What an absolute nightmare, I think.

'Well, dear, I just did. There wasn't really any other option. It was tough, at times, don't get me wrong. But you were such a good boy, always knuckled down at school and you never gave me any cause to worry. You saved that for your twenties,' she laughs and I smile apologetically as I recall the backpacking trip I took across South America with my friends in the summer after I graduated, before I met Lisa. I shudder to think of Emilia in some of the situations I managed to get myself into in those few weeks on the other side of the world. I guess you never stop worrying about them.

'I just don't know how we're going to do this, practically I mean.' It dawns on me that I haven't broached the subject of me spending the foreseeable weekends here, when Lisa's back from London. I ask the question, looking down at my hands.

'Darling, you know you are always welcome, anytime, for as long as you like. Emilia too, of course. It's a joy to have her around. And you, obviously. And anyway, it might only be a temporary measure whilst Lisa has some time to think things through and figure out what it is she wants.'

I admire Mum's optimism. But I realise she's probably just telling me what she thinks I want to hear.

CHAPTER TWENTY-NINE

As I lie awake in the darkness of my mum's spare room, I try to retrace my steps back to when I first noticed things not being right between Lisa and me. I find it hard to pinpoint a defining moment, an event, but it seems instead there has been a gentle drifting over time, a shifting of the tectonic plates of two people in a long-term relationship. With the drifting come the inevitable tremors of differing views, clashing needs and unspoken grievances that, left unchecked, eventually result in the seismic tumbling down of everything that you've built up around you.

I think of all the opportunities I should have taken to talk with Lisa, that might have opened up the lines of communication to help save our marriage. All the times I felt the pinch of her behaviour, slowly eroding my self-worth until deciding it was easier to keep my mouth shut for fear of descending into an argument. Or until I talked myself round full circle to believing it was actually me being unreasonable. If only I had taken the bull by the horns, been less passive, actually spoken my mind about how her behaviour was making me feel. Perhaps she would have had more respect for me, and I would have more respect for myself. Maybe I wouldn't have found myself spiralling back into my OCD and self-loathing. I could have been an easier person to be around, easier to live with.

The radio alarm clock in Mum's guestroom shows me it's nearly a quarter to one in the morning. My despair reaches new depths in the dead of the night. The perfect conditions for a personal best. I'd forgotten how cold it feels, to sleep alone. I'm exhausted yet my mind won't give in, constantly playing the weekend's conversations with Lisa over and over to the point of analysing every syllable, examining every stress of intonation of what she said, for some hidden meaning. Some clue that indicates she doesn't really want to leave me. I need something to break the silence which allows my head so much space to ruminate. I fumble around to flick the radio on and wait to see what station it's tuned into. A piece of waltzing classical music crackles through the airwaves before coming to a slow and gentle crescendo. It's instantly recognisable to me as the sound which soothed so many sleepless nights during my teenage years.

'And now, the shipping forecast issued by the Met Office on behalf of the Maritime and Coastguard Agency...' the softly spoken presenter announces in a near-whisper, fitting for this time of night. I lie my head back on the soft down pillow and close my eyes. I just need to sleep. The rhythmic nature of the broadcast helps to calm my mind, as I follow the poetic recital of the shipping areas and their forecasts. *Where are these places? Who else is listening to this, I wonder.*

'Viking, North Utsire, South Utsire... southerly or southwesterly, five to seven, increasing gale eight for a time in Viking, drizzle, moderate, occasionally poor...'

The words wash over me like a bedtime story. When Mum

and Dad were splitting up, I'd put on the radio on my bedside table when I couldn't sleep. When I first tuned into this mysterious broadcast I thought I'd accidentally stumbled upon some secret code being whispered across the airwaves. It was only when it was rounded off with the national anthem, before switching to the World Service, that I realised it was the shipping forecast. It soon became part of my nightly ritual, a way to try and get some sleep after the exhausting compulsions I'd have been giving into since getting into bed. The intrusive thoughts about what might happen to my mum would be too brutal to be able to ignore, the nighttime winning the battle with my rationale. Desperate, I'd let myself imagine sitting by the sea in one of these mysterious places, watching the push and the pull of the tide. Fishing boats bobbing gently, waves crashing violently. When I was listening to the shipping forecast, there was no space in my mind for anything else.

'Tyne, Dogger, Fisher... veering westerly, three or four, increasing five or six in Dogger later, occasional rain, moderate or poor...' I start to feel my eyes getting heavy.

I wake to the silvery twilight of the mid-February morning creeping in through the shutters, just before the sun starts to rise. Somehow, I've managed to sleep through the night since my late-night lullaby of the shipping forecast and I notice that the radio is still on. Despite having slept for a solid six hours, my body feels heavy as I prop myself up against the wooden bedframe with a pillow behind my back. The fogginess that was a permanent resident in my head a few weeks ago has returned and there's a dull ache behind my eyes.

I get up and head slowly to the bathroom across the hall, my legs leaden. I run the tap and splash some cold water on my face before searching in the mirror for any hint of the man I thought I was. Where is he now? I don't know who I am anymore. Who I'm supposed to be. I was a husband; can I still call myself that? What happens when one person wants something so badly but the other doesn't? I want the description of my identity to include 'husband' but it seems my wife has detached herself from that and taken a part of me with her. We were more than the sum of our parts, at one point.

'Martin Taylor,' Martin answers cheerily after I dial his direct line. I feel sick.

'Oh hi, Martin, it's Paul.' I want to tell him about Lisa and the shitshow that is my life at the minute but the words stick in my throat again. 'I, er... I won't be in today I'm afraid.' Perhaps if he asks the right question I'll give him a truthful answer.

'Oh, sorry to hear that, Paul. That shoulder of yours playing up again, is it?'

I clear my throat. 'Err, yeah, that's it, I think I aggravated it at the weekend wrestling Emilia into her pushchair. Toddlers, hey?'

'Indeed,' he laughs as though he remembers but I doubt he does. 'Well, rest up and see how you go for tomorrow. Keep me posted though, won't you?'

'Yeah, course, thanks Martin. Sorry to leave you in the lurch. I'm sure I'll be alright for tomorrow.' I'm anything but sure.

'Not to worry, Paul, these things happen. Nearly half-term, eh?'

'Yeah,' I laugh. 'Right well I'll see you tomorrow then, hopefully.'

'Right you are, cheerio.'

I breathe a sigh of relief that the conversation's over but berate myself for not being honest. *You're going to have to tell him at some point*, I think. I'm just not quite ready to face up to the fact that my wife is leaving me. '*Is leaving*' or '*has left*'? At what point does it become definitive, moving through the tenses from the present continuous to the present perfect?

Mum comes into the kitchen and puts a hand on my shoulder. 'Morning, darling. Did you sleep?'

'Err, yeah, I think so, eventually. I feel like shit though,' I rub my eyes. 'I just called in sick at work. I might see if I can bring my appointment with the therapist forward to today.'

'Well, that sounds like a good idea,' she agrees as she fills the kettle at the sink. 'Tea?'

'Ah, yes, please,' I pick up my mobile phone and punch out a message to Julia:

'Hey Ju, I'm not in today. Weekend did not go well. Will fill u in when I can but am at my mum's at the minute. P. X'

Despite the day starting off as a vast expanse of time opening up in front of me, I find myself rushing to leave the house to make it to the bus stop in time. Thoughts of Emilia stopped me in my tracks whilst trying to get ready for my appointment and I found myself giving in to compulsions to try and neutralise the thoughts.

I'm constantly checking my phone for anything from Lisa. I just want to know Emilia is OK. No news is good news, I reassure myself. Lisa would tell you if anything was wrong. And why would anything be wrong? But my catastrophising mind reels off all the possibilities of what might have happened to Emilia between now and the last time I saw her, when Lisa picked her up from my mum's yesterday evening.

My pace quickens as I try to focus on getting to the bus stop. I just have to walk through the park to the main road, it's only ten minutes. I breathe in through my nose and the coolness of the air tingles in my nostrils. Breathing out through my mouth, I see my breath in front of me. I should have brought some cigarettes, I think. Pulling my phone out of my pocket, I check the time. 10.25am. Emilia will be at nursery.

Would they call me if she died at nursery, I think. No, no. I shake my head to eradicate the thought. My heart pounds faster. *Think about it though, what's the protocol for that kind of thing? They could hardly break the news over the phone, could they? Would they call and tell you to go to nursery, then tell you? Or would they visit you at home? What if you were at work?* My thoughts descend into chaos and I stop in my tracks, take a deep breath and turn around to retrace the steps I just took whilst that imagined horror show was unfolding. I search for the point in the path where the thought first entered my mind and start again. Breathe.

Keep her safe, keep her safe, I plead with whoever it is in charge of these things. It can't hurt, I kid myself. I look down at my feet, making sure I'm pushing the intrusions firmly out of my mind whilst retracing the same path. You just need to get to the bus stop. I notice someone approaching me in the opposite direction.

I look up to offer a friendly greeting, figuring that's what normal people do. The woman looks up to meet my eyes and I'm paralysed by Laura's gaze. The sight of her takes my breath away, a dizziness taking over me as she smiles and waves gently with her fingers.

I spin around as Laura walks past me and I call her name. The woman turns around with a quizzical half-smile and I realise it's not her, just her phantasmal figure that seems to follow me around these days.

'Sorry,' I breathe, shaking my head. 'I thought... I thought you were someone else. Sorry.' I try and compose myself, masking my odd behaviour. She smiles before turning back around to carry on walking.

Despair comes to join me. As I turn the corner out of the park gates and onto the main road, I notice the bus approaching and pick up my pace to a jog, flagging it down as it pulls in to a stop and the doors jolt open in front of me.

CHAPTER THIRTY

'Hillsborough Road, please,' I say, placing a pound coin on the tray.

'Cheer up mate, it might never happen!' the bus driver chirps as he returns my twenty pence change.

I look up with uncharacteristic contempt and put the change in my pocket, unable to paint my usual smile across my face today. I want to tell him to mind his own fucking business. But that really would be out of character. There should be some sort of badge that grieving people can wear. Yet here I am, on the bus, operating like a normal human being when inside I'm in turmoil, tormented by the thoughts in my own head. It's such a lonely place to be.

It was in those few months after dad left that I learned how to paint my face. The imaginary brushstrokes sweeping across my lips, creating a more pleasing picture for others to look at. Hiding the reality of what was going on behind the façade, giving nothing away. Maybe the paint is finally starting to peel away.

I press the button as I approach the stop for Jeremy's office and I get to my feet. A wave of cold air wakes me up as the doors open and I step out onto the pavement to take the short walk to the office. I press the buzzer, which is still broken, and announce my arrival before the door clicks and I push it open. It feels heavier than last time.

Sinking into the seat, I breathe in slowly, trying to steady the thumping in my chest.

'Hello, Paul,' Jeremy says softly as he enters through the double doors. 'Come on up.'

I smile and follow him up the stairs in silence. I wonder where the hell I'm going to begin.

Jeremy holds the door open for me as I walk through and take a seat on the familiar sofa. The hazy sunshine is filling the room with an ethereal light. I pour myself a glass of water from the jug, out of habit rather than thirst. Jeremy closes the door behind him and makes his way quietly to his chair, taking a sip of his own water as he sits down.

'How are you?' he asks gently.

The question wrestles me to the ground and pins me down. My eyes start to panic as I'm locked inside. An involuntary groan escapes from my throat and I cover my mouth before the tears rush out of my eyes and down my face.

'Take your time,' he offers a compassionate glance and places both hands on his knees in front of him.

'I'm err, I'm not great, actually,' I manage to admit, if there were any room for doubt.

Jeremy nods sympathetically. He listens attentively and without interruption, taking occasional notes, as the dam containing my feelings about everything that happened in the last 48 hours bursts violently into the room.

'That must have all come as a huge shock to you, Paul,'

Jeremy says kindly, in his gentle but affirming tone. 'Do you have friends nearby?' he asks.

I think about who I'm in touch with from my closest friends. *Where did they all go*? I answer with my eyes and Jeremy nods.

At primary school, it was always me and Dave. We bonded over our matching *Superman* lunchboxes on the first day. He commented on how shiny and new mine looked, compared to the hand-me-down version he'd got from his older brother, the paintwork scuffed along the corners of the metal box, the handle slightly grubby. There are some perks of being an only child, I thought.

Dave lived around the corner so we'd often go round to each other's houses for tea, kicking the ball against the kitchen wall, carefully avoiding the window. Dave was always the chattier of us two, always the one to recruit others into our games, invite new faces onto our lunch table. As we grew, I'd stick with him, too shy to branch out and never wanting to anyway. It was no effort.

'What is it that first attracted you to Lisa, do you think?' Jeremy continues his attempt at unravelling the story of how we arrived here.

It feels like such a lifetime ago I don't know where to start. I sometimes can't remember my life without her. I puff out my cheeks as I breathe out, bracing myself.

'She's... quite different to me, I suppose,' which feels like I'm stating the obvious. 'I guess she's always been so... confident, so at ease with herself. I'd often just let her do the talking, she's very easy company. Being with her, it gives me... light, I guess. She leads the way.' I think back to all the dinner parties and drinks we've been to together over the years, me happy to cling to her side and let her lead the conversation. Without her it feels like I've lost my light, lost my voice.

'And what do you think your next steps are, in terms of moving forward?' Jeremy asks, surreptitiously checking his watch.

'Honestly, I have no idea.' I sigh. I feel like I've got a mountain to climb just getting out of bed. And tackling the intrusive thoughts has become a Sisyphean task.

'OK, well, let's look at how you're feeling, day-to-day. What makes your symptoms most manageable? What does a good day look like to you?' he asks as he presses his fingers together and rests them on his lips.

'Well, on Friday, my friend came over and we had a drink and some food, nothing crazy but it was nice. And, Saturday I had a run through the park. That felt really good, getting some proper exercise.'

'Good, that's great. Exercise can be a good way of clearing your head and it releases endorphins which make us feel positive.' Jeremy reaches for a leaflet from a pile on the coffee table. 'Running is good as it gets the blood pumping and you're out in the fresh air. Perhaps you could also try an exercise that involves meeting other people, too? Yoga is good as it has lots of physical benefits but the meditation and breathwork side of it can also help with some of the symptoms you're experiencing.' He hands me a leaflet with some details of a local class.

'I don't know... I might just stick to running, at least I know what I'm doing,' I protest, weakly.

'Well, I'd recommend something out of your comfort zone and which helps you to meet other people, perhaps without too much of a competitive edge,' he seems to stress the 'meeting other people' point. 'I know it's not going to help you in terms of how you get your life back on track, but you'll be better placed to deal with practicalities and discuss those big decisions if you're able to manage the symptoms of your OCD. And of course, anxiety about your situation is bound to exacerbate the OCD, so anything we can do to alleviate your pain in the short term will help us to get to the root of the problem, give us the clarity we need. But, of course, it's up to you.'

'OK,' I say, taking the leaflet. 'My mum's a big yoga fan, actually.'

'Great, you might get some tips from her then,' he laughs. That's the first time I've seen him laugh. 'It's important to make time for things that make us feel good. It's not a panacea but it might make the road to recovery a little smoother.'

I'm not sure how I feel about yoga. What do I wear? But my mum has been trying to get me to do it for years. Can't hurt to try it, I guess.

CHAPTER THIRTY-ONE

On the bus back from my appointment I have a sudden need to speak to Julia.

I call her number and the line rings. It occurs to me that she's at work – where I'm supposed to be – and I check my watch in case she's in lessons. 12.10pm. It's lunchtime so she'll probably be in the staff room or over at the park.

'Ay up, love,' she answers cheerily. 'Sorry, my phone was at the bottom of my bag.'

I don't really know what to say. I think I just wanted to hear her voice.

'You there, Paul?' she asks.

'Yeah, sorry. I'm here... Are you on lunch?' I manage to stammer.

'Yeah, just having a stroll round the park seeing as it's a nice day. How's it going?'

'Er, yeah, a bit shit really...' My voice starts to break and I clear my throat. 'I, erm, I told Martin my shoulder was playing up but... erm, well, Lisa's left me, so...' I don't really know how

205

to succinctly articulate everything that's happened since I last saw Ju on Friday night. But I do my best to fill her in with the headlines.

'Fucking hell, mate... sorry,' her voice is sympathetic but not pitying. 'Are you OK?'

'Not really,' I fight back a tidal wave and realise I need to get off the bus. I've no idea where I am but it's not like I've got anywhere I need to be. I press the button and leave quickly when the bus comes to a stop.

'Where are you?' Julia asks, an urgent concern to her tone.

I wipe my eyes on my sleeve. 'I've just got off the bus. Sorry... for ringing you. I just, I don't know, I just wanted to tell you... how much I value our friendship,' I'm fighting back tears and conscious I'm probably not making much sense.

'The feeling's mutual Paul, believe me. And don't apologise for ringing, OK? Listen, it's a fucking nightmare now but it'll get better, alright? I promise.'

'Everything's just so... heavy, Ju.'

'Course it is, you've had a really rough few months. And now all this. It's no wonder. You going to take the rest of the week off?' she asks, but it feels more like an order.

'I don't know, I feel like just sitting around thinking about stuff probably isn't helping me. I might just take tomorrow off to go and see Lisa and then come back in on Wednesday.' Making plans makes me feel more normal.

'Well, if you're sure, but maybe see how you go, eh?'

'Can I ask a favour, Ju?' I don't wait for her to reply. 'Could you bring Martin up to speed for me? I feel like he needs to know what's going on if I'm going to get through the next few weeks, but I'm not sure I can face having the conversation with him.' Every retelling of the story of my failed marriage is like a kick in the bollocks.

'Of course,' she sighs, and I can almost feel her warmth. 'Whatever makes it easier for you.'

'Thank you,' my breathing is less laboured now. 'Listen, I'll let you get on, I'll probably see you Wednesday.'

'OK, see you then.'

I've made it to the park gates and I'm suddenly exhausted. I drag my aching body back to my mum's, kick off my shoes at the front door and head upstairs to bed.

I wake up to gentle knocking on the bedroom door. I panic, having no idea what time – or even what day – it is. I scramble up and Mum pokes her head around the door.

'Are you ready for something to eat, darling?' she asks quietly.

'What time is it?' I ask, rubbing my hands down over my face.

'It's twenty to seven,' she replies, looking at her watch.

'In the morning?'

'No, dear, in the evening,' she chuckles then sighs through her nose. 'Come on, let's get you some food.'

I get up slowly and realise I'm still fully dressed. I wonder how on earth I can sleep so heavily for so long when my mind is working overtime. I suddenly think of Emilia – this is the longest I've been away from her since mine and Lisa's night away last month and I have an urge to see her. Why hasn't Lisa called me?

'I'm going to give Lisa a quick ring, I want to speak to Emilia,' I hunt around the room for my mobile phone and find it on the chair next to the bed. 'I'll be down in a minute.'

'OK, love. I've got soup on the hob so it's ready when you are.'

I have no idea where I would be without my mum right now.

I scroll down to Lisa's name in my contacts and dial. The line rings but she doesn't answer so I leave her a voicemail.

'*Oh, hey, Lis... I, er, I was just ringing to check in with Emilia and... and you, obviously. Erm, so yeah, I was wondering if I could pop over tomorrow... if you're free? OK, well, let me know... Give Emilia a kiss for me. Bye.*'

She's probably busy putting Emilia to bed. There's an ache in my heart from not seeing her for a whole twenty-four hours. I've no idea how I'll be able to cope with doing this on a regular basis.

I wake up early and can't get back to sleep, probably from having slept a whole six hours during the day yesterday. I roll over to check my phone and there's a message from Lisa. I squint at the bright yellow-green glow from the screen.

'*Sorry was putting Ems 2 bed. She's fine, had a good day. I'm busy 2mrw but mayb pop in after work? U cld collect Ems from nursery & bring her here? Let me know.*'

I'm buoyed by the idea of picking Emilia up and start typing out my reply straight away. Lisa obviously assumes I'm well enough to be at work. I wonder what she'll be 'busy' doing but figure it's none of my business, anymore. Maybe I should just get up and get myself to work instead of sitting around feeling sorry for myself.

I look at the clock. 5.53am. I can walk to work from my

mum's and I've got a shirt and some smartish trousers with me. I think about what Jeremy said about exercise and decide to go for a run. I'll have time for a run round the block and a shower before breakfast then the half an hour walk to school. It's only a few more days until half-term and it'll be good to get back to a bit of normality, I think. Plus I'll have seeing Emilia tonight to look forward to.

I pull on my jogging bottoms and a t-shirt then creep downstairs so as not to wake my mum. I slip on my trainers, grabbing my hoodie from the coat stand in the hall before heading quietly out of the door.

There's something liberating about running in the dark silence of the early morning, when no one else is around. Feeling the shockwaves from my feet pounding on the pavement, up through my legs, meeting the thump of my heart in my chest. The energising inhalations and refreshing cold air on my face cleansing my mind. The purposeful exhalations of breath leaving my body and taking some of my pain with them. When I'm running, it feels like I might just make it through.

I get back and head straight to the bathroom for a shower. I open the tap until it runs hot and steam fills the room, shrouding me like a warm hug. The hot water pricks my cold skin like needles. It's strangely comforting, as if the sensation helps me understand what's real. A defiance washes over me, as if it's being pumped directly out of the shower head, and tells me that it will be OK. I can make this work, whatever *this* is. I am a good person – a good dad – and I've done nothing wrong. If my wife doesn't want to be a part of our life then that's on her, not me. A piece of the puzzle falls into place which I think might be key to me starting to make strides towards getting better: I can't control how people behave or feel or respond to things. I can't control anything. *Anything*. And the harder I try, the harder the struggle in my mind becomes. Suddenly, it all seems so obvious.

CHAPTER THIRTY-TWO

'Morning, Ju,' Julia spins around and looks surprised to see me as I walk across the car park towards her.

'Paul! How you doing?' she asks, putting a hand on my upper arm. 'Wasn't expecting to see you today.'

'Well, I figured I'd be better keeping busy'.

'Take your time though, won't you,' she looks me straight in the eyes. 'I filled Martin in yesterday about... things.'

'Thanks, yeah I was going to ask if you'd managed to speak to him,' I swipe my pass and we head in through the double doors. I lower my voice. 'It's good to know he's been... brought up to speed.'

'No problem, mate. I'm going to grab a quick coffee before class, do you want one?'

'Nah, I'm alright thanks. I'm going to pop in and tell Martin I'm here. I'll catch you at lunch though, yeah?'

'Yeah, sounds good. Hope this morning isn't too tough.'

I smile and head for Martin's office down the other end of the hall.

Martin's door is ajar but I knock, before poking my head

around. He's sitting at his desk and looks up, greeting me with a wide smile.

'Paul, come on in,' he gestures to the seat in front of him.

I hesitate, not wanting to get drawn into talking too heavily about everything he's already heard from Julia.

'I won't keep you, Martin,' I gesture, raising a hand, to politely decline the seat. 'Just thought I'd let you know I'm... here. And I gather Julia filled you in yesterday, about... things.'

'Yes, she did, she did. Very sorry to hear about your... troubles, Paul. But you know where I am if you need anything, don't hesitate.' He eyes me over the top of his glasses again.

'Thank you, I appreciate it. I'm, er... I'm better when I'm busy, I think.' I assure him.

'Right you are, Paul. Good man.'

I nod him a friendly acknowledgement and step back out into the hallway, letting out a sigh of relief. That wasn't so bad.

If you think your morning is going OK, there's nothing like three hours of trying to teach English to a load of unruly teenagers to bring you back down to earth. First lesson wasn't so bad, being powered by caffeine and residual optimism, but by the end of second lesson I was wading through treacle. And now, after lunch, I'm starting to feel the effects of the last three days of disrupted sleep. My eyes ache and I'm irritated by the unnecessary noise the kids are making as I sit in the office opposite our tutor group classroom, waiting for afternoon registration. I'm pulling my lesson plans together for the last two periods and see I've got my own tutor group for last lesson and we're carrying on with our Romeo & Juliet analysis. The bell sounds and I neck the last of my coffee before stuffing the papers into my satchel and heading next door to the classroom.

As I walk in, Andy has one of the girls in a headlock, two of the boys are lobbing a squash ball around before it bounces off the back of Manny's head, who is tangled in an inappropriate embrace with Shaun Leverton. My eyes roll as I consider what tactic to employ to bring them back. I opt for sarcasm, they seem to like that.

'I see you're all ready...' I raise my voice above the din and pause until I have their attention. '...for a thrilling afternoon of education?' I finish quietly. 'Put Shaun down, please Manny. And Andy, if that's your attempt at flirting, I think you're going the wrong way about it, mate. Seats now please, guys, let's go.'

Andy shoots me a disapproving glare and someone throws the squash ball in my direction which I manage to catch, met by some laughter. 'Unlucky,' I grin sarcastically before placing the ball down on my desk.

'Right, try and calm yourselves down will you before next lesson?' I implore them after taking the register. 'And you lucky lot have got me for fifth period so let's try and end the day on a high, shall we?' I shout above the row as they all file out for fourth lesson.

———

By the time last lesson comes around my head is banging and I'm ready for a lie down. At least I've got picking Emilia up to look forward to, I think. I take a sip of my tea as the kids file in and take their seats in the classroom. There's a last lesson lethargy in the air but I can also sense some tension between Erin and Andy. He seems to be in a provoking mood this afternoon and I'm pretty sure I heard Erin telling him to fuck off as she came into the classroom.

'Alright guys, let's get to it shall we? Can you open your books up at act five, scene three and we'll pick up from there.' I give them a minute to shuffle about finding their books.

'So did everyone manage to untangle what was going on here, in that last scene?'

There is a mixture of tentatively affirming mumbles and some blank faces. I don't have the energy for this.

'OK, well let's look at the film and see if that helps us get to the bottom of it,' I suggest, wheeling the TV across to the front of the room and closing the blinds before pressing play on the VHS player.

We watch the final fifteen minutes of the film and by the end I feel my eyes starting to close. Just half an hour left, I think. I open the blinds and everyone begins to move around in their seats.

'So, that didn't go quite to plan, did it?' there are a few laughs and I open up my book and perch on the edge of my desk in front of the class.

'Let's have a look at lines 118-121,' I start to read aloud. '"Oh, here / Will I set up my everlasting rest, / And shake the yoke of inauspicious stars / From this world-wearied flesh." Who wants to try and translate that for me?'

Erin's hand goes up. 'Yes, Erin.'

'So, he's saying he's going to kill himself, to leave his body behind and shake the burden of his unhappy fate.'

'Very good, Erin, nicely put.'

'Ohhh Romeo, Romeo, wherefor art thou, *Romeo*!' Andy mockingly calls over in Erin's direction.

'Piss off, Andy!' she snaps, her cheeks bright red.

'Andy,' I intervene sharply, 'I don't know what you're getting at but that's enough, alright?'

'She fancies you sir, is what I'm getting at.'

'I said that's enough!' I shout, slamming my hand on the desk in front of me and a wave of shock ripples through the classroom. Andy sits back in his chair with a smirk on his face. I haven't got the patience for his bullshit right now.

'Well you might be in with a chance now his missus has left him,' Andy laughs as the room gasps and a rage I can't control descends on me. I march over to his desk, pick him up by the lapels of his blazer and push him up against the closed door. 'Get the fuck out of my classroom!' I scream into his face before opening the door and pushing him hard out into the hall. He stumbles backwards and steals a provoking glance at me before rising to his feet and straightening up his clothes. I slam the door behind me and close my eyes, resting my head against the door and taking a deep breath in through my nose. I breathe out into the thick silence of the room, and anticipate twenty-eight teenagers staring at me as soon as I open my eyes. A cold bead of sweat forms just below my hairline. What the fuck have I done? Panic chases me, like when I kicked that ball into the art block window when I was twelve, the deafening smash, shards flying. Only this time I've attacked one of my students, a child I'm charged to protect. I'm pretty sure that's against the law. I take another breath before facing the room.

'Sorry... about that,' I say as I loosen the collar of my shirt and lower myself into my chair. What if his parents call the police? 'I shouldn't have reacted like that, I'm sorry.'

Manny Dhindsa breaks the quiet. 'It's alright, sir. He was being a prick. He has been all day.'

'That's no excuse, though,' I admit, as the classroom door opens and Martin fills the doorway.

'Everything alright in here, Mr. Johnson?' he says quietly and I nod towards the corridor, heading for the door.

'Right,' I clear my throat, 'carry on with annotating those last lines of act five, scene three, please. I'll be back in a minute,' I address the class as I head out of the door with Martin. Andy is standing there looking smug.

'I'm sorry Andy,' I say, not quite able to meet his eyes. 'I shouldn't have reacted like that. But I'd appreciate it if you kept your remarks on my personal life to yourself, OK?'

'You,' Martin addresses Andy in a voice so soft yet stern that it sends a chill down the back of my arms. 'Collect your things and make your way to my office, now.' Andy sheepishly retreats into the classroom to get his bag.

Martin turns to me. 'I heard a commotion from my office so I thought I'd come and see what was going on. Come and talk to me after class, would you?'

'Yeah, I will do,' I sigh, as I realise I've probably tried to rush back into normality a little too early. Andy comes out into the hallway and follows as Martin leads the way to his office.

My stomach churns on the way to Martin's office after last lesson finishes and I wonder how I'm going to explain what happened this afternoon. I was never called to the headteacher's office while I was at school, I kept myself to myself most of the time. And I'm livid at myself for rising to a teenager's pathetic games.

I can't imagine this is going to do my head of department chances much good. What if I lose my job? People have lost their jobs for less serious things in the past. How will I get another job with something like this on my record? *I'm sorry*

Mr Johnson, we can't accept applications from teachers who have had disciplinary action around safeguarding issues. I swallow, smoothing down my tie as I reach Martin's door.

'Come in,' Martin bellows from his desk and I step inside. 'Paul, come and take a seat.' His face is grave.

'So, do you want to tell me what happened this afternoon?' he asks, taking his glasses off and resting them on the top of his head.

'I, er... I lost it, Martin, I'm sorry,' I take a breath and recount the events leading up to me picking a student up by the scruff of his neck. 'He just pushed my buttons, you know, announcing to the class that my wife's left me. I don't even know how he knows! But anyway he was winding Erin Robson – and me – up and, well... I should have just taken him outside before it got to that point, he'd been winding everyone up all day. And obviously I shouldn't have roughed him up like that, I'm sorry. I think maybe I bit off more than I could chew, coming back today.'

'Yes, probably. And as for *roughing him up*, well, if it were me, I think I'd have clouted him. So it sounds like he got off lightly by all accounts,' I laugh through my nose and close my eyes. I can't quite believe I acted the way I did and it scared me. I didn't know I was capable of behaving like that, in front of the kids. It felt like I was watching someone else react. 'I gave him a good talking to and I don't think you'll be getting any more trouble from him for a while. In terms of your reaction, I witnessed your apology, which he says he accepts and unless we get a complaint from the parents – which I think is unlikely – then, as far as I'm concerned, that's the end of the matter.'

I sigh and put my head in my hands, considering myself lucky to have someone like Martin on my side. I look up, bringing my fingertips together and resting them under my nose. 'Thanks, Martin. It won't happen again, I can assure you.'

'It can't, Paul. OK? I'm on your side here. And an isolated incident in the circumstances you're facing is one thing, but if it happens again, I'll need to be seen to be taking further action.'

'I know, I know. I'm sorry... to have put you in this position.'

'You're under a lot of strain at the minute, I can see that. I suggest you take the rest of the week off and come back after half-term, *if* you're feeling up to it,' he says firmly, leaning back in his chair as if to say that's the end of the matter.

I feel a cool dampness creep across my forehead. 'I don't know, I mean, they've got their mocks in a couple of weeks. It's hardly the best timing! I'd feel a bit like I was abandoning them, it doesn't feel right,' I protest. Maybe he's just trying to keep me out of the way so he can put his case together for firing me.

'I admire your diligence, Paul, but really you need to be in a fit state in order to be any help to them. And life doesn't stick to a timetable I'm afraid. I'll step in as their form tutor for now and I can organise cover for your other classes from the supply agency this evening.' Martin jots something down on his desk pad and looks up at me from under his eyebrows. 'OK?' he asks.

I know they'll be in good hands with Martin but it still leaves me anxious to think I won't see them until after half-term. 'Yeah, I suppose you're right. I shouldn't be running before I can walk.'

'Now, there's something else I wanted to talk to you about,' Martin starts and I freeze. 'Don't look so worried,' he laughs. 'I read your application and I was very impressed with your ideas about improvements for the department. But I've had to inter-view two other external candidates.'

'OK,' I say, filling the silence of his dramatic pause. I know what's coming.

'I need you to get back on top form, Paul. So we can interview you and get you lined up for September, OK? I want you to take as long as you need to get yourself well and we'll get that interview set up for when you're better. But I cannot have a repeat of this afternoon, do you hear?'

I sit up in surprise. 'Yep, yeah of course, it absolutely won't happen again Martin, you have my word. And I'm working on getting myself better, I really am. I'll keep you more up to date, from now on.'

'Right you are, Paul. I'm sorry you're having a tough time of it but let's put our tin hats on, eh? And I'm here to help, if I can.'

CHAPTER THIRTY-THREE

I'm distracted when I collect Emilia from nursery, replaying the events of the afternoon over and over in my mind. I can't let Lisa find out, what would she think if she knew I'd assaulted a student? She'd probably stop me from seeing Emilia. And if I lose my job how on earth am I going to pay the mortgage? What if Lisa takes her to London with her? Sets up home down there, I'll only get access visits on birthdays and Christmas. I can't believe I've been so stupid, put everything even further at risk.

My heart sinks as I notice Lisa's parents' car on the drive when I arrive at the house. I wonder if it's odd that I refer to our home as 'the house' now instead of 'home' but it hardly resembles home if we're not living in it together. I stand in the porch and knock, waiting to be let in. I wonder if Emilia finds it odd, for us to be knocking on our own front door. Or whether she realises that it's been nearly a week since we all slept under the same roof, probably for the last time.

Lisa answers the door, her face pallid and clammy. She greets Emilia quietly and ruffles her hair as she runs through the door and down the hallway.

'Hi,' I'm not sure whether to go in for a peck on the cheek.

'Hey,' Lisa utters. I catch her eyes, despondent, before she looks away. She looks exhausted. 'Come through,' she says. Even she seems to baulk at the weirdness of inviting me into my own house. I follow her in, noticing her posture shrunken and hunched, her movements slow and cautious.

'I didn't know your parents were going to be here,' I mumble from behind her. I can hear them in the kitchen making a fuss of Emilia.

'Shall we go in the front room?' Lisa suggests, pointing. 'Mum and dad are only staying a bit longer. They wanted to stick around to see Emilia before they head off.'

'Ah OK,' I say, relieved. I hadn't psyched myself up for facing them too. I take a seat on the sofa while Lisa perches on the armchair. 'Have they been here today then?'

'Yeah, Mum came over this morning and dad popped by this afternoon. I'm having a miscarriage, so...'

Her words slice through me and send a stabbing pain deep into my chest. She's never been one to beat around the bush. Always straight to the point. But her directness still catches me off guard. 'Oh Lis, I'm sorry,' I move over to her and take her hand. I'm heartened when she gives mine a squeeze back. I feel myself starting to choke up. I clear my throat. 'Are you sure? When... did it start?'

'I started feeling unwell last night and noticed some bleeding so I called the hospital. They said it might not be anything to worry about, but I should go in for an early scan just to see. So I went today, with Mum, and... well, they're pretty sure that's what's going on, so...' She looks down at her feet and lets go of my hand. Something strange happens inside my head as if part of me might have left the room, dissolved like particles through the air, escaping through the walls and out into the atmosphere. I try and bring myself back.

'How are you feeling?'

'Yeah, a bit shit to be honest. The bleeding has got a lot heavier and the pain's started to get more intense. Mum's going to stay here tonight but I said you might want to put Emilia to bed, so you get to spend a bit of time with her. If you want? They're going to head out and get something to eat and then Mum will come back later.' She shifts her position and closes her eyes as she breathes in slowly.

'I could stay, instead?' I suggest hopefully. I'm broken by the thought of Lisa going through this without me being there to help her. And there's something about the situation that makes me even more sad than if she'd have gone ahead and organised the abortion she wanted. Although I suppose it just wasn't meant to be. I wonder if it's made it easier for her but I'm not foolish enough to ask.

'I don't know Paul, I think it might be easier if you go back to your mum's. Thanks though,' she smiles. 'I appreciate the offer.' There's a softness to her that wasn't there at the weekend and I feel a tiny glimmer of hope.

'So, are you still going to London on Monday?'

'Er, Sunday, I think. And yes, still planning to go, if I'm well enough. They said the worst should be over in a couple of days so I'm just going to try and rest up for the rest of this week.' She talks as if she's getting over a cold. Perhaps that's easier than the reality of what it is. The loss of a baby.

'Do you think that's wise? Could you not just postpone it a week?' I forget for a second that how she lives her life is no longer my business.

'Well, like I said, I'll see how I feel. Nothing's set in stone but I think it'd be best to carry on with the plan.'

• • •

'Can I just ask, Lis, for how long was this part of your plan?' I ask, with an ounce too much bitterness in my execution.

'Can we not do this now Paul? Please?'

'I'm sorry, I just... I don't know, I feel like it's all happened so fast. Like if we could have sat down and talked about stuff, properly, instead of just getting on with things and ignoring the elephant in the room until it's become too late. Don't you think we could give some counselling a try? You can still go to London, if that's what you want, but don't give up on *us*?' I feel like I'm pleading.

'I think we want different things, Paul, long-term, I mean. Your reaction when I told you I was pregnant was the complete opposite to mine when I found out. That speaks volumes about where we are as a couple – it seems we want entirely opposing things. Different lives. It's not fair on either of us to pretend that we'd be happy going along with it. I can't see that any amount of counselling is going to bring us back onto the same page, if we stay true to ourselves.'

'So, what, we just give up, just like that? All those years together, all this?' I throw my arms out in exasperation, gesturing at the house we made our home.

'Surely it's better to quit while we're ahead rather than limping on towards a life of bitterness and resentment? One of us *will* lose out. But right now, we're still young, we can make the lives we want, just not together. You can find someone to give you the family you want. I'm just not that person. I thought I was, but I'm not, I'm sorry.' She looks down at her feet.

'It's just such a waste, Lisa! Such a fucking waste! We were so good together, once. We could be even better, if we tried?' I've got nothing left, my head's in my hands.

'People change, Paul,' she says quietly. 'This whole thing, I just don't think it's for me. We're told we need to settle down, buy the house, get married, have the kids. It's like I'm a piece of a jigsaw puzzle being forced into a space I don't fit into. It might seem like it fits for a while but, before long, when the other pieces fall into place, you start to realise it's not going to work.'

We sit there in silence, the weight of loss hanging heavy in the room. *Loss.* Loss has followed me around like a dark cloud over the last three months. First Laura, now my marriage, and our unborn child. My family as I knew it and my family as I imagined it, lost.

———

Walking back to Mum's there's an emptiness sitting in the pit of my stomach from having left Emilia. And Lisa. Should I be trying harder? But it seems to me that any chance of making her see sense will come from giving her space, rather than stating my case over and over again.

My phone vibrates in my pocket and I pull it out to see a message from Mum.

'At yoga tonight darling so won't be back until later. Soup in the fridge if u haven't eaten. See u later on X'

The prospect of going back to an empty house doesn't fill me with joy but I figure I'm going to have to get used to my own company for a while. I start to count my steps as I walk back through the park.

———

The house is cold and in total darkness except for the porch light. I turn the key in the door and notice how differently it sounds to the door of my own house opening. I flick on the hallway light and a sudden hunger reminds me I should eat.

The flagged floor in the kitchen is cold and I remember I should bring my slippers. Maybe I'll pop over tomorrow, just to see how Lisa is getting on. And get my slippers. Maybe I could put Emilia to bed again. I'm not entirely sure how I'm going to fill my days between now and Sunday. I take my food into the lounge, dialling the central heating thermostat up a couple of notches as I walk past.

I sit down on the sofa facing the window and look out onto the street. Is there anything sadder than a grown man eating alone in his mum's house, I wonder? Then I realise, yes there is. It could be worse, I tell myself. It might not feel like it right now but it really could be much worse. A sharp pain stabs me just below my ribs as I think of Emilia. I need to pull myself together, for her, I think. I can't let what is currently unfolding in front of me – happening to me – ruin the life I can have with her.

I finish my soup and remember the yoga flyer I stuffed into my pocket, pulling it out as I place my empty bowl on the coffee table in front of me. Classes every day, it tells me. See timetable for details. I turn over and see there's a class tomorrow at 10.30am. The pictures show people doing yoga. They're wearing jogging bottoms and t-shirts. And there are men. Everyone is smiling. Maybe it's worth a try, I think. I've nothing better to do at the minute.

The silence is unnerving so I head over to Mum's record player and browse her LPs. Roxy Music, Crowded House, Fleetwood Mac; she's got such good taste it's hard to choose. I go for The Human League's *Greatest Hits*, carefully tilting the sleeve to allow the record to slide out. Placing the record down on the turntable, I press start and it begins to spin, the arm clicking then whirring before moving itself into position. There's a loud thudding noise before the crackling of the dust on the vinyl, then the unmistakable synth of *Together In Electric Dreams* kicks in. I realise I've started it on Side B, but never mind.

I sink back down onto the sofa and close my eyes, following the drumbeat by tapping it out on my thigh. A wave of warmth fills the room, the heating must have finally kicked in, I think. I open my eyes and Laura is sitting on the sofa opposite me. Her presence is becoming less and less of a surprise, but still she startles me.

'You're too good for her, you know,' she says, raising her eyebrows as she sits back in the sofa, folding her arms across her front. 'I just think you should know that.'

It's the first time I've had a conversation with her when she's not in school uniform. She's wearing a faded grey Nirvana t-shirt and light blue flared jeans, frayed at the bottom, with red hi-top Converse trainers. Her chestnut hair sits in a long bob, the gentle waves resting on her shoulders.

'And what makes you say that?' I ask, curious as to how she's come to that conclusion. I suppose I need someone to massage my ego after the last few days.

'She's not been treating you properly, she could have at least given you a chance to work things out.' She swings her legs onto the sofa and lies back, resting her head on the arm. 'I love this song!' she exclaims, beaming as she turns to face me.

'Me too,' I smile back. I think about what she said. 'But she's made up her mind. And like she said, people change. What they want changes, where they see themselves heading changes, what they're interested in changes...' I realise I'm defending Lisa's point of view.

'You guys don't seem to have much in common? Does she even *like* music?' She looks baffled that mine and Lisa's tastes are so dissimilar.

'She does, just different music, I guess...' I laugh at the observation. 'She's not a mad Radiohead fan, put it that way.'

'That blows my mind,' she turns to look up at the ceiling, shaking her head.

'But, you know, opposites attract and all that.'

'Yeah, to begin with maybe, but... I mean you've got to have *something* in common to make a lifetime of it together, right? But hey, what do I know?' She laughs through her nose.

'Maybe that's where we went wrong... Got swept up in the moment. Then you can kind of get lost in the daily grind. If you're not careful.'

'You deserve someone who takes an interest in *you*, like you did with her. It has to work both ways.' She wanders over to examine my mum's LPs on the shelf. 'You can be happy again, though. When you're ready.'

The maturity of her awareness never ceases to amaze me and I shake my head gently, smiling to myself. She catches me in her gaze and holds up The Cure's *Boys Don't Cry* LP. 'Can I put this on?' she asks excitedly.

'Yeah, course,' I laugh. 'Are you *trying* to make me cry?'

'It's OK to cry, you know. Oh and don't worry about Andy Smithurst. He's such a twat. I sent him some karma by way of a flock of pigeons shitting all over him on his way home. So he's been dealt with.'

I burst out laughing, both at the prospect of this either being real or a creation of my imagination. I come to the conclusion that it doesn't really matter which is true.

Laura replaces the record on the turntable and carefully moves the arm, lowering the needle down at exactly the point where the title track starts to play. She takes a seat next to me on the sofa and invites me to rest my head on her shoulder.

'Thank you,' I whisper, closing my eyes as the music takes hold and I drift away.

CHAPTER THIRTY-FOUR

The morning light streams into my mum's spare room, through the gap where the curtains don't quite meet, hurting my eyes. The radio is still on from last night's lullaby. It must have been gone 1am before I managed to get to sleep, thoughts of my conversation with Laura rolling through my mind. The warmth I felt as she entered the room, I miss that. An emptiness swells in my stomach as I remember I'm not due into school today. I roll over and reach across the cold side of the bed to pick up my phone from the bedside table. No messages, although I don't know who I was expecting to have heard from. 7.15am. Is it too early to message Julia? I remembered last night that I wanted to check in with Manny after last lesson, see how her extra Maths sessions are going, but I didn't have a chance after what happened with Andy. Maybe Ju could have a word with her. A hot panic washes over me as I realise there's so much that only I know about the kids, stuff I carry around for them. How will this set them up for their exams, especially the ones who need extra help? This is their future. I punch a quick message out to Julia, asking her to call me before class. The only other thing I have to achieve today is my appointment with Jeremy. I lie back, and wait for time to pass.

———

'I just feel like I'm losing my mind,' I manage to say between gulping sobs, my nose running down onto my top lip. I dab it with the back of my hand before taking a tissue from the coffee table in Jeremy's office. I take a deep breath in through my nose and hold it in my chest for as long as I can, until it feels like drowning. Jeremy offers a sympathetic smile but says nothing, waiting for me to continue.

'I don't know where I'm heading and, sometimes, it all just feels completely pointless. I know Lisa is better off without me, I was making her completely miserable. I've not exactly been much fun to be around over the last few months. But I don't know where that leaves *me*.'

I pause again, glancing around the room. How did I get here? I wonder for a second what it would be like to be Jeremy, his calm exterior, ability to consider things so carefully before passing comment on them. I steal a glimpse in his direction and catch sight of his wedding ring, a thick band of either gold or silver, the shine dulled. Funny how these symbols become part of our bodies, no longer noticeable to ourselves but giving away clues to others about who we are. Is he happily married I wonder? Maybe he's a widower. He knows so much about me yet I have only fragments of him.

'It's like a whole part of my identity has been snatched away,' I continue into the silence. 'I can't call myself a 'husband' anymore. I don't know where I belong, in the world, which box to tick. It's just all slipping away from me, everything that I hold close, and my mind is constantly taunting me. I'm just so tired. And so lonely.'

The word 'lonely' sticks in my throat. As the tears flow again I realise this session has just been a continuously rolling tide of monologue from me. With every deep breath in, another wave of self-loathing is spewed out of my mouth, until I can barely breathe, and the cycle repeats. Push and pull, in and out, each wave dragging me further out. It's painful and exhausting but somehow cathartic to vocalise everything I hate about myself and my life right now.

'You mention *belonging*, Paul,' Jeremy's eyes narrow sympathetically. 'And this has been a bit of a recurring theme since we started our sessions together. Do you want to talk any more about that perhaps?' he suggests gently, looking up from his notebook. It feels like he's just managed to get enough purchase on something that, until now, has been out of reach, but now might be the time to start teasing it out.

I wipe my eyes on the heel of my hand as I breathe out through my nose. 'I guess I've always struggled with the idea of fitting in, since I was a kid, I suppose.' He nods encouragingly as I pause. 'I always felt a little bit different to the other boys in my class, not in a good or bad way, just *different*. I was never one of the really sporty lads, I'd join in but it wasn't really my thing. I liked music, but not always the sort of stuff everyone else was listening to.' I laugh, but I don't know why.

'Everyone was friendly enough with me – I wasn't bullied or anything like that – but I never had any particularly close friendships with anyone... Just a few mates that I'd knock about with, you know... to go round and play on the Atari or hang around at the rec with. I always felt like they just kind of... put up with me, like they were indifferent about whether I was there or not. We didn't talk about stuff, properly I mean. And I guess that was one of the things I missed out on – not having my dad around, growing up. No brother or sister to confide in, or whatever. I mean, Mum was always there for me. But there are some things you just can't talk to your mum about when you're fifteen, you know? So, I guess I found it harder and harder to come out of my shell, like I'd left it too late.' A deep sadness that's new to me, like a grief for my younger self starts to bloom in my chest. If only I could go back and tell him it's alright to be different. *You don't need to be something you're not.* I wonder if I might have turned out more at ease with myself. My thoughts turn to Andy and whether he has anyone he can talk to at home. Him winding me up in class is probably just his way of seeking attention, a cry for help. And I respond to that by physically assaulting him. Hardly Head of Department material.

'That all makes a lot of sense, in terms of what you've said previously about seeking acceptance and people-pleasing. You said earlier that you don't know where you belong *now*, in the world. But you know, Paul, everyone's identities, their sense of self, are multi-faceted and, whilst you might feel that your identity as a husband, as you put it, has been taken away, there are still so many important and valuable elements to who you are. A father, for example, to your daughter. You're a son, a friend, a *teacher*. We can't be defined by one single element of our lives, whatever that may be.'

'I suppose not,' I admit, knowing that he's right. 'But I feel so... *ashamed*, I guess, that I've let my marriage slip away. I can't bring myself to tell people that my wife has left me, left *us*... it just feels so... I don't know, it's embarrassing, like people will think there's something wrong with me. And then I feel bad that I'm having those feelings, you know. Why should I feel ashamed? I tried my best. I didn't do anything wrong. But also, would I feel so awkward about it if it was the other way around? It seems more socially acceptable for a man to walk out on his wife and kid. And then I end up hating myself for even *thinking* that, judging women – my own wife – by different standards. It's not what I actually think, or at least I don't want to believe I think that, but maybe subconsciously I do.'

'We all have subconscious prejudices that, when we hold a mirror up to ourselves, we don't like the look of. But it's important not to dwell on them or tell ourselves that we're bad people because of these ideas. They're often ingrained in our upbringing, for generations – your father leaving you, for example – and society generally. That's not to say it's OK to just go along with them. But what's important is that we can identify them and, with good intentions, challenge ourselves to think differently, recognise other perspectives and grow as a result. Progress doesn't have to equal perfection.'

I consider this for a while, before picking up the miniature Newton's cradle on the coffee table and taking one of the tiny metal balls between my fingers. I pull it back on its string then let go, the ball crashing into the next with a loud clicking sound, sending the ball at the other end of the row of five flying like a pendulum and back again, repeating the process in reverse. Click, click, click, click. Something about cause and effect, action and reaction? I can feel Jeremy watching me closely. The constant clicking quickly becomes irritating so I stop the motion of the balls with my hand, holding them still.

'I just can't seem to get out of this cycle of blaming myself. For the breakdown of my marriage, for Laura's death. Even though the rational part of my brain knows I didn't do anything wrong in my marriage. Laura's death wasn't my fault. Maybe it stems from blaming myself for my parents' divorce? I don't know,' I blow out an exasperated sigh. 'But I just feel like a failure, like everyone is pitying me. And when I fall into this paranoia, that's when the intrusive thoughts get hold of me. It's such a horrible, vicious cycle and I struggle to see a way out.'

'Recovery is an ongoing process, Paul, with many ups and downs along the way,' he smiles knowingly. 'But you should be proud of yourself for how far you've come, although at times it might not feel like it. You've taken the brave first steps to getting help. And you've got your friend Julia and your mum to lean on in an emergency, when it all gets too much. As well as the crisis contacts I've given you.' His eyes widen and he holds my gaze with a slow nod, to labour the point. 'You will get there, we just have to take it one step at a time, whilst expecting some relapses along the way. Did you try a yoga class, after we last spoke?'

I sigh and my shoulders drop. 'No,' I confess, shaking my head. 'I'd talked myself up to it but... I don't know, I bottled out.'

'Well, what if I were to set you a challenge? To try a yoga class before our next session? You're doing great work, Paul, but if we were to inject a little gentle enjoyment into this process I wonder if we'd make even bigger strides towards you feeling better? I don't want to force you to do something you don't want to do but, perhaps ask yourself – what's the worst that could happen?' He raises his eyebrows and gives a little shrug of the shoulders.

'I know, I know,' I laugh through my nose, shaking my head. 'I guess I'm just worried about making a tit of myself, doing something wrong.'

'Well, I'm sure if you do do something *wrong*,' he says, with air quotes, 'then the teacher will guide you in the right direction, don't you think? And isn't that how we learn, by making mistakes?'

'I guess so,' I mumble, like a petulant child.

I roll a mat out onto the cold community centre floor and glance cautiously to both sides of me, checking I've done it right. Is there a wrong way to roll out a yoga mat? *Probably not, get a grip of yourself, you might actually enjoy it.* Nerves are knotted up in my stomach as I sit cross-legged in the centre of the mat, straightening up my back. I look at those in front of me – I strategically chose a space in the middle row, not wanting to expose myself as a beginner at the front, but also not having the confidence for a back row spot – some are lying on their backs with their eyes closed, some stretching their arms overhead. I move my head from side to side to loosen out my neck and pull my fingers back to stretch out my wrists, for something to do with my hands. I look around at the other participants, they're mostly female but there are a couple of guys amongst the fifteen or so of us in the room. At least I'm not the only one, I think.

'Morning, everyone,' a cheerful but calm voice sings from the doorway at the back of the room. A few people mumble hello and I look over my shoulder to see the instructor enter the room, carrying a water bottle and a small hand towel. *Shit, did I need a towel?* I panic. *God, I'm about to make a massive twat of myself. I knew this was a bad idea.* She makes her way gracefully tiptoeing between the mats along the floor to the front of the hall, her long black braids swinging between her shoulder blades, before taking a seat on her mat which is placed perpendicular to everyone else's.

'So we'll start class today in child's pose, just to settle into our breathing,' she soothes, as she manoeuvres her body across the mat. I watch nervously, trying to remember what shape she's making, as I attempt to mimic the pose as effortlessly as possible. I glance sideways to my fellow students, trying not to make it too obvious I haven't a clue what *child's pose* is. *Am I in the right class?*

'I see we've got a couple of new faces in today, so if anyone needs any help with any of the poses just pop your hand up and I can come over and make adjustments,' she reassures the newbies, although I'm certain that was aimed solely at me. She's probably sniffed out my sheer terror.

'Just one more breath here before we gently unfold up into mountain pose,' she says quietly in her soft, muted Manchester accent. I catch a glimpse of her face as she demonstrates the movement to the class. She looks about my age, maybe a few years younger, and as she uncurls her body into *mountain pose*, I notice how tall she is. She seems to have a fixed gentle smile, like she knows something about life that the rest of us don't. I realise I don't know her name.

'Now we're going to take our right foot forward, bend the knee and step the left leg back to come into our warrior two. Make sure that right knee is stacked over the ankle and keep your weight even through both legs... then bring your right arm out in front, left one behind and stretch... really reach out as far as you can and bring your gaze beyond your fingertips.'

She moves her lithe limbs into the pose effortlessly and I watch, while bringing my right foot forward, trying to keep it in line with my left foot behind. As I shuffle my feet into position, my right foot catches on the sticky surface of the yoga mat and my heart leaps as I lose my balance, wobbling slightly towards the person to my right.

I recover myself and glance over at my neighbour, mouthing 'sorry' as I catch her eye. She smiles with a gentle shrug and whispers 'don't worry' as she moves further into position. I follow everyone else's lead and am surprised at how good the stretch across my chest, shoulders and hips feels, as if I'm opening myself up.

'Make sure the crown of your head is stacked on top of your pelvis, and your shoulders are over your hips. Now try and reach a little further into your fingertips... Don't forget to breathe...' the teacher guides us followed by a long outbreath through her nose. I do the same and ease into the stretch.

'You did great,' the soft voice approaching me says as I roll up my yoga mat. I look up and see the instructor standing next to me, sipping from her water bottle. 'Was this your first class?'

'Err... yeah, could you tell?' I laugh, trying to release my nerves.

She laughs. 'No, I just noticed I'd not seen you at this class before,' she says kindly. 'I'm Rachel, by the way.'

'Paul,' I smile, as I rise with my mat rolled under my arm. Should I shake her hand? 'I was a bit nervous, to be honest. I've never done this kind of thing before, but I really enjoyed it, thank you.'

'Well you know where we are, now. The first class is always the hardest. I'm trying to get a few more classes going in the week but this one is always popular. Maybe see you next time?'

'Yeah, cheers,' I nod awkwardly as she heads off to talk to another one of the newcomers. I breathe out quietly. Well, that wasn't so bad, I suppose.

CHAPTER THIRTY-FIVE

Sitting in the corridor in my best suit – the one I wore to Laura's funeral – I suddenly feel like an outsider in my own school. It seems to possess a different energy, an air of unwelcoming hostility, as if I'm about to get found out. For what, exactly, I can't quite put my finger on. The evening sun is streaming in and bouncing off the sheen of the parquet floor.

Why are you so hell bent on making a fool of yourself? I try and breathe through the voice in my head, telling me I have no right to be doing this. *They'll all know about what happened, before.* I frown, shaking my head. I really want this. I didn't do anything wrong. I touch both of my cufflinks and run a hand through my hair. *You think you're going to get a promotion, after you basically assaulted one of your students?* My stomach churns. Extenuating circumstances, Martin had reassured me. *Not to mention your creepy dreams about the one you pretty much sent to her death.* It was an accident, everyone says. But I do still feel guilty about the dreams.

They'll see right through you. You're nothing special. You can't even hold down your marriage. For fuck's sake. This is all I need.

Passing clouds, leaves in the wind, I tell myself. I try counting my breaths to calm my heart. *You left them when they needed you most, just before their exams, you disappeared. Hardly Teacher of the Year, are you?*

I try and remember the questions Julia asked me in our mock interview last night. I was sceptical – is there anything more awkward that role play? – but she insisted it would help prepare me.

'Come on,' she said, taking our empty plates over to the kitchen side. She came home with me after the staff meeting at work and I'd made a pasta bake. 'I'll be one of the board and you can be... you, obviously. I'm going to ask you some questions.'

'Oh Ju, do we have to? I'm not very good at this sort of thing.' I pulled a face.

'It'll be good practice, you want to be prepared don't you?'

I sat down opposite her at the table and we both tried not to laugh.

'*Paul,*' she said sternly, looking at me over her glasses with a raised eyebrow.

'Sorry, OK, let's do it,' I cleared my throat.

'So, Mr Johnson, tell me about your teaching experience so far,' she started, pretending to look down at her notes.

I reeled off my CV, settling into the scenario as I got into my stride. We went through my development plan.

'And what do you think makes you the right candidate for Head of English?' Julia asked casually, but the question struck panic into my stomach. I still don't know the answer.

'Oh God I don't know, Ju! I don't think I am, if I'm honest!' I sat back in my chair in a huff, like one of the kids when I ask them to analyse Shakespeare.

Julia lifted her glasses, resting them on her head. 'Come on, mate, you were doing great. You're *definitely* the right person for the job. Those kids love you. You're everyone's favourite teacher. And you care about them, anyone can see that.'

'Paul?' Martin bellows cheerfully, springing from the door opposite with a wide smile. 'We're ready for you.'

I startle, smiling with pursed lips as I look up and rise from my seat. Smoothing down my tie, I take a sharp, silent breath in through my nose.

'Don't look so nervous,' Martin whispers with a wink as he holds open the classroom door for me. As I enter, I realise it's the classroom I was in during my dream of Laura, when she was talking to me about *Romeo & Juliet*. I smile at the panel of two school governors sitting in front of me as I walk over to the lone chair behind a single desk. I extend my hand and introduce myself, my voice shaky. Martin resumes his position in the middle of them and takes his seat.

'Hello, Paul,' the man to Martin's right says as he grips my hand firmly, his expression stony and cold. 'David Jenkins, I'm the local authority governor on the board. This is Louise Platt, our safeguarding governor.' *Safeguarding. They must know all about you.* I smile weakly as she shakes my hand, smoothing my tie again as I take my seat.

'Martin speaks very highly of you and your abilities as a teacher,' Louise says, her tone measured. 'So we're here to understand a bit more about your skills and what you think you have to offer the school as Head of English,' she looks down at what I assume is a copy of my application and I feel my cheeks flush. 'Perhaps you'd like to start by talking us through your department development plan?'

I try and steady my voice with another deep inhale through my nose before I begin presenting the plan I'd set out in my application all those months ago. I've rehearsed what I need to say so many times but suddenly my mind's blank. I close my eyes momentarily before taking out my own dog-eared copy from my satchel and referring to all the sections I'd highlighted as important to mention. As I start to speak my confidence grows, I know exactly what needs to be done, having watched the school evolve over the last five years. I've done my homework.

The governors are unmoved by my presentation. Martin catches my eye and discretely gives an encouraging nod. My mind wanders to the other candidates. They're probably more experienced than me, better educated. Less emotional baggage. I wish I had something to do with my hands.

'We'll move on to questions now, Paul, if that's OK,' David says, looking down at his notes. I reply with a half-smile, sitting forward in my seat. The less I say the better.

'It says here you studied English at Sheffield Hallam University; did you grow up in the local area or move here when you came to study?' David asks. I wonder what he's getting at.

'Er, yes, I grew up here, in the suburbs but across the other side of town,' I'm not sure how I'm supposed to elaborate on that. 'I enjoyed my time at Sheffield Hallam. It was very... rewarding.'

A series of similarly uninspiring questions about my background follow and I'm not entirely sure where it's going. Is it important where I grew up? Are they going to ask what my parents did for a living? I wonder if they've written me off already and are just filling the time with polite chit-chat.

'It's been a difficult year, hasn't it, Paul?' Louise asks, her eyes locking on mine. My stomach flips as her question knocks the wind out of me. *They must know everything.*

I swallow hard. 'It has, yes,' I manage.

'You must have found it quite a challenge, at times, to cope with what's happened over the last few months?' David chips in.

'There have been some challenging times, certainly. But I'm fortunate to be well supported by my colleagues and, of course, Martin,' I nod in his direction.

'And what do you think makes you the best person for the Head of English role?' Louise smiles curtly, the first smile I've seen from either of them.

I clear my throat. The classic question that you think you've prepared yourself for answering.

'Well... as you say, it's been a very difficult few months, particularly for my tutor group. And, being a father myself, I've felt the loss particularly keenly. There have been days – I'll be honest –' I figure I've got nothing to lose now, 'when I've struggled to get out of bed. And I did need to take some time, to get myself in better shape, because I wanted to be there for the kids. To be the best I could be, for them. It's been tough, really tough, but we've all been in it together.' I pause before continuing, whilst I gather my thoughts. 'There were one or two teachers in my school as a teenager who really shaped my attitude to education and helped me through some difficulties I was facing at the time. I lacked a father figure for much of my time at high school and you might say that that, coupled with my working-class background, meant the odds were stacked against me. But they saw my potential and encouraged me to follow my own path. There's no doubt that they inspired me into teaching. And, you know, these kids in my tutor group, I've had the privilege of watching them grow since I started with them in Year 7. I've got to know them and tried to understand their individual needs and challenges. And across the wider school, every single one of them that comes through my classroom doors is important. I want to see them *all* thrive. Because, at the end of the day, there's no such thing as someone else's children. They're all so precious. They're the future, aren't they?'

I hold my breath as I look first to Martin, for his reaction. He nods and I notice the muscles in his jaw clenching as he shoots me a steady smile, his nostrils flared. The others on the panel look to each other as David puts down his pen and says 'Thank you, Paul, we'll be in touch.'

CHAPTER THIRTY-SIX

THREE MONTHS LATER

My arms shake as I push my weight down into my palms and lengthen my neck, moving my shoulders away from my ears. The backs of my hamstrings are tight and I feel the stretch as I adjust my feet and push my tailbone up to the sky. My first downward dog of the practice and it feels good. I follow the instruction and take a long, slow breath in through my nose, moving deeper into the pose with my outbreath.

It's been three months since I accepted Jeremy's challenge to my first yoga class and I have become completely addicted to my new routine. The release in my body with each new pose, and in my mind with the meditative breathwork. Maybe I should have listened to my mum all along.

Rachel walks around the studio adjusting poses slightly but with great effect. Her feet stop next to me and she leans down and gently presses on my shoulder blades, guiding me further into the stretch.

'On your next outbreath, I want you to walk your legs out to plank position and hold it there...' She guides the class with her gentle tone. 'Don't forget to breathe… you can come down onto your forearms if that feels better. Listen to your body.'

The studio is warm, with soft lighting and a subtle scent of unidentified incense. It might be sandalwood. I'm still learning the ropes.

'Now lower onto your forearms – if you weren't there already – and then slowly down onto your front…' I breathe out as I lower myself down. 'Take a deep breath in… and as you breathe out lift your head, your neck, your chest into baby cobra. Breathe… Really push down into your forearms to feel that stretch… Good.' The release of tension across my chest and lower back feels so good.

'And on your next outbreath, bring your knees up and stretch your arms out in front, gently lowering your front body down into child's pose. We'll take a few breaths here to finish our practice.' Rachel says gently, returning to the front of the room.

'Bringing your attention back to the room, gently guide yourself back up to seated and take some nice deep breaths in through the nose… and out through the mouth…' she smiles and brings her hands down in front of her, as if in prayer. 'Thanks for joining me today, hope you all enjoyed that and I'll see you again soon.'

I head out into the warmth of the late spring morning and the breeze is carrying the scent of the rhododendrons and azaleas on a wave through the park. The mid-morning sun is creeping higher in the sky and I pull my sunglasses out of the pocket of my hoodie.

'Are you joining us for coffee, Paul?' Brendan calls as he emerges from the studio and swings his yoga bag over his shoulder.

'Yeah, that'd be nice, thanks,' I'm quite enjoying the slowness of my weekends these days although I do miss Emilia. And Lisa, sometimes.

'Cool, so, we've got... me, you, Craig, Rachel and Josie, I think,' he counts our heads like we're on a school trip. 'Sarah, are you coming?'

'Nah, I've got to get back for the kids, Tom's off to football. Next time though!' she waves as she walks off towards the park gates.

'So, are you back at school then on Monday, Paul?' Josie asks as she puts her coffee cup back down on the table. She's squinting as the sun streams through the window right into her eyes, and shuffles to the end of the bench she's sitting on to avoid it.

'Yeah, back to normal for me on Monday,' I feign a groan and roll my eyes.

'It's a tough gig, isn't it, all those holidays...' Craig smirks.

'Well, someone's got to do it...' I retort, taking a sip of my coffee. 'But, yeah, my tutor group have got their GCSEs these next two weeks then they're all done for the summer. So it'll be a bit quieter after that and then it's only a few weeks 'til a glorious six weeks off...' I stretch my arms out behind my head and they all laugh.

'It's alright for some, hey?' Rachel nudges me with her elbow. 'What do you do with all that... *time*?' she asks, eyes wide, shaking her head in disbelief.

I laugh and try to think of something witty to say but my nerves get the better of me. They've all known each other for quite a while and I'm the new guy, so I'm still trying to figure out the group's sense of humour. But they've all made a real effort to get to know me and make me feel welcome over the last few weeks.

'Well, I'll be hanging out with my daughter for most of it – she's only in nursery during term time. So it'll be trips to the swings and finger painting for me from Monday to Thursday each week. And I start a new position as Head of English in September so I'll have a bit of prep to do at some point.'

'Ah congratulations, that's exciting!' Rachel toasts me by clinking her coffee cup against mine.

'Thanks, yeah it's a big step up plus I'll have a whole new Year 7 tutor group too so that'll be... different,' I raise my eyebrows.

'How old's your daughter?' Josie asks with a smile.

'She'll be two in September. Such a fun age. But yeah, that's the real work,' I laugh. 'You've got a little one haven't you?'

'Yeah, Freya, she's coming up to 18 months. It is a fascinating stage. They sure do keep you on your toes though.'

'Ain't that the truth!' Brendan joins in. 'My three-year-old is like a force of nature. I don't know where he gets his energy,' he shakes his head as he takes a sip of coffee. 'At least he sleeps now though, thank *God*! But we're expecting number two in October so I'll be needing a lot more of this,' he says, holding up his cup.

A fleeting image of Lisa enters my head as it dawns on me that our second baby would have been due in October. *It wasn't meant to be*, I tell myself.

'Ah mate, I remember those days,' I give him a friendly pat on the shoulder. 'I think my bloodstream was ninety per cent coffee just after Emilia was born.' Brendan laughs as he finishes the rest of his Americano.

'Yeah, Gemma's coming to my pregnancy yoga classes over the summer, isn't she?' Rachel smiles, her face open and warm.

247

I notice the depth in her brown eyes as the sunlight catches them.

'She is,' Brendan nods as he gets up from his chair and reaches down for his bag. 'She's really looking forward to it. I think she's starting to struggle a bit with her back,' he says, wrinkling his nose. 'Right guys, I've got to dash, bon weekend everyone!' he waves and heads for the door.

'Yeah, I'd better be off too, actually,' Craig looks at his watch. 'Dan and I are off to the outdoor jazz festival in town this afternoon,' he says, with a jazzy little shake of his shoulders.

'Sounds good, enjoy!' I give him a wave and check the time on my phone before putting it back in my pocket.

'Cheers, catch you guys later!'

There's an awkward pause before Josie reaches for her hoodie and the three of us remaining start mumbling things about needing to make a move. I grab my bag and pick up my own hoodie from the back of my chair as I get to my feet. We all head out into the midday sunshine together and Josie says her goodbyes before heading to the car park.

'Well I'm heading off this way,' I say to Rachel, pointing in the direction of the path through the park towards the main road. 'That was a great class, thank you.'

'Glad you enjoyed it,' Rachel replies with a wide smile. 'I'm heading that way too actually, if you don't mind me walking with you?' she asks, as she bunches her long braids together.

'Yeah... I mean, no, I don't mind...' I let out a little nervous laugh. 'I'm, er, I'm just over on Derwent Terrace so I'll head up to the main road.'

'Ah it's nice up there,' she says with a nod. 'You might know my friend Becky then, she's on Derwent too!'

'Well I'm, er, I don't actually live... I'm staying at my mum's at the minute, so... that's where I am this weekend,' I catch her stealing a sideways glance at my wedding ring. It's the first time that it's occurred to me that I'm still wearing it. 'My, er... my wife and I are separated, so...'

'Oh no,' she winces then offers a half-smile. 'I'm sorry.'

'No, it's OK, it's all good, we're just... you know, figuring out... logistics,' I laugh to try and soften the mood. 'We're selling the house at the minute so I'm in the process of getting my own place, just waiting for the paperwork to get sorted.'

'Ah that's good, then,' she says. 'It's nice if you can still be amicable.'

'Yeah, it makes life easier,' I think about how far Lisa and I have come over the last few months, despite our differences of opinion. 'Our house is on the new estate just out of town so I stay there with Emilia for part of the week while Lisa – my... er, Emilia's mum – works in London. Then she comes back on Thursday night and we all have a changeover day dinner together and I head off to my mum's for the weekend. Until we finalise the sale of the house and stuff, that is.'

'That's a really grown-up way of going about things. And it must mean much less disruption for your little one.' She shields her eyes from the sun as she turns to face me.

'Exactly, that was the most important thing. I mean, it's taken us a while to figure it all out but it's made this transition period a bit easier. And we're lucky enough to have our own rooms in the house so it doesn't make it too weird. There've been a few raised eyebrows when we've explained to people how we're doing things but it seems to work for us, so...' I wonder if I'm oversharing but I find her so easy to talk to.

'Well, if there's one thing I've learnt over the last few years, it's that how you live your life is none of anyone else's business. You've got to figure out your own ways to be happy. Other people's expectations can do one as far as I'm concerned.'

'Too right,' I laugh. I'm conscious of talking about myself too much. Talking about my situation does come a little easier though, these days. Jeremy would be impressed. 'So, how long have you been teaching yoga?'

'Erm...' she exhales and raises her eyebrows as if trying to remember. 'About 18 months now, I think,' she nods slowly. 'Yeah... I had a bit of a tough breakup, so I took myself off to India for a yoga retreat and came back a qualified teacher.'

'Oh wow, that must have been amazing!' I enthuse, then realise she mentioned a tough breakup. 'Not the breakup bit, I mean, sorry...'

'It's OK, it was for the best,' she catches my gaze. 'And yeah, it was pretty special. Yoga had always been my escape so I figured I had nothing to lose.'

'Yeah, yoga's really helped me through these last few months. Yoga and music.'

'A magical combination! I'm pretty jealous of Craig and Dan going to that jazz festival this afternoon,' her eyes light up. 'Sounds amazing!'

'I know, I love a bit of jazz. That club in town is good, we used to go down there a bit, before we had Emilia...' my voice trails and I wonder for how much longer I'll refer to Lisa and me as a 'we'.

'Yeah, we went there for my friend's hen night a few months ago. The music was *unreal*. Food was nice too.'

I could talk to her all day. She has such an enthusiastic warmth about her, as if she's hanging on your every word. We reach the park gates and she pauses just outside.

'Well, this is me, I'm heading this way,' she points behind her shoulder with her thumb. 'Hope Monday isn't too much of a shock to the system!' she laughs, with a playful wink.

'Oh I'm sure I'll manage,' I laugh. 'Thanks... for... this morning,' I stumble awkwardly.

'Yeah, it was nice,' she grins and her eyes glisten. 'See you next week?'

'You will,' I wave with a smile and head off in the other direction, before stealing another glimpse of her over my shoulder.

CHAPTER THIRTY-SEVEN

'So you're finding that the yoga helps then, with management of your symptoms?' Jeremy asks kindly as he retrieves his glasses from the top of his head and flicks back through his notebook.

'Yeah, it's really helping, on a number of levels, actually,' I nod and realise how much more confident I am sitting here now compared with even just a few weeks ago. 'I'm not getting as many intrusive thoughts now but, if I do, I use my breath work to help me let them go, instead of it leading to a compulsion and spiralling out of control.'

'So you're still getting some intrusive thoughts, but fewer than before? And you're able to manage your compulsions easier?'

'Yeah, far fewer than before. Before I could barely do a simple task without some horrible image barging into my head. Now I just get the odd few, if I'm tired or whatever, but it's like a switch has flipped and I know not to dwell on the thoughts. I know that that's all they are, just thoughts. We all get them and I just need to acknowledge them, and let them go. Like passing clouds.'

Jeremy looks up and smiles before making more notes in his book. I hadn't realised until now that he's left-handed.

'And I think the CBT helped me to get out of the habit of letting the compulsions get the better of me. Knowing that I can think things, but it doesn't mean they're going to happen,' I continue, almost as if I'm making a case to Jeremy to prove I'm on the mend. 'That was the turning point for me. Realising that I can't control anything – which alarmed me at first but then it sort of put me at peace, knowing that me thinking something awful – involuntarily – wasn't going to have any effect on the world whatsoever.'

'So the lack of control doesn't alarm you anymore?'

'No, it's... liberating, if anything. That doesn't mean to say I'm reckless with my choices. I know that there are consequences to my actions. But I also know that I can't control events with my thinking.'

Jeremy nods with a knowing look. 'And in terms of your family life, have things settled down a bit?' He peers at me in that way that he does, over his glasses.

'I think so, yeah. I got the keys to my new place last week so that's another door opening, so to speak,' I laugh at my own accidental joke.

'That's great,' Jeremy laughs along politely. 'How is it going, living on your own now?'

'It's OK. I mean, I'd rather still be living with my wife and daughter but... here we are,' I shrug and raise my eyebrows, accepting. 'It was hard, leaving our home for the last time. Closing the doors on all those memories. And I guess it'll take a while to settle in properly to the new place and make it feel like home. I'm still sleeping on an airbed and living out of my suitcase at the minute. But at least I've got my own space now. I'm worried I might find it lonely when I don't have Emilia but yoga's been keeping me busy and I'm throwing myself back into work a bit more.'

I think back to my first night alone at the new house. Loneliness seemed to be ingrained in the exposed floorboards of the bedroom as I lay on that airbed. It felt so cold. Rushing to unpack things was a mistake. But the few boxes stacked up in the hallway felt like a sad reminder of how little I had to show for a thirty-something, about-to-be-divorced man. I'd brought some books and records with me, my old turntable as Lisa never really used it. But it was when I opened up the box containing my old photo albums that the reality of how my life has taken a massive U-turn hit me. This was life now, for the foreseeable.

'And things are going well then, at work? A bit more... stable?' he flicks back through more pages of notes. 'You start the new job in September, is that right?'

'Yeah, that's right. It's been a lot better... But I don't know, I feel like any day they're going to pull me into the office and tell me actually, we made a mistake, you're not really cut out for this... Like they can see right through me.'

Jeremy nods with a half-smile. 'You know, there was a paper published, around twenty years ago now, about something termed *imposter phenomenon*,' he takes a sip of his tea before placing it down on the table next to him, looking like a grandfather about to tell an important tale. 'There's still a lot of ongoing research around it, but this experience can typically manifest as denying one's ability – putting achievements down to luck, for example – as well as fears of being exposed as a fraud or feelings of being undeserving of success. We can begin to feel guilty about our achievements, that we don't deserve any better than someone else. This often goes hand-in-hand with other mental health issues such as those that you have experienced, as well as low self-esteem and feelings of inadequacy, which I think perhaps ties in with some of the themes we've discussed around your friendships and your marriage.'

As he describes all of this, it's as if he's opened up my skull and riffled through all of the feelings swirling around in my mind over the last twenty years or so. Knowing there's a name for it – and that other people apparently experience it too – makes it slightly easier to accept.

'That pretty much sums it all up to be honest,' I laugh. 'I've got my last day with my tutor group next week, so I guess I've been anxious about that.'

'Anything you want to talk about?' he ventures gently.

'It's hard to describe but it feels a bit like everything's... coming to a close,' I clear my throat. 'And I guess I feel a bit guilty about it. I'm obviously keen to draw a line under this year but I don't want to forget about Laura. I still miss her. And I feel guilty about getting on with my life when she should be starting the next stage of hers. But then I've not seen her in a while and I wonder what that means. I mean, you know, in my dreams... or whatever,' I wonder if I'm making any sense.

'Well, there are different stages of grief that we move through – and there's no set timetable – but it sounds like you might be at acceptance, which is good,' Jeremy pauses and I ease into the silence while I wait to hear his thoughts.

'Whether we believe in an afterlife or an ability to contact the dead doesn't really matter. Because, it seems to me, that these visions you've had of Laura - whether they're *real*,' he says with air quotes, 'or simply in your imagination – they've helped you move through the stages of grief and her loss. And whilst, in the early days, when you were struggling with your OCD, they were perhaps disturbing to you, all of these encounters have helped you to understand some of your complex feelings and, latterly, it seems, have provided you with some comfort. So, it appears to me, the fact that these visions are becoming less frequent perhaps demonstrates an acceptance, that it's time to let go and move forward, would you agree?'

I'm blown away by the power of being heard and understood. How one person listening to you unravel your thoughts then summarising them so succinctly back to you can validate everything. I clench my jaw as I feel tears of relief – gratitude, maybe – rising up within me. 'Yes,' I nod slowly and smile. 'I think that's it.'

Jeremy smiles back warmly, raising his glasses back on top of his head. 'Do you feel like you've got what you need, for now, from our sessions, Paul?'

'Are you breaking up with me?' I joke to try and release my nerves. He laughs. 'Yeah, I think I have,' I answer. I hadn't really thought about when or how our sessions might come to an end but this seems to be a natural juncture.

'You seem to be coping much better with things than you were when I first saw you nearly six months ago. And it sounds like you've got some exciting things on the horizon. But you know where we are if you need us again,' he rises from his chair and I do the same.

'Thank you, Jeremy,' I say offering my hand. 'For everything. It's really helped.'

'I'm pleased to hear it,' he takes my hand and shakes it gently. 'Take care, Paul.'

Rachel gently pushes down on my hips as I lie face down on the yoga mat, arms outstretched in front of me and knees tucked up underneath, in child's pose. Her hands are warm and seem to give off a healing energy.

'Take a few breaths here while you release that tension in your lower back,' she soothes as she walks slowly around the room adjusting people's positions. There are only a handful of us here this evening, the Friday night class being one of the least popular. But I like it when it's quiet.

'Allow your mind to be still in these few moments before we bring our attention back to our bodies,' I open one eye and see Rachel taking a seat on her mat at the front of the studio, her long legs stretched out in front of her. She takes a forward fold, grabbing hold of her toes and pulling herself down to meet her outstretched legs before lowering her head down into her shins, her braids bunched on top of her head flopping down in front of her. 'And as we reawaken our bodies, let's take one long breath in through the nose... and sigh it out through the mouth.'

As I curl myself back up to a seated position, I notice how free my neck and shoulders feel. I move my head slowly from side to side and stretch my arms out above my head. I'm more confident now to move my body in a way that feels good to me, rather than watching nervously and following everyone else's lead. Rachel catches my eye and a smile creeps across her lips.

'Well done everyone, thanks for joining me and I'll see you next time,' she says in her soft lullaby tone before reaching for her water bottle to take a sip. I suddenly realise I'm thirsty and do the same as I get to my feet. I pull my hoodie on and step out into the mild evening air.

'Right, who's up for a pint?' Craig calls, rubbing his hands together as the others emerge from the studio and Rachel locks the door behind her. 'I promised Dan I'd meet him for a drink after work but he'll be with his worky pals so I'll need some back up.' He wrinkles his nose into an unimpressed face. He has one of those faces that makes it impossible to know how old he is.

'I'd love to, but I'm still trying to get everything unpacked at the new place, so I should get off really and sort a few things out,' I say unconvincingly. A few of the others make their excuses and head off towards the car park.

'Oooh so you've moved in then? All the more reason to celebrate then, hey?' Rachel suggests, pulling a thin sweater over her head and flicking her hair out from underneath.

'Come on, just a quick one!' Craig insists, pulling me along by the elbow in the direction of the pub. 'They're only meeting in the Coach & Horses round the corner.'

'Go on then, you've twisted my arm,' I laugh as we walk through the park and towards the pub. It's actually on the way back to my new place and it's a nice evening to sit outside with a drink.

'So where've you moved to then Paul?' Craig asks, pulling out a cigarette and perching it between his lips to light it. He offers the pack to Rachel and me but we both decline. 'Levelling up to make space for more sprogs are you?' he laughs as Rachel looks at me in apologetic horror.

'Er... no, downsizing, actually,' I smile awkwardly as I give him the short version back story of how I've arrived where I'm at.

'Oh shit, sorry,' he takes a long drag on his cigarette. 'I'm an idiot.'

'No, it's all good. One door closes and all that.'

'Yeah, and you're back on the market now, I'm sure Dan's got some single colleagues we can hook you up with!' He gives me a cheeky wink and slaps me on the back a little too hard.

'Craig!' Rachel laughs incredulously, shaking her head. 'Jesus!'

'Nah, I'm, er, I'm not quite there yet mate,' I laugh, wrinkling my nose as I look down at my feet.

'Fair enough, fair enough,' he laughs and stubs his cigarette out on the pavement under his shoe. 'Here we are, Dan's on his way. What we having then?'

'I'll have a gin and tonic please,' Rachel smiles gratefully. 'Thanks Craig.'

'Yeah, I'll have the same please, cheers.'

Craig wanders off into the pub while Rachel and I take a table outside and pull up a couple of extra chairs. It's a warm but overcast evening and the bar is busy with groups of people having post-work drinks.

'Craig can be a bit... er, *direct*, sometimes,' Rachel breaks the silence as we sit down at the table. She frowns apologetically on his behalf. 'Hope he didn't overstep the mark, just then?'

'It's alright,' I say with a laugh and a shrug of the shoulders. 'I just haven't really thought about... *that*, yet. My mum's always telling me I should get out and 'meet people',' I say with air quotes and raised eyebrows. 'I've been telling *her* that for twenty years!'

Rachel nods with a hint of a smile. 'We're all ready at different stages, I guess,' she looks down at her hands, stretching out the fingers on her left hand. I have an urge to ask her something, but I'm not sure what. I wish I was one of those people that can just ask questions without overthinking, like Craig. Sometimes I think I come across aloof or uninterested because I'm afraid of asking something too personal.

I'm relieved when Craig returns with our drinks. 'G&T for three!' he announces placing three tall glasses down, ice tinkling. 'Cheers!'

'Cheers!' we both join in, clinking our glasses.

'How was the jazz festival the other week?' I ask.

'It was so good!' his eyes widen as he raises his palms out in front of him enthusiastically. 'They had some amazing musicians and the weather was glorious. Dan and I had a bit too much of the rum punch they had on at the bar!' he laughs loudly, throwing his head back and nudging my arm with his elbow.

'Sounds fun, I'll have to look out for the next one,' I say, taking a sip of my gin and tonic.

'We've got a few music fans in the class, haven't we?' Rachel says, putting down her glass. 'I was going to ask you actually, Paul,' she turns to face me, tilting her head to one side with a soft smile. I notice she has a habit of closing her eyes while she considers what she's about to say. She opens them and locks into mine. 'Brendan organised a night out a while back... there's this guy David Gray playing in Derby in a couple of weeks and there's a spare ticket if you're interested? It's on a Friday night so we were going to get the train and then the venue's only across the road from the station. Jump on the last train home?'

'That sounds great,' I nod, fidgeting with my fingers. 'In fact, my mate from work saw him in Sheffield a couple of months ago, said he was really good.' I think back to when Ju came into work one Monday morning in the spring, raving about a gig she and Anthony had been to at the weekend. She'd brought me one of his CDs he was selling afterwards and said she thought I'd like his stuff. She was right.

'Yeah, Brendan was at that gig, that's how he heard about this one!' Craig says, lighting another cigarette. 'Derby will be a laugh, I don't think I've ever been to *Derby*,' he pulls a curious face.

'Yoga squad on tour!' Rachel laughs as she stirs her drink with her straw and glances up at me. 'So shall I tell Brendan you're in then?'

'Yeah,' I smile. 'I'll look forward to it.'

CHAPTER THIRTY-EIGHT

I push open the window as the steam builds in the tiny kitchen and I'm suddenly way too hot. I've just about got sight of Emilia standing at her play kitchen in the corner of the adjacent dining area, mirroring my every move with her saucepans.

'Mummy will be here soon, poppet!' I call over to her as I stir the Bolognese sauce bubbling away on the hob. I take a sip of the merlot I picked up on the way home – Lisa's favourite – and right on cue, the doorbell rings.

'Mama!' Emilia shouts with an excited squeal and waddles through the hall towards the front door.

'Shall we go and see?' I say, turning down the gas burner to a low heat. I grab a tea towel to wipe my hands and throw it over my shoulder as I make my way to open the front door. Lisa is standing on the front porch with her weekend bag and greets us with a warm smile. 'Hello, sweetheart!' she squeaks as she scoops Emilia up and holds her close, breathing in her scent and kissing her forehead.

'Hello,' she smiles and leans in to give me a kiss on the cheek. 'What's cooking?'

'Bolognese,' I announce as I let her through and close the door behind her.

'My favourite!' she declares, more to Emilia than to me. 'Smells amazing.'

'Do you want one?' I ask, holding up my wine glass.

'Ooh yes please! It is Thursday after all.' She crouches down next to Emilia's play kitchen. 'What have we got here then?' she asks, pretending to stir whatever Emilia imagines is in her saucepan.

I hand the glass to Lisa. 'Take a seat,' I say, gesturing to the dining table. It feels a little odd, inviting my wife to take a seat in my new house.

'Thanks,' she smiles. 'This is nice!' she gestures around the room. 'You settling in alright?'

'Yeah, getting there, I think,' I drain the pasta and serve it into bowls, with a tiny one set out for Emilia. 'We'll give you the tour later. Could you just cut up this spaghetti for Emmy, please?'

'Yeah, course,' she takes Emilia's bowl from me and heads over to the table.

'Right, tea's ready poppet,' I call. 'Let's eat!'

———

Lisa helps me to clear up after dinner and we put a Teletubbies video on for Emilia to sit and watch while we catch up. I pour her another glass of wine and we take a seat in the lounge.

'How are you feeling about tomorrow?' she asks gently, knowing it's my last day with my Year 11s. She takes a long sip of wine.

'Emotional,' I nod with a half-smile. 'I'm going to miss them. Don't think it's quite sunk in yet that I won't be seeing most of them again after tomorrow. Just hope I can hold it together.'

'Yeah, I guess it'll be a tough day for all of you,' she wrinkles her nose and smiles through pursed lips as she squeezes my shoulder.

'But, I don't know, I think I'm looking forward to drawing a line under the year to be honest,' I swallow down hard on the lump forming in my throat as I think about what we've all been through this year.

She smiles sadly and puts a hand on mine as she turns to face me. 'I'm sorry, Paul, I can't imagine,' her face crumples and tears start streaming down her face.

'Hey, it's OK... I'm alright!'

Lisa wipes tears from under her eyes and pulls a tissue out of her sleeve to blow her nose. 'I'm just so sorry I wasn't particularly supportive, you know, after... Laura... died. I can't imagine how you must have felt, dealing with your own grief and that of all the kids. And I was so dismissive. I just, I don't know, I wasn't in a good place. But that's no excuse. I feel like I let you down right when you needed me most.'

I'm heartened by her admission that she wasn't in a good place. She doesn't owe me it, or anything but it's nice to know she acknowledges her part in how we got to this point. But I hate to see her upset.

'Neither of us were in a good place, Lis. It wasn't your fault. But thank you.' I put my other hand on top of hers. It reminds me of our wedding day. We were so young. It feels like a lifetime ago now.

'There's something I wanted to tell you, actually,' Lisa looks away first. 'I've been seeing a therapist. For the last couple of months.' A pained expression creeps across her face, as if she's telling me she's met someone else.

'That's great,' I smile, recapturing her gaze. 'That you've been talking about things, I mean. Have you found it helpful?'

'Yeah, I suppose. I guess I've learnt a lot about myself, since... you know.' She looks up from her hands.

'Good, I'm glad it's helping. I've learnt a lot about myself too,' I laugh. 'And, to be honest, I never said it to you but I had my suspicions about you and Richard so... neither of us are blameless.'

'Richard!' She almost chokes on her wine. 'You know he's gay, right?'

'Really?' I ask with genuine surprise, annoyed at myself that the possibility had never crossed my mind. 'Wow. Well now I feel like a total dick.'

'Don't blame yourself, Paul. This is the fucking problem with society!' we both glance over at Emilia, but she's still engrossed in Teletubbies, oblivious. 'It feeds us this *bullshit*,' her eyes narrow, 'that a relationship is only acceptable or valuable if it involves a heterosexual couple producing 2.4 children and living happily-ever-after in white middle-class suburbia. It's *horrible*.'

'You're right, it *is* horrible,' I finish my wine but cover my glass as Lisa tries to top me up.

'Sometimes I feel so ashamed,' Lisa blurts out, in an uncharacteristic admission.

'About what?' I ask, with a frown.

'About leaving you. And Emilia. It's not what women do. We're not supposed to put our careers first. We're not supposed to leave our families. Or be selfish, or do anything for ourselves. But I had to. It would have driven a wedge between us anyway, in the long run. And I couldn't carry on as we were. So what's worse? We'd probably have ended up hating each other,' she looks down at her hands and I notice she isn't wearing her wedding ring. Her eyes look so sad.

'Listen, Emilia adores you and I think you and I are getting on better now than we have done in years. We're talking more. I'm so pleased we've managed to find our own way of making this work for us, you know, without falling out completely. People can say what they like but I think it's testament to the strength of the basis of our relationship, our friendship. I'd have hated us to have lost that. And as long as we're all happy with our situation, who cares what anyone thinks?'

'Yeah, there've been some interesting faces pulled at work when I tell them how we've been doing things. But fuck the system! Speaking of which, I've been looking at some places nearby, for me and Emmy when I'm not in London. Not sure how much longer my mum and dad can cope with us in their spare room every weekend!' she laughs, finishing her wine.

'Ah nice, that's exciting,' I smile but there's an ache in my stomach as I remember our excitement when we first started house hunting together.

'Yeah, well now the house is sold I've got a bit of a better idea about what I can afford, so...' her voice trails and I wonder if she's finding this as hard as I am, underneath it all.

'Yeah, I guess so,' is all that comes out.

'OK, well I'd better get this one off to bed. My dad's on his way to pick us up. Thanks for dinner, it was lovely,' she says, squeezing me on the arm. 'Come and say bye-bye to Daddy, poppet. We're off to Granny and Grandad's!'

I head over to where Emilia is snuggled up on the sofa and scoop her up to give her a sleepy cuddle. 'See you later, angel. I love you.' My heart hurts knowing I won't be reading her bedtime story for the next few nights.

I grab the weekend bag I'd packed for her earlier from the

hallway and hand it to Lisa, who's holding Emilia snuggled in between her neck and her shoulder. 'Thanks for tonight,' I smile, kissing her on the cheek. 'It was really nice, to talk... properly.'

'Yeah, it was,' she smiles back. 'See you Sunday, then.'

CHAPTER THIRTY-NINE

Friday 18 June 1999 is the last day of term with my Year 11 tutor group, as the last of their GCSE exams finishes at lunchtime. We've arranged to have a leaving picnic to celebrate and there are some mixed emotions: relief, excitement, sadness. To say it's been a challenging year would be an understatement.

We gather on the school playing field under the pink hawthorn tree, still colourful with some lingering blossom. There's lots of excited chatter about next steps; a handful are staying on at Melbury High for their A-Levels, some are heading off to college in Sheffield, a few have got apprenticeships lined up and then there are some that haven't quite made up their minds. They're a good bunch and it dawns on me that I'll really, really miss them. Even the likes of Andy Smithurst. Five years is a long time to watch a group of kids grow up through their formative years and I can't help but wonder what the future will bring for each of them. I just hope I've done my best to guide them through.

I work my way around the small groups to chat to them about how they think their exams went and what they've got planned for the summer, as they all sign each other's shirts in marker pen. I've written them all a personal note in a 'good luck' card and I hand them out while some of them pull me into photographs taken on disposable cameras. I wonder what they'll tell their kids about me. Will they remember the residential at the end of Year 7, when I lost the bet that I could get to the top of the climbing wall in under thirty seconds and they got to push me in the lake? Or when they voted to custard pie me in the face as their prize for our class winning sports day in Year 10. I wonder if they'll remember anything about the books we read together, the plays we studied, how it all made them feel.

It brings back such vivid memories of how I felt leaving school after I finished my O-Levels. Some teachers had more of an impact on me than others. And whilst I generally enjoyed school, despite never quite feeling like I fully fitted in, I was excited about moving on. The independence, the next steps of the journey – it's one of those defining moments during a lifetime that you're aware you probably won't forget. The sounds, the smells; the faintest hint of these in the future will take you straight back to that time. Someone has a portable stereo and I can faintly pick out the distinctive chorus of *The Day We Caught The Train* by Ocean Colour Scene. I wonder what sort of memories hearing this in twenty years' time will evoke. For me, as well as them. The world feels so different now, to when I was that age. Now they have mobile phones in their pockets, email and something called MSN Messenger, whatever that is. It wasn't so easy to keep in touch with each other when I left school. Will it make it easier or just make them lazy in the long run, assuming their friends will always be there, behind the screens? I don't know. But as a generation, there's no doubt their young adulthood will be very different to mine.

I have a sudden urge to go and speak to Andy to try and make amends for our little bust up earlier in the year.

'Andy, can I have a quick word?' I ask quietly, as I approach him sitting with a couple of the others. He looks up at me from under his mop of black hair flopped over his eyes, before standing up to my level. He's already as tall as me. They're almost adults now.

'Look, I just wanted to apologise, properly I mean, for what happened before,' I try and meet his shifting gaze. 'I was going through a really tough time at home, but it's no excuse for how I reacted, I should know better.'

'It's alright, sir. I know I was being a bit of a dick,' he shuffles on his feet, hands plunged into his trouser pockets. 'I can't help myself sometimes.'

'You've got a lot of promise, Andy. I feel like maybe I never told you that enough, over the years. But I just want you to know. Everyone says we need to enjoy our school years, they're the best of our lives and all that. But it's not like that for all of us. Usually the best is yet to come. And what one person's idea of success is, won't necessarily be the same as the next person's. So don't be afraid to do things your own way, OK?'

'Thanks, sir,' he mumbles, with an awkward half-smile. 'You're alright, you know. I always liked you, even though I used to wind you up.'

'Good man,' I laugh, giving him a friendly pat on the back.

'We got a little something for you actually, sir,' Manny announces as a hush descends on the group, some nudging and whispering going on amongst them. 'Close your eyes!'

I close my eyes with a quizzical smile. I'm not good with surprises. They could be about to stitch me right up, I think.

'James,' Manny calls beyond me. 'Bring it over here. Keep

them closed, sir…' I sense them placing something by the tree in front of me and I'm still none the wiser. 'OK, open them!'

I blink my eyes open and my jaw drops as I see the walnut Fender Squier acoustic guitar propped up against the hawthorn tree. I'm blown away. Tears start to prick my eyes. 'Guys, what… is this for me?' I ask, trying not to give away that I'm choking up. 'This is way too much!'

'Well, you're always banging on about the sort of music we should be listening to!' Manny laughs. 'And, anyway, James' dad was selling it so we thought we'd all chip in a couple of quid rather than you end up with twenty-odd 'World's Best Teacher' mugs…' she explains as I pick it up and play the open strings gently to check it's in tune. It is. 'Do you like it?' she asks, with a wide smile.

'I love it. It's… amazing, I'm speechless,' I laugh, shaking my head as they all watch my reaction. 'It's so thoughtful… thank you so much. I'll treasure it.'

'You've been so good to us, sir,' Jo Shaw joins in as she hands me an envelope which I slowly open. 'We know we've not always been the easiest group to deal with,' they all laugh. 'But… well, we've all been through a lot together, especially this year, and we'll really miss you.'

'Oh, I'm going to miss you lot too, all of you,' I smile sadly as I open up the card that they've all written a message in. I clench my jaw to stop the tears from escaping. 'I'm going to read this later, else it'll set me off,' I laugh, holding up the card. 'Thank you.'

I spot someone walking towards us across the field and remember that the school photographer is coming to take the class portrait. 'Right,' I say, taking in a deep breath through my nose. 'We've got our team photo now, so get yourselves ready.'

The photographer heads over and tests the light in front of

the laurel bushes where we've all planned to assemble. I brought out a couple of gym benches earlier for the back row to stand on and the front row to sit on. I recruit a couple of students to move them into position.

'Who's got Laura's rose?' I shout above the chatter as the photographer organises them into three rows.

'It's here!' Erin shouts, holding up a perfect single yellow rose before reaching over to hand it to me. We wanted to honour Laura in the photo and the class decided on a yellow rose, symbolising friendship.

Everyone assembles into their places as the photographer makes some adjustments to positions. A space in the middle of the front row is cleared and I fight back tears as I place the rose down on the bench. Quiet descends on the group and the rippling undercurrent of Laura's absence that has been building amongst us all day threatens to take us all under. I breathe in deeply through my nose and let out a steadying exhalation through my mouth.

'Let's do Laura proud, hey?' I break the silence, as I take my position to the left of the middle row and the photographer prepares to shoot. 'Here's to the class of ninety-nine!' I beam proudly as the flash fires.

The group disperse and some console each other as they're reminded once again of the loss of their friend. They'll get many reminders, over the years. I'm so proud of how they've helped each other through what must have been some of the toughest months of their lives. I glance over at the pink hawthorn tree and see Laura standing there bathed in dappled sunlight, her shirt still crisp white, a soft smile resting on her lips. She waves to me and her smile broadens. I wave back, instinctively, and blink away warm tears. When I open my eyes, she's gone.

ACKNOWLEDGMENTS

Huge thanks to Damien Mosley and everyone at Indie Novella for all the support, advice and encouragement in writing this book. I am so grateful for the opportunity and your expert editing and guidance. Thanks also to Kika Hendry for the wonderful cover design and marketing brilliance. I appreciate the extraordinary efforts involved in making it happen, as well as the important work Indie Novella are doing to improve diversity in publishing, making it accessible to everyone. Thank you, I will be eternally grateful.

Thanks to readers of early drafts for patiently helping me work through the process of bringing Paul's story to life.

To the artists that shaped my formative years through the power of words and music, whose works are either referred to in these pages or have provided rich inspiration – Neil Finn (Crowded House), Robert Smith (The Cure), Jarvis Cocker (Pulp), Thom Yorke (Radiohead), Tim Booth (James). And, most of all, Nick Cave – your artistic genius, beautiful words and spiritual wisdom guide my life and inspire me every day.

The piece of light music referred to in chapter twenty-nine, which precedes the 12.48am shipping forecast on BBC Radio 4, is Sailing By composed by Derby musician Ronald Binge in 1963. It holds a very special place in my heart.

The academic paper referred to in chapter thirty-seven, in which the term 'imposter phenomenon' was first coined, is "The Imposter Phenomenon in High Achieving Women:

Dynamics and Therapeutic Intervention" written in 1978 by Dr Pauline Clance and Dr Suzanne Imes.

To anyone quietly suffering with obsessive-compulsive disorder, know that you're not alone and help is out there. Mind (mind.org.uk) is a great place to start.

To my wonderful parents, sister and brother-in-law, brother and sister-in-law for unending love, kindness and encouragement. You berries are the best, thank you for always being there and for all you do.

To Sarah Marshall for being my biggest cheerleader, thank you, for everything.

To Immy and Theo, for bringing the joy and light to every day. You are my sunshine.

And to James, for everything. I couldn't have done this without your love and support. There's no one I'd rather be on this wild ride with.

ABOUT THE AUTHOR

Tori Beat is an advocate for working class writers and working class stories. Tori is a former lawyer turned writer from Derbyshire, where she lives with her husband and two young children. Tori rediscovered her love of writing after leaving her career in law to study an Arts & Humanities degree, which led her to submit her first novel, *Class of '99*, to the Watson Little x Indie Novella Prize in 2023, for which it was shortlisted. Through her writing, Tori explores the taboo surrounding mental health, inspired by her own experience of obsessive-compulsive disorder, as well as issues of social and gender inequality and the impact and complexity of human relationships. Tori Beat shines a light on both mental health and class stigma in this poignant debut novel.

THE ROCK 'N' ROLL OF INDIE PUBLISHING

We're Indie Novella and we were founded by a group of friends with one mission, to make publishing more accessible to everyone.

We love literary fiction, but we don't love the snobbery that gets associated with it. Great literary fiction comprises of stories that capture our imagination and resonate with us. Stories that shed light on modern issues, which use relatable and understandable language, which are about characters who speak for the communities we live in.

That's why we're publishing novels which make literary fiction less elitist and get readers as passionate about books as we are. We're also revolutionising publishing by doing something so few others are. Levelling the playing field. Our writing course is funded by the Arts Council and has been designed in collaboration with leading literary agencies such as Watson Little, David Godwin Associates and Georgina Capel and is completely free.

When it comes to writing and storytelling we believe there are so many voices that go unheard. Therefore we made a vow: We won't sit down. We won't shut up. We will commit to being our authentic selves. Just like our authors.

Stories of identity, community, belonging, and being proud of who we are. Our authors write the stories that represent what they stand for, in a truly authentic voice.

If that's not Rock 'n' Roll, I don't know what is.

indie
NOVELLA